W9-BIF-805

Death and Daisies

Death and Daisies

A MAGIC GARDEN MYSTERY

Amanda Flower

NEW YORK

Copyright © 2018 by Amanda Flower

Published in the United States by Crooked Lane Books, an imprint of The Quick Brown Fox & Company LLC.

Crooked Lane Books and its logo are trademarks of The Quick Brown Fox & Company LLC.

Library of Congress Catalog-in-Publication data available upon request.

ISBN (hardcover): 978-1-68331-781-4
ISBN (ePub): 978-1-68331-782-1
ISBN (ePDF): 978-1-68331-783-8

Cover illustration by Ken Joudrey
Book design by Jennifer Canzone

Printed in the United States.

www.crookedlanebooks.com

Crooked Lane Books
34 West 27th St., 10th Floor
New York, NY 10001

First Edition: November 2018

10 9 8 7 6 5 4 3 2 1

Dedication to

Reepicheep & Mister Tumnus

"I am sure there is Magic in everything, only we have not sense enough to get hold of it and make it do things for us."
—Frances Hodgson Burnett, *The Secret Garden*

Chapter One

"**I**'m going to drop it! Help, they're slipping!" my younger sister called.

I dropped the bunch of sunflowers I was arranging on the polished driftwood counter and ran around it.

I snatched the two boxes of vases from my sister's arms just as she was letting them go. I knelt and gently set them down.

I looked up at her from my spot on the floor.

Her full-cheeked, heart-shaped face was red, her dark-blue eyes were wide, and wisps of feathery blonde hair stuck to her clear brow. She appeared to be bracing for impact, and I was afraid that impact might come from me.

"Isla, why on earth did you carry *both* those boxes at once?" I shook my head.

She tilted her head up to the white ceiling. "I'm just trying to finish. Fi, we've been here *all* day. Can't we go home? The storm is rolling in, and I don't want to be caught in it! You know I hate storms!" she said in a notable Tennessee accent, though nowhere near as pronounced as our mother's.

I stood and walked to one of the large display windows at

the front of the shop. Each window was five feet across on either side of the front door. Isla was right; the storm was closing in. Gray, angry clouds churned in the sky. It was time to return to my cottage at Duncreigan. I wanted to check the garden and make sure it was secure before the storm hit, and if I wanted to do that, I had to leave now. I could make the final touches to the shop tomorrow before the opening.

I moved away from the window. "I'm sorry for snapping at you. There is just a lot to do for tomorrow."

She brushed her hair back from her face. Even when she was sweaty, my sister was beautiful. Unlike me, she was petite and had plenty of curves. She hated her curves because the fashion magazines told her to. She had the perfect hourglass figure, which I, who was tall and narrow, had always envied. She was spunky, eight years younger than me, fresh out of college, and ready to conquer the world. I didn't so much want to conquer the world as make my profit margins for my new business, the Climbing Rose Flower Shop in Bellewick, Aberdeenshire, Scotland.

I had chosen the name Climbing Rose after the three-hundred-year-old rose growing in my garden back at Duncreigan. No, roses don't live for three hundred years . . . usually. Unless magic is involved. The name was a reminder to me. The flower shop might be the place I worked, but being the "Keeper of the Garden" was my real purpose. My godfather was counting on me to do it right.

"It's okay," she said, and gave me her bright sunny smile, which couldn't have been more different from the blackening sky outside. She removed her phone from the back pocket of her purposely ripped jeans and scrolled through the screen. Her rosebud mouth puckered into a frown.

"Something wrong?" I asked.

She shoved the phone back into her pocket. "No. I mean, other than the storm. I hate storms," she said, repeating her earlier sentiment.

"I know you do," I said gently. "Let me finish up these sunflowers, and we can leave. Everything else can wait for the morning."

She picked up the top box of vases. "Do you want these in the workroom?"

I nodded as I gathered up the sunflowers once more.

My sister went around the counter into the workroom, and I admired my shop. It was perfect with its cool, whitewashed stone walls and wide, pegged floorboards. One wall had a refrigerated flower case full of new arrangements, much like a cake decorator would have in her shop. I hoped that many of those arrangements would sell at the opening so I could fill that case with the custom flower orders I envisioned rolling in after the shop opened.

I'd paid a local carpenter to make the sales counter out of a large piece of driftwood. It had been a splurge to have a custom-made sales desk, but I hoped this was my last place of business, and I wanted it to be exactly how I wanted it. An iPad was docked on a stand at the counter in place of a cash register. It took up so much less space than a computer, which allowed more room to show customers their flower options instead of taking them back into my workroom. I glanced behind me at the second half of the shop. Shelves lined two opposing walls and were filled with all the materials I needed to run my business: wire, brackets, cloth, burlap, and twine. In the back of the room were the flowers sitting in large water-filled buckets waiting to be arranged. I'd decided to install a half door instead of a regular door because most of the time I would be the only person in the shop, and I wanted to be able to see what was going on out front when I had to work in the back.

Isla was in the middle of the workroom messing with her phone again, frowning. I assumed she was texting with someone back home. She didn't know many people in Aberdeenshire yet. She had been in Scotland only two weeks to the day when she showed up on my doorstep and declared she was spending the summer with me because she needed one last fun summer before she flung herself fully into adulthood. Knowing Isla, she would tell me all about the text messages later. She was a talker and made a point of letting everyone know what was on her mind, whether they wanted to or not.

The shop was better than anything I could have imagined. For ten years, I had run my own flower shop back in Nashville. I had done a good business until year eight when a chain flower shop had opened on the same street as mine. When I'd finally locked the door to my shop for the last time, I'd thought my career as a flower shop owner was over, but here I stood.

Much of my business at this point was based on hopes, dreams, and lots of hard work. I'd moved to Scotland two months ago to accept my unique inheritance from my godfather, Ian MacCallister. The bequest was unique indeed because it included a charming moorland cottage and a magical garden. The garden had been under the care of Uncle Ian's family

4

for centuries, and without any direct heir, he had passed the garden on to me. By my calculations, I was the twelfth Keeper of the Garden. The first Keeper had been Uncle Ian's ancestor, Baird MacCallister.

Baird had been a merchant sailor who lived in the early 1700s. He had no love for his homeland, and he planned to leave Scotland on a shipping voyage, never to return. But the sea had other plans. Baird's boat took off from Aberdeen harbor as planned, but a terrible storm whipped up over the sea and he never made it past the rocky cliff of the Scottish coast. Baird's ship was wrecked. All lives were lost expect Baird's. The sea spared him.

As he was tossed in the raging waves, he made a promise to the sea that if she let him live, he would remain in Scotland forever and help others, though at the time he didn't know how. He swore he would no longer be a selfish man. The sea accepted his vow and spit him onto the land. He landed at what would become Duncreigan, but at the time all that was there was the menhir, an ancient standing stone, with its yellow climbing rose wrapped tightly around it. Baird took the menhir and the rose as a sign that this was where the sea wanted him to remain, and to protect the stone and it's rose, he built a garden around them.

In the garden, the flowers and plants flourished year-round, living off the magic of the standing stone and the sea. Over the generations, the standing stone had bestowed gifts onto the garden's Keeper. Each gift was unique and was to be used only to help others. Hamish, my godfather's friend and the garden's caretaker when Uncle Ian was away, had been the one to tell me all this when I first arrived in Scotland. I wished I had heard it directly from my godfather, but I hadn't the chance, as he, a career solider for the Royal Army, had died in combat in Afghanistan. The only explanation my godfather had left me was a letter containing a set of three garden rules. Everything else I would have to learn on my own. It had been a steep learning curve, to say the least, and I hoped that opening this flower shop with the money my godfather had left me wasn't my first huge mistake as Keeper.

I shook these worries from my head. It was too late to second-guess now. I put the last sunflower in the vase and moved it to its spot at the end of the counter as Isla took the second box to the workroom.

I had spun on my heel to follow her when the small chime on the front door rang. Isla must have forgotten to lock the door behind her.

Pivoting back around, I prepared to tell the would-be customer that the shop wasn't open until the next day.

My friendly shopkeeper smile melted from my face when Minister Quaid MacCullen stepped through the door. Minister MacCullen happened to be the local parish rector for the village, and he also happened to hate my guts. He vocally disapproved of the MacCallister family and their garden, and since I was now the Keeper of the garden, he disapproved of me, too.

He wore black trousers and a shirt with a clerical collar under a black woolen coat and a perpetual scowl. Around his neck was a golden medallion the size of a silver dollar with a cross overlaid with intersecting rings in the middle of it.

The last time I had seen the minister had been exactly one week before on a Sunday morning when I had made the mistake of going to church. St. Thomas's, the parish church where Minister MacCullen was the pastor, had also been my godfather's church. In my quest to understand my godfather better, I had decided to attend, but I had been turned away. The minister met me at the church door and said, in front of his entire congregation, that I wasn't welcome. I had thought everyone was welcome at church, but in this case, I was not. I left without arguing with him, but the rejection and embarrassment cut deep, making me long for my church back in Nashville. Because of that whole experience, I didn't have the faintest idea what the minister was doing in my store this evening. It seemed it was the very last place he would want to be.

"I had heard the flower shop was reopening." He had a deep Scottish accent and spoke as if he were shouting from the pulpit.

"What can I help you with, Minister? I'm afraid we aren't open until tomorrow. The entire village is welcome to the opening. You are welcome as well," I managed to say with a straight face, although I hoped he wouldn't show.

His eyes formed into narrow slits that disappeared in his wrinkled face. "I didn't come here to see the shop. I have no interest in it."

"Then why are you here?"

He studied a grouping of canna lilies by the front window and wrinkled his nose. "I wanted to see with my own eyes if the rumors were true and you were opening a business in my village."

I dug my fingernails into the palm of my hand. "The village doesn't belong to you."

He shook his head. "That is where you're wrong. I am the village minister. Everyone who lives in the village, whether they come to Sunday morning services or not, is a member of my flock, and I don't want you confusing or corrupting them."

That hurt. A lot. I had neither expected nor deserved the minister's hostility, and while I understood that his intentions came from a good place, my Christian upbringing inspired me to look for the good in people rather than the worst. Okay, so maybe the rumors about my garden *were* true, and maybe my uncle hadn't exactly done anything to dispel them and the magic surrounding Duncreigan. But corruptors of the flock we were not.

My nails dug a little deeper, and I had to stop myself from pressing so hard I broke the skin. The minister had been worried about me corrupting the village from the moment I'd arrived in Aberdeenshire. He had an old grudge against Duncreigan and the MacCallister family, since we'd tended the garden at Duncreigan for so many centuries. Even though I wasn't a MacCallister, that grudge had been extended to me now that I had inherited the cottage and garden. There was nothing I could say that would change his mind about the MacCallisters and me, so I had stopped trying weeks ago.

But I'd never been a victim of such intense, unprovoked loathing before.

I caught sight of the top of the sheath of papers he held in his hand. In bold letters, it read, SAVE THE CHAPEL! The minister must have been out rustling up funds to conserve the village's first church building. I pointed at the stack of fliers. "Would you like me to hang one of those in the Climbing Rose?"

He curled up his bulbous nose. "No, I would not want this cultural project to be soiled by anyone from Duncreigan."

"Then I think it's time for you to leave. You have satisfied your curiosity and know I have a business here in the village. If that's all you were here to do, mission accomplished," I said. Behind him the sky outside grew even darker. "And I think it would be best if we both went home before this storm breaks. It looks like it's going to be a bad one."

The minister peered over his shoulder out the window and then back at me. "It won't be as bad as the fate you face, Fiona Knox. I can promise you that." He opened the front door to the shop, and one of the planters toppled over by the force of the wind coming through the opening. A small amount of dirt fell from the pot.

I didn't move to put the pot upright just yet. I was too taken aback by his words. "What do you mean by that?" I asked the minister.

He smiled at me in a *Grinch Who Stole Christmas* kind of way and went out the door without a word.

I grabbed the front door before it could close and held it open against the wind. "What do you mean?" I shouted at the minister's receding back, but my words were lost in a crack of thunder that didn't seem that far off. I had turned to go back into my shop when movement across the narrow cobblestone street caught my eye. A slender young man slid into the alleyway between two buildings, but I caught sight of him before he disappeared.

What was Seth MacGregor doing back in the village of Bellewick, and why did I find his appearance as foreboding as the minister's threat and the oncoming storm?

Chapter Two

"Just tell me. Are we going to die?" a muffled voice asked from under the stack of blankets draped over my bed.

A streak of lightning played across the lone window in the tiny bedroom that had barely enough space for the double bed on which I perched, a large wardrobe, and one chest of drawers. Not to mention my sister's three half-opened suitcases and my still-packed boxes. A crack of thunder so fierce it made my tooth fillings ache was almost immediately followed by another flash of light. The wind and rain pummeled the two-hundred-year-old cottage, and, if I was being honest, it sounded like the slate roof might be torn from the rafters above us.

But I placed my hand on the lump in the middle of my bed and said with as much confidence as I could muster, "No, we are not going to die." Because that's what big sisters always tell their baby sisters, even if they don't know it to be fact.

Isla wriggled under the covers as if she was finally considering coming up for some air. I knew that she had to be hot under all those blankets. But another crack of thunder came before she surfaced, and she wriggled back down into her fetal position.

I shook my head. If I hadn't been so worried about the storm myself, I would have laughed. But I was just as frightened as my sister, just not for the same reasons. I didn't think the storm advancing from the North Sea and over the black cliffs to the glens of Scotland would rip the cottage from the earth and toss us *Wizard of Oz* style into the land of Munchkins—or at least that was my hope. The cottage had been in the same place for centuries and had faced many storms just as fierce as this one, but how was the garden, *my* garden, faring?

I wondered because the garden was my responsibility. I was its Keeper. The Keeper of the Garden was the title my godfather, Ian MacCallister, had placed on me in his will, and tending his garden had a lot more to it than watering and weeding. It was of paramount importance that I keep the garden safe from storms that might ravage it and from people who might want to hurt it, such as the minister. His thinly veiled threat earlier that day still floated in the back of my mind. What had he meant when he'd said, "It won't be as bad as the fate you face"? What did he have in store for me or for this place I had grown to love?

I looked out my bedroom window in the direction of my garden. I prayed that it would be all right. It was too dangerous to go out and check just then, as much as I wanted too. There was a real risk of becoming lost in the storm, and if I abandoned Isla in that way, she would never forgive me.

Another crack of thunder shook the cottage, and Isla moaned in her hiding place. The wind howled outside and the windows rattled in their frames. The fox head–shaped knocker on the forest-green front door banged against the weathered wood over and over again.

I patted the lump that was my sister. "Are you going to come out of there?"

"No," she said in a muffled but defiant voice. "Not until it's safe. I'm too young to die, and we haven't even made our shopping trip to Edinburgh that you promised me we would take before I went back to Tennessee. It's so not fair! I could have at least passed on knowing I had bought the perfect outfit on Princes Street! It's just not fair."

I was about to console her when Ivanhoe, my gray striped Scottish Fold cat, jumped onto the bed and on top of my sister. Isla screamed.

Ivanhoe hopped off her and walked the length of the bed until he was sitting next to me. The cat tilted his head as if to ask, "What's wrong with her?"

"The storm," I whispered to him.

He gave me a slow blink, which I knew meant he understood me. Like all cat lovers, I believed my feline was particularly brilliant.

"Are you talking to the cat about me?" Isla demanded from the recesses of the blankets.

"Isla, he's worried about you and wants you to come out from under there." I patted where I thought her head might be.

The cat meowed as if to reinforce my statement. I smiled at him and gave him a thumbs-up sign in return. I appreciated the support.

The lump in the bed began to wiggle again, and finally, after what seemed like forever, Isla's sweaty head appeared from under the covers. She glared at me. "I can't believe you got me to come all the way out to the middle-of-nowhere Scotland only to die. What kind of big sister are you?" Her honey-blonde hair stuck up every which way, like she had taken a balloon and rubbed it all over her head to see how static electricity worked.

"First of all, if I remember correctly, I didn't *make* you come here. You just showed up on my doorstep and yelled, 'Surprise! I'm going to live with you for the summer!'"

She threw back the blanket. "You don't want me here?"

I sighed and pushed my wavy black hair out of my face. "I never said that. Of course I want you here, but you can't blame me for you being here. It was your idea."

"What did you expect me to do, stay at the farm with Mom and Dad? And wasn't I a good surprise? I'm your sister. Your only sister."

I tucked a lock of her hair behind her ear, just as I had when she was a little girl. Because Isla was so much younger than me, I was much more like a favorite aunt than a sister to her. "You were a good surprise," I said. "It's been hard to be this far away from home. It's nice to have someone from my old life here."

"Old life?" she asked. "You sound like you never plan to go back home."

I didn't, at least not permanently, but I wasn't going to confirm her fears when she was already upset by the storm.

Bang! Bang! Bang! The fox knocker thudded against the front door, but the rhythmic knocks did not sound like they had been caused by the howling wind.

Isla screamed again and made a dive back under the blankets.

I caught her before she could fully submerge. "If you go back under there, you will suffocate. It's just the knocker hitting the door in the wind."

Bang! Bang! Bang!

"That's not the wind, Fi!" Isla shrieked.

I stood up and started toward the bedroom door.

Isla shot up in the bed and grabbed my wrist. "You can't go out there! It could be a madman, a mad Scottish man, think Braveheart—not in a hot kind of way but in a he-could-kill-me kind of way."

"Isla, seriously, get a grip. There is no Scottish madman at Duncreigan," I said.

Ivanhoe walked up and down the bed with his gaze fixed on the open bedroom door. If I hadn't been sure someone was outside the cottage before, my cat's reaction convinced me.

I extracted my hand from my sister's death grip. "Ivanhoe, stay here with Isla."

Isla moaned and slid back under the blankets. As I was leaving the room, her arm snaked out from under the covers and pulled Ivanhoe under the blankets with her.

There was a meow and hiss in protest, then nothing. I entered the main room of the cottage, which was a living room, dining room, and kitchen combination. The largest feature of the space was the stone fireplace. Above the mantel, the painting of Uncle Ian's ancestor Baird MacCallister, the merchant sailor who had washed up on this land, hung. Some days, I wasn't sure how I felt about Baird, since he was the one who had tied the MacCallisters and now me to Duncreigan all those centuries ago.

At the moment, the view of the hearth was obscured by a stack of boxes that came up to my waist. There were similar piles in every corner. After I had decided to move to Scotland permanently, I'd asked my mother to ship my clothes to Scotland. It seemed that my mother had gone to my storage space in Nashville and shipped as many boxes as she could afford. I had yet to find an actual box of clothing, though.

The banging on the front door intensified. I grabbed a poker from the fireplace and approached the door, keeping my stance wide and grounded as if I planned to hit a home run at SunTrust Park. I didn't agree with my sister that it was a madman at the door. The poker was merely a precaution. "Who's there?" I called.

There was a howl in response. Whatever words there might have been were lost in the storm. I adjusted my grip on the poker. "What do you want?"

Again, the wind grabbed the words and took them away.

There was only one way for me to find out what was on the other side of the door. I took a deep breath, unlocked the door, and pulled on the handle with my right hand. The poker was in my left hand, raised and ready to strike.

I cracked open the door.

"Miss Fiona?" A tired voice asked.

I dropped the poker onto the worn wood floor. "Hamish, oh my God! What are you doing out there on a night like this?" I grabbed the wet sleeve of his raincoat and pulled him inside. After Hamish was safely in the cottage, I slammed the door closed and locked it.

Hamish MacGregor, Duncreigan's caretaker, stood in front of me dripping on the floor. Hamish was a stout, elderly man with a puglike nose who had worked for the MacCallister family for as long as anyone could remember.

He removed his yellow raincoat and specks of water went flying every which way, including on me. It was as bad as a dog shaking out his coat after a bath. "Miss Fiona, you are all right?"

I wiped water from my face. "I'm fine, Hamish. What are you doing here?"

He removed his yellow rain hat. "I came to check on you and Miss Isla. This is the worst storm we've had since you've come to Duncreigan. I was worried sick about you, so Duncan and I came here to check." Hamish reached into his fisherman's sweater and came out with a damp-looking red squirrel. Duncan blinked at me, then scrambled to the top of Hamish's shoulder.

Isla stepped out of my bedroom with an unhappy-looking Ivanhoe tucked under one arm and a curling iron in the other. Clearly she was approaching the situation armed and ready should the need arise.

Duncan's tail puffed up as soon as he saw the cat. The two animals were always at odds, mostly because Ivanhoe wished to eat the squirrel and spent a large portion of his lazy days plotting a strategy to accomplish that life goal.

"As you can see, all three of us are fine," I said.

Hamish nodded. "Good, good. Now that I see you are all right, I had better be back on my way home."

"You are not going back out into that storm," I said. "You can stay here tonight if you don't mind bunking on the couch. Isla and I can share the bed."

He started to argue, but I held up my hand. "Please, Hamish." I picked up the poker and put it back on the stand beside the fireplace. "I'll gather up sheets and blankets and make you up a nice bed." I turned to my sister. "Isla, can you make Hamish a warm cup of tea? That will help get the chill off from the rain."

She hoisted Ivanhoe onto her shoulder. "Sure, but I'm going to need something harder than that to recover from tonight."

"A nip of whiskey would do me better, miss," Hamish said.

Isla grinned. "I knew that I liked you, Hamish." She set the cat on the floor and made a beeline for the kitchen cabinet where I kept provisions for just such a time.

I shook my head and went into the bedroom for the extra sheets and blankets. When I came back into the front room, Hamish and Isla were sitting on the moss-green couch sharing a nip of Scotch.

Hamish sipped from his tumbler. "We used to say on a night like this that the sea wants a life, and she will take it."

Isla's mouth fell open. "You mean like someone is going to die?"

"The sea always gets what she wants. Always." Hamish stared into his drink as if he were considering the ocean itself.

Another bolt of lightning lit up the cottage, followed closely by a crack of thunder. Isla whimpered.

I dropped the load I was carrying on the arm of the couch. "Hamish, please don't tell my impressionable sister any ghost stories tonight. Save them for a sunny day."

He nodded, but his brow stayed furrowed in worry. "The sun will come again in the morning. We should all get some rest."

We finished our whiskey to that.

Later, when I lay on the bed next to my sister, I chewed my

lip and worried over whether or not I should tell Hamish I'd seen his great-nephew Seth in the village. Seth and Hamish had a complicated relationship and as far as I knew were the only family either of them had. Hamish had promised his dying brother that he would care for his grandson. Duncreigan's caretaker had taken that vow to the extreme and even gone to drastic measures to support Seth through medical school. However, Seth had dropped out of school to follow environmental pursuits and used Hamish's money to support his gambling habit. Hamish had been hurt when he learned the truth. But when Seth had promised to return to school, Hamish had yet again agreed to support him. At that moment, Seth was supposed to be in medical school in Aberdeen, the capital of Aberdeenshire.

The county seat of Aberdeen was only thirty minutes away. It was an easy trip. There was no reason for me to suspect Seth was up to something or cheating Hamish again. Maybe I was just projecting my own trust issues left over from my broken engagement onto Seth. Hamish believed his grandnephew when he said he would go back to school, and the wisest thing for me to do would be to stay out of it.

I pulled my phone out from under my pillow. There was a text message. That was odd; not many of my friends back home in Tennessee had my new UK number.

The text said it was from Chief Inspector Neil Craig, and my heart fluttered. I had met the police officer the day I arrived at Duncreigan and discovered a dead body in my godfather's magical garden. Craig had wrongly assumed my guilt in the murder but had eventually come around to see I was innocent after a little sleuthing by yours truly. Since the incident, I had seen him around the village off and on. Bad storm, the text said. Checking in to see if you are okay.

The text had been sent over an hour ago, and Craig had been waiting all that time for a response from me? Or he hadn't. Craig was chief inspector in Aberdeenshire working out of the city of Aberdeen. As an officer of the law, he must have been hard at work on a night with such a terrible storm. It would be all-hands-on-deck at the police station in Aberdeen to make sure everyone was safe, but he had still texted me to see if I was all right. He had texted *me*.

I stared at the screen for a long moment, trying to craft the perfect response that would sound interested but not *too* interested. If Isla were awake, she would have accused me of over-thinking again. Isla never overthought. That's how she had ended up in Scotland. She'd bought a plane ticket with her college graduation money and had been on the flight eastward the next day. There were very few times in my life when I had done something without weighing all the pros and cons, and that included texting a handsome Scottish chief inspector.

"Get it together, Knox," I whispered to myself.

Before I could change my mind, I texted, All is well at Duncreigan. Thanks.

The immediate response back was Good. And that was all. The simple Good left me feeling slightly disappointed, and I worried what that Good meant all night long as the rain and wind pelted the slate roof of my cottage.

Chapter Three

Before dawn, while my sister was still sleeping, I slipped out of bed. In the main room of the cottage, I found Hamish and Duncan gone. The pair must have left sometime in the middle of the night when the storm died down. I wasn't surprised—Hamish would have been so uncomfortable with the idea of sleeping on my couch that I doubted he'd gotten a wink of sleep all night, and Duncan was never at ease in Ivanhoe's vicinity. Speaking of the cat, the Scottish Fold wove around my legs, requesting breakfast even though it was much earlier than when I normally fed him.

"Since I'm up, you think that I should feed you, don't you?" I asked.

The round-faced cat looked up at me and meowed. As if to say, "You got that right, Human."

I sighed as I opened a can of cat food and placed it in his dish. "Sometimes, I feel like little more than a human can opener for you." I set the dish on the floor.

Ivanhoe didn't bother to reply. He already had his flat face buried in the bowl of food. I left the cat to his meal.

Outside the cottage, the fir tree that stood by the cottage was upright. The fox-head knocker that had rapped against the door all night long remained intact, and the area immediately around the cottage seemed to be fine. Leaves and branches were scattered over the grounds, but a little raking would make short work of that. I was relieved to see that the cottage was also in one piece, but the house wasn't my primary concern. The garden was. The garden always was.

I was careful not to step on any of the granite rocks that peeked out from the glen that separated the cottage from the garden. Over the last several weeks, I had learned I could make the trek from the cottage to the garden without stepping on a single one.

I glanced behind me and back at the cottage and stared. A man walked behind the cottage and away from the garden. It wasn't uncommon to see hikers wander through Duncreigan. There was a hiking path through the mountains only a half mile from here, and from time to time, hikers would wander off the path. But I didn't think it was a hiker.

The person faced away from me, as he was going in the opposite direction, but I couldn't help but wonder if it was Seth MacGregor. He was the right build and height. Was I thinking that just because I had seen Seth in the village the evening before? And was he on his way to speak to Hamish? Part of me wanted to go after him and ask him what he was doing there. In the short time I had lived in Scotland, Hamish had grown very dear to me, and I hated to think how his great-nephew had hurt him.

I shook my head. It was up to Hamish and Seth to figure

out their relationship. I had nothing to do with it. Seth—if it was Seth—disappeared out of view and I turned back in the direction of the garden.

While I stood there in indecision, dampness soaked through my sneakers and into my socks from the wet grass. I should have thought to wear my puddle boots to visit the garden, but I had been so eager I'd grabbed the first pair of shoes I could find.

My toes curled in from the cold, but there was no way I was going back to change my footwear now as the stone wall that surrounded the garden, eight inches thick and seven feet tall, came into view.

Lush green ivy crawled along the wall's length in every direction. The round, centuries-old wooden door that I knew was there was completely blocked from view by the ivy. When I reached the garden, I removed the skeleton key that was my entry into both the cottage and the garden from my pocket. Pushing my hand and the key through the tangle of vines, I searched for the lock and fit the key into place. I turned my wrist to the left, once, twice, and pushed the door open.

I ducked my head under the ivy and stepped into my garden.

The first thing I noticed about the garden were the colors. The English-style flower beds that grew in complementary bunches around the garden were bursting with colors. My eyes were assaulted with pinks, purples, yellows, oranges, blues, and so, so much green. The garden shimmered with green. The large willow tree, which marked the halfway point in the garden and was the overseer of all the other growing things, glistened with raindrops on its millions of tiny drooping leaves.

This place took my breath away, just as it always did. When I had visited Duncreigan as a little girl, my godfather had taken me into the garden, and I had fallen in love with it and all its flowers. It was his magical garden. Now, it was mine.

As much as I had thought the garden was magical when I was a child, I hadn't known that it *actually* held magic until recently. Now I had the burden of caring for the garden and using the magic that it contained to help others. Unfortunately, except for a brief letter from my godfather telling me that I was the Keeper and a list containing a handful of guidelines, the magic and the garden didn't come with an instructional manual. It seemed that I would have to figure out how to use the magic on my own. I hoped I was up to the task. My godfather seemed to believe I would be, but I wasn't so sure. I'd had a string of failures that were constant reminders of my shortcomings. One was my failed flower shop in Nashville. The second was my failed engagement, the one where my wannabe country music star fiancé left me for our wedding cake decorator. I'd had a strong aversion to cake after that incident, and there would be no cake at my flower shop opening.

After observing the garden's beauty, I noticed minor damage from the storm. Flowers bent on their thin stalks, some with their blossoms touching the ground, and tree branches and leaves had been thrown every which way. It might be a magical garden, but it was still a garden in the truest sense of the word, a living entity that had to be cared for as such. My godfather had been very clear on that in the few instructions he left me.

It would take some work to clean up after the storm, but

I didn't think it would take more than a day. Hamish would be here in less than an hour and set straight to work. He cared as much about the garden as I did.

I had bent to pick up some of the fallen sticks when I heard a stick snap. I looked up and found myself eye to eye with the resident fox.

I smiled. "Hello, Uncle Ian. I'm glad to see you are all right."

The fox blinked his blue eyes at me. I wasn't sure how I knew that the fox was my godfather, but I knew it down to my bones. I had tried to convince the animal speak to me many times, but apparently he had nothing to say or the magic didn't work that way. The stone hadn't given me the ability to speak to animals, which was a pity.

"I was afraid something might have happened to you in the storm." I left the sticks where they were on the ground and straightened.

The fox took a step closer to me. The fox had my godfather's eyes, which I know sounds crazy. And, if I was being honest, I could have sworn that the fox didn't just have traits of Uncle Ian—those inquisitive looks and blue eyes, that mischievous grin. I reached out my hand, but he pivoted away toward the hedgerow and around the side of it.

Around the hedge, the menhir stood with its faded triskele, a three-pronged ancient Celtic spiral, carved in the stone, and the yellow rose entwined around it. By looking at the menhir alone, I never would have known that there had been such a fierce storm the night before.

Something about the stone drew me to it, and I held out

my hand as if to touch it. The fox jumped between me and the menhir. That was when I saw the two withered rose petals at the foot of the standing stone. I shivered. What could this mean? In the time that I had been taking care of the garden, the rose had always bloomed. Nary a petal had fallen from the vine in all that time, but now those two petals lay in the bright green grass.

I bent to pick them up, and the fox growled at me softly. I wasn't afraid that he would hurt me, but I pulled my hand back in any case. The fallen petals meant that trouble was coming. I wasn't certain how, but I knew it in my bones just as I knew the true identity of the fox. But what kind of trouble, I didn't know.

Perhaps the menhir could tell me, but I was hesitant to touch it. I remembered the instructions my godfather had left me in the letter before he died.

Rule #1: It's important that you and the garden stay connected. You must visit it as much as possible in your early days. In time, you will be able to leave it for longer periods, as I did.

Rule #2: The garden should be cared for and treated like any other garden. You must water, weed, and feed it. The better cared for the garden is, the stronger your connection with it will grow. Hamish will help you as he helped me.

But the most important rule was the third and final one.

Death and Daisies

Rule #3: The menhir and the rose are the heart of the garden and the source of the magic. They were there first, and everything else grew up around them. They are your true connection to the magic. To know what the garden wants you to know, you must touch the stone. Do not approach this task lightly. You will see things that you may not want to see.

I had to take care when touching the stone because I might have visions I didn't want. And it seemed the fox version of my godfather wasn't ready for me to see any at the moment. Today was the opening of the Climbing Rose. Whatever trouble was coming for me, it could wait.

I nodded. "All right. All right." I stepped back from the stone.

I wished I could spend all day in the garden trimming, weeding, and planting, but I had a flower shop opening to get to. I said good-bye to the fox and left the garden.

Three hours later, Isla sat in the passenger seat as I drove my car under the stone arch that marked the entrance into the village and around the roundabout with the seven-foot-tall bronze unicorn in the middle of it. I drove my new silver Astra over the stone bridge into the residential part of the village, parking on a side street that had free parking. It made for a bit of a walk to the flower shop, but as a new business owner, I had to save every penny I could. I couldn't be feeding a parking meter every couple of hours.

"I'll never get used to sitting on the wrong side of the car," Isla said as she opened the passenger door. The car was a third

27

of the size of the SUV I'd owned and sold back home in Nashville. However, it was much more practical for the narrow roads and tight parking spots in Scotland. I would have been terrified to drive anything larger than a toaster in the United Kingdom.

"You would be surprised what you can get used to." I opened my own car door. I had been living in Scotland for less than two months, and Duncreigan already felt like home to me.

Isla shivered and rubbed her bare arms. "It's freezing this morning. Doesn't the calendar know it's July?"

I laughed. "This is July in Scotland, Isla, not in Tennessee. It's never going to be as hot here as it gets back home. You should have worn a jacket."

"I refuse to wear a jacket in July. It goes against everything I stand for."

I simply shook my head. There was no arguing with my sister when she made a statement like that.

I opened the car's trunk and removed the boxes of supplies that I wanted to take to my shop. I handed two of the boxes to my sister.

She eyed the boxes. "Those look heavy."

I laughed. "It's mostly tulle and wire for flower arranging. You're not going to break your back carrying them to the shop."

She sighed. "I guess not."

We walked back over the bridge into the main part of town. The creek that ran under the bridge was high and the water moved swiftly under our feet. I wondered if perhaps the bridge troll that I imagined lived there had been washed away in the storm. The unicorn statue that reared up on the roundabout didn't look any worse for wear after the storm. A troll bridge and a unicorn in the town center. The Scots liked their legends, which made me smile, thinking that Duncreigan was a part of that lore too.

A tree that had been overlooking the creek lay in two pieces, its top doused in the debris that filled the creek. Damp leaves and tree limbs were scattered all over the cobblestone roads and the sidewalk. Two village workmen collected fallen branches along the roads, while a third revved the engine of his chainsaw and approached a fallen tree.

"Looks like there was a little storm damage after all," my sister said over the grind of the chainsaw. "I think Duncreigan got off easy."

I bit my lip, praying that my shop was intact. Part of me feared a tree limb had sliced through the front window, allowing the wind and rain inside. I'd put everything, including the entirety of my savings and a large portion of the money I'd inherited from my godfather, into opening the shop.

I adjusted the boxes in my arms and hurried past the small Tesco and the laundromat. I knew I wouldn't relax until I knew that everything at the Climbing Rose was all right.

As the shop came into view, the bright-yellow awning that I'd added to the facade jutted out from the building and shaded the large front windows. It had taken some convincing of the village council to allow me to vary the building, but they'd finally agreed. The awning protected the flowers in the front window displays from the heat of the afternoon sun, which would be too direct in the west-facing window. I wasn't going to sell any flowers if the only ones that passersby could see were wilted by the sun.

Villagers made their way to the Twisted Fox, the local pub on the corner just beyond my shop, for breakfast. I made a mental note to stop in later for a scone and a bit of tea once I checked to make sure my shop was okay. I always like to say hello to Raj Kapoor, the sixty-something barkeep owner of the pub as well as the owner of the only laundromat in the village. He and his kind twin sister, Presha, had become two of my closest friends since I'd moved to Scotland. It also helped that they owned two of the best eateries in the village. Presha owned and operated Presha's Teas. I never had to worry where I would find my next meal in the village.

I had been lucky to find the space right next door to the Twisted Fox, which was the most popular place in all of Bellewick. In addition to the Twisted Fox and Presha's Teas, there were two walkup food stands in the harbor. One sold meat pies and the other fish and chips. For a full breakfast, lunch, and dinner menu, the Twisted Fox was it.

I came to a halt in front of my shop. The yellow awning was safely in place with THE CLIMBING ROSE FLOWER SHOP emblazoned in black letters across it. My blue-and-white window display of hydrangeas, peonies, daisies, canna lilies, and bachelor buttons was just how I'd left it. The bright-blue front door was also intact, and the rose-shaped knocker, which I had installed myself, was still there. Everything was how we'd left it the evening before the storm hit. All was well.

Isla caught up with me on the sidewalk. "Is there a reason we're running? I'm carrying boxes here."

"We only have a few hours before the party. There's a lot to do," I said. "I think—"

"Look!" Isla interrupted me and pointed at the door. There was a piece of parchment paper tucked between the closed door and the doorjamb.

My sister plucked the paper from the door and showed it to me. Across the back, my name was written in precise lettering. I reached for the paper, but my sister held it away from me.

"It could be from the adorable chief inspector who has a crush on you." She danced on the sidewalk. "You will have your own Scottish love story a la *Outlander* without the hassle of time travel." She pressed the back of her hand against her forehead as if in a swoon.

"Chief Inspector Craig does not have a crush on me." I tried to grab the note from her hand, but she was too quick. The text message Craig had sent me the night before came to mind, but there was no way I was telling her about that. It hadn't meant anything. Craig was just a nice police officer, checking in on a new citizen under his jurisdiction. That was all. I held out my hand. "Isla, please give me the note."

She shook her head and dropped her hand from her forehead. "I won't read your love note. I just want to know if I am right in guessing who it might be from." She started to unfold the parchment.

"Isla! Mom would be very disappointed in your manners right now." I set my boxes down.

"Mom's back on the farm feeding the chickens. She'll never know." She raised her brow. "And why do you care if I know who it's from? I thought sisters aren't supposed to have any secrets. Is Craig your secret from me?"

"Shh," I hissed, and looked around me.

Villagers strolled up and down the street. It was Monday morning, and many of them were on their way to work or out on an early walk. The last thing I wanted was a rumor to circulate about Craig and me in the village. Although Chief Inspector Craig no longer lived in Bellewick, he'd grown up in the village and was here often.

Isla unfolded the note and began to read.

"Isla, you shouldn't read other people's notes!"

Her usually pale face blanched until her skin was the same shade of white as a boiled egg.

"Isla, what is it?" I asked.

She looked up at me with huge eyes. "It's not a love note."

Chapter Four

M y brow wrinkled, and I took the piece of folded paper from her shaking hand. "Let me see."

I unfolded the note. It read, *The garden is not what you think. It will destroy you as it has others. Let this be a lesson to you. I write this for your sake.* The note was signed, *The Reverend Quaid MacCullen.*

My stomach clenched, but I forced a laugh. "It's just a message from Minister MacCullen. He's not a fan of Duncreigan or the garden." I waved the note. "Maybe he's trying to be nice."

"Not a big deal? He cursed you! Like for real!" She took a step back from me. "He put some Scottish voodoo on you. I had better keep my distance."

"No one has the power to curse someone. That's absolutely ridiculous. Minister MacCullen is all talk, and I'm certain that he would be offended if he knew that you called his supposed curse Scottish voodoo. There's nothing of the kind." I said this as much for my own benefit as for Isla's. "I'm not going to let him ruin opening day."

She stepped closer to me. "That's right, sister, and I'm here to help you." She paused. "But if your hair starts falling out or something, I bounce."

I rolled my eyes. "Thanks for the support, Sis."

I unlocked the door and was happy to see that everything was just as I had left it. The flowers were arranged to perfection and ready for their big debut. The light coming through the two large windows played off their brightly colored petals and shone off their waxy leaves.

I would make this shop a success. I promised myself that as I crushed the folded note from the minister in my hand. It would be much easier to do if I didn't have outside complications, such as a minister who thought that the garden, and me by extension, were somehow evil. It seemed to me that the minister was the only one who felt that way about Duncreigan. All the villagers knew Baird's story, the history of the place, and that the garden's flowers continued to grow even in the deepest and darkest moments of winter. They just accepted that was the way things were at Duncreigan. Apparently, the minister could not.

I walked into the workroom with my boxes and set them on the island. I dropped the note from the minister in the middle of the work island as well. I would deal with it later or not at all. Minister MacCullen had hated Duncreigan long before I came along. I didn't know what I could do to make it any better.

"Where should I put these?" Isla stepped into the room, still carrying her boxes from the car.

"Set those there," I told my sister. "One of them has tulle inside. I would like to use it for some of the last-minute arrangements I'm making."

Isla dropped the box in the general area I asked her to. "Have you heard from Mom and Dad?"

I shook my head.

Before she went back into the showroom, my sister said, "I think it's lame they aren't here for your opening. They should be."

I winced because I had thought the same thing more than once. I wanted my parents to be here to see what I had been able to accomplish in a very short time. But they had seemed more distant than ever since I'd moved to Scotland, and I didn't think it was the geographical distance that was making them hold back. There was something more to it than that. I just didn't know what. "You know July is a busy time on the farm. It's hard for Mom and Dad to get away," I called after her.

My younger sister popped her head into the workroom and snorted. "They could have gotten away if they wanted to. If you ask me, they didn't come because they don't want to face the fact that Uncle Ian is dead. He was like a brother to them both. They just can't deal with it, and maybe they thought they should have inherited Duncreigan and not you."

I didn't want to think that any possible resentment lingered from Uncle Ian's will. I knew my parents were happy for me. Although I also knew they would much rather have me living close by in the States. As for the shop opening, I tended to think it was their grief over Uncle Ian's death that kept them at bay. Rather than sharing my thoughts, I turned to Isla and quirked a brow. "Those are pretty deep ideas, Isla."

"Hey, I'm a college graduate. I think deep thoughts." She removed her phone from her pocket and frowned at the screen.

I stifled a smile because I didn't want her to think I was laughing at her. "Let's get ready for the opening," I said as I inhaled the sweet fragrance of the flowers and immediately felt my body begin to relax.

I hoped to do flowers for weddings, parties, and social events throughout the county. The toughest part was going to be getting my name out there—so far no one in Aberdeenshire had ever heard of me.

The shop opened at ten, so I had to have everything ready for the party before then because I would have to be available in case any customers wandered in. The party was set for two o'clock. It was time to get to work.

Around one in the afternoon, I tucked another vase full of blue hydrangeas in the large window display and stepped back, admiring my work. It was perfect.

I was in the middle of patting myself on the back when Presha floated in. My friend pushed a metal cart that was stacked high with white bakery boxes with one hand. In the other hand, she held a large paper cup of her fragrant chai. She handed me the chai. "I thought you could use this."

I held the drink under my nose and inhaled the sweet and spicy scent. Presha's chai was strong, much stronger than any I'd had back in the States, but over the last several weeks I had become accustomed to it. If I ever ordered chai back home again, I knew it would be too weak for my taste.

Presha was a sixty-something Indian woman who had been living in Bellewick for over forty years. She and Raj had left their home country for the United Kingdom decades ago, and somehow landed in the seaside village. Bellewick was certainly off the beaten path, and I had never heard the full story of how they had picked this tiny fishing village when they had so many other choices.

She had long black hair that had thin streaks of silver running throughout, and like her brother, she had high cheek-bones and deep-set brown eyes.

I held up the cup. "Thank you. I really did need it."

"I thought you might." She winked at me. "Where's your sister? I thought she'd be here with you helping out."

I glanced around. Isla wasn't there. I moved to the back of the room and peeked in the workroom. She wasn't there either.

Normally, this wouldn't have bothered me. But I was wound so tight over the opening and the note that the minister had left that I was more than a little irritated.

I forced a laugh. "She probably got bored and went for a walk. Or maybe went to call one of her friends back home. She's been playing with her phone a lot."

Presha studied me with her dark eyes for a full minute. I did my best not to squirm under her closer scrutiny.

Just when I thought she was going to ask me what was really going on, she asked, "How was the garden after the storm?"

I gave a sigh of relief. Talking about my magical garden was far more comfortable than talking about Minister Mac-Cullen. "All is well."

"And Ian?" she asked.

"He was okay too."

Presha was the only person with whom I'd shared suspicions of the fox's true identity. As a Hindu, she found the concept of my godfather returning in the form of a fox less alarming than others might have. Heck, *I* still found it alarming.

She smiled. "You saw him again."

I nodded. "This morning. I wonder if he will always be there when I go to the garden. Part of me is afraid that one day I'll go back and he will be gone."

She wheeled her cart to the long table I had set in front of the wall opposite the refrigerated case and started to move the white bakery boxes to the table. "Ian will stay as long as he feels you need him. When he feels all is well, he will move on."

I wasn't sure how I felt about that. I wanted all to be well, but I liked seeing the fox every day when I visited the garden. At the same time, I didn't like the fact that he was still around because that meant that things were not well. The question remained, would things get worse before they got better?

Presha arranged the pastries and cookies she'd provided from her tea shop for the opening on the table. When I offered my help, she shooed me away, and I floated back to fussing over my display window and prayed that villagers would show up for the party. There would be nothing worse than if no one showed up at all.

Just before the party began, my sister reappeared, coming into the showroom through the back door.

"Isla, where have you been?" I asked.

She blinked at me. "I went for a walk."

Presha made last touches to the table and glanced over her shoulder at us. I smiled at her, and she turned back around.

I lowered my voice to a whisper. "Why didn't you tell me you were leaving?"

"You had everything under control. There really wasn't

anything for me to do." She shrugged. "Sorry. Next time I'll say something."

"Where did you go?" I asked. I couldn't help but notice that her cheeks were pinker than normal. It was the way they got when she was keeping something to herself or when she was outright lying. Why would my sister be lying to me about going for a walk?

"I went to the harbor." She stiffened. "I don't know why it's such a big deal." She folded her arms. "I know I'm your little sister, but you act like I'm always up to something. Is that really fair?"

I pressed my lips together in a straight line. "I—I didn't know that you felt that way."

She wouldn't make eye contact with me. "Well, I do. Not all of us can have our lives all put together like you do. You need to let me be me. I already have one mother, I don't need a second one."

"I wouldn't say I have my life all put together. I'm starting over here."

She shook her head. "But you have a plan of how to start over, and sometimes I feel like you're frustrated with me because I don't always have a plan."

"I didn't know that you felt that way," I repeated quietly.

She looked at me with her big blue eyes again. "I have always felt that way, Fi. You would know that if you took the time to pay attention."

I winced. Her words stung. I thought I *had* been paying attention to Isla. I certainly had paid more attention to her than our parents had over the years.

Our parents were wrapped up in each other to the point that they often excluded their children. And if it wasn't each other, it was the farm that came in second place. The farm that had been in my mother's family for generations, and she was determined to keep it viable. Both Isla and I had been a great disappointment to her when neither of us showed any interest in continuing in that tradition.

I shook my head. "I'm sorry. I'm just a ball of nerves over the opening. I shouldn't have snapped at you like that."

She frowned. "You worry too much, Fi. You're over thirty now; you should really try to calm down. You need to worry about you blood pressure at your age."

"Fiona," Presha said in her soothing voice. "The village is here."

I turned away from my sister and back in the direction of the front of the shop. My heart swelled as I saw two dozen villagers come through the front door. Many of them carried cards and gifts. It was far more than I had ever expected. Minister MacCullen might not want me in Bellewick, but the rest of the village was welcoming me with open arms. Their warm smiles and cheerful congratulations warmed my heart.

I knew the opening would be a success. Isla had been right. I had been worried for no reason. It wasn't until later that I realized I had all the reason in the world to worry.

Chapter Five

The visitors milled around the shop, smelled the flowers, and munched on the scones, cookies, and cupcakes that Presha had been so kind to provide. To drink, I had lemonade, Presha's chai, and coffee. I even made a few small bouquet sales. I hoped this would be just the beginning of my sales in the village. It was far too early to tell, and I tried to follow my sister's advice and put those worries out of my head.

"Everything looks so beautiful. You should be so proud," a round and red-cheeked woman said to me.

I thanked her.

She held out her hand. "My name is Mary Macintosh. My daughter is getting married in the fall, and as you can imagine, we are in the midst of the planning, which can be quite a challenge because she and her fiancé live in London. However, they are getting married here in Bellewick. I was wondering what you charge to do flowers for such an event?"

My pulse quickened. This was what I had hoped would come out of the party. One big event could be just the thing to put me on the map. I tried to sound eager about the job, but

I didn't want to come off as desperate. "My prices vary, of course, on the number of flowers and varieties that you would like. I would be happy to meet with you and your daughter to have a flower consultation, free of charge."

She clapped her hands. "Would you? That would be just delightful. I'll call my daughter tonight and ask her when would be a good time for her to come up. There is so much to do for the wedding; she will be back and forth between here and London quite a bit this summer."

I handed her one of my cards. "Just give me a call when you're ready."

Mary smiled. "I most certainly will."

"I was wondering the same thing for the price of arrangements," a voice said behind me. "Your work is so lovely."

I turned to find a slender woman with silky brown hair that fell in perfect waves around her oval face. She wore a pink blouse and tweed pencil skirt. She completed the outfit with nude pumps and silver beaded necklace. On her right arm was a gorgeous bright-pink Valentino purse. In her left hand she held a basket that was full to bursting with tea, honey, spun wool, and handmade cards.

"I'm Emer Boyd. I'm the official chairwoman of the village's welcome committee. We are so happy to have you in our little village. This flower shop has stood empty for far too long. We are delighted that someone with so much experience has come here to revive and start a new business. This is for you." She held out the basket. "It's just a little welcome basket from the community. Everything in there is made by local shopkeepers."

"Thank you so much. That's very kind of you."

"It's my pleasure. The village is so pleased you're here. My husband and I were very happy to hear that the flower shop was reopening as well. There were many times that Douglas wished there was a place nearby to purchase flowers for the school, and it's too much of a hassle to drive all the way to Aberdeen City to purchase the flowers. Your being here will be a great help!"

For the first time, I noticed a man standing behind her about an arm's length away. He was bald, at least five inches taller than Emer, and outweighed her by thirty pounds. Even so, he was the more diminutive of the couple. Dark circles hovered under his gray eyes. He stood back and let his wife do all the talking.

She beamed at her husband. "Douglas is the head teacher at the school. The children and parents absolutely love him." She squeezed his arm.

Douglas's face turned beet red. "Emer, please."

I couldn't imagine him overseeing an entire school. Perhaps he was one of those people who was just better with children than adults.

I held out my hand to him. "It's nice to meet you. I would be able to provide any flowers you need for the school."

He shook my hand, quick and firm, much firmer than I would have expected from this man who seemed to almost cower. "School is out now for summer term, but we do need flowers often, usually for special programs and at the end of school for award ceremonies and the like. My wife is right that I will be grateful to have a flower shop right here in the village. Although you will work with the school secretary much more than with me personally."

"That would be fine," I said. "I'm happy to help in any capacity that I can."

He nodded and looked away. Oddly, I felt like I had just been dismissed from school. Perhaps I had misjudged him at first and he was the perfect head teacher for the village.

"I was also interested in flowers for St. Thomas's as well," Emer said, pulling my attention back to her.

"The parish church?" I did my best not to wince thinking of my last visit there. To arrange the flowers every week for the local church would be stable work for my business. There was just one problem. St. Thomas's was Minister MacCullen's church. "I'm not sure that the minister would want me to do the flowers for St. Thomas's . . ." I trailed off.

She shook her head. "You must be thinking of the incident outside our church last Sunday."

"When the minister didn't let me inside the building?" I asked. "That does come to mind."

"I was there and saw the entire ugly scene," she went on to say. "On behalf of the church, I am so sorry that happened. The minister should never have spoken to you that way. I was hoping that by hiring you to provide the chancel flowers, we could make up for it."

"I don't know why he would want me to handle the flowers if he doesn't even want me inside the building." I smiled. "It's very kind of you to make this offer, but I certainly wouldn't want to put the minister in an uncomfortable position when he feels so strongly about me."

She winced. "Please know that the church doesn't always

agree with the minister's stance on certain things. The church elders reprimanded him for turning you away. They sent him a letter asking him to apologize to you just two days ago."

I raised my eyebrows. Now the reason that the minister had stomped into my shop the night before made a little more sense. He was clearly furious over the church elders' rebuke. He had most certainly not done what they had asked. I bit my tongue from saying that. I didn't want to have anything to do with their inner-church dispute.

Even so, I couldn't turn down this chance to expand my business. "I would be honored if the church would consider me to provide their flowers every week, but I really need the minister's approval to do it."

She beamed. "Good. I'll speak to Minister MacCullen and the church elders about it at first opportunity. I don't see it being a problem. The minister typically leaves such minor decisions about the budget to me, especially right now. Furthermore, I am certain that he will agree it is the best way to make amends with you. I wouldn't be the least bit surprised if he hasn't already put the incident out of his head. Now he's all caught up in the chapel restoration project. I'm sure you have heard of it."

"I've seen the flyers," I said.

She nodded. "The church is trying to raise money to save what is left of the original chapel that was built in the twelfth century. St. Thomas Church, as it stands today, is much younger. It was built in the seventeenth century." She said this like the seventeenth century was last week. If anything was over one hundred years old back in Nashville, they turned it into a museum and built a fence around it. In Scotland, "old" had quite a different definition than I was accustomed to.

"The chapel is crumbling as we speak," Emer went on. "A historian is here this summer to do an assessment. Based on his recommendation, we will be able to determine how much money it will take to save what is left of the structure. Even without knowing the costs, the minister has been aggressively raising funds for the restoration." She smiled. "So, he is far too preoccupied with that to worry about where the church finds its flowers for Sunday morning services."

Clearly Emer didn't know how the minister felt about Duncreigan or me. Either that or she was a much stronger woman than I would have guessed.

She patted my arm. "It was lovely to meet you. I will be in touch soon."

I nodded and was about to thank her, but my words got caught in my throat when the door opened again.

Chief Inspector Neil Craig stood in the doorway of the Climbing Rose. The six-five, broad-shouldered chief inspector filled the entire doorway, blocking out the sun for a moment. My heart flipped in my chest. Craig scanned the room like he always did when he entered a new place. I thought that behavior had something to do with being a cop. Absently, I told Emer I would be happy to talk to her about the church flowers anytime and then excused myself before walking over to Craig.

He looked down at me. I was tall for a woman, but I wasn't tall by the police inspector's standards. It still felt odd to have to crank my neck back in order to look him in the eye.

I blinked up at him. "What are you doing here?"

He grinned. "Well, hello to you too, Fiona."

My face felt hot. "I'm so sorry that came out wrong. I'm just surprised to see you here is all."

"I thought the entire village was invited to your grand opening." He smiled, and his straight white teeth appeared from behind his dark auburn beard.

"Well, yes, but . . ." I searched for the right words. "I—I didn't know you liked flowers."

"Can't a man like flowers?" he said in mock defense.

I could see that this line of questioning was going nowhere fast. "Of course, but I just didn't expect to see you here. It's just I know that you're busy, and . . ." I trailed off. "It's a surprise."

"It's a nice surprise, I hope." Before I could respond, he went on and said, "It may astound you, but I do in fact like flowers. However, I like flower shopkeepers more."

I swallowed. I might have been slow on the uptake when it came to men. The fact that my fiancé had been able to carry on an affair while we were planning our wedding without me knowing was proof of that. But even I knew that Craig was a little bit interested in me when he made a comment like that.

I blinked at him a couple of times. Eloquent to the very end, I said, "Oh."

Craig laughed. "Go entertain your guests. I don't need you to babysit me. The place looks brilliant; you have done a great job."

"Thank you," I murmured. "Take a look around. Even the

back room is open to view. I wanted everyone who came to the party today to get a real sense of my business."

He nodded. "You've done a wonderful job. You should be proud of yourself. I know that I'm very proud of you."

I didn't know what to say to that, so I said nothing and turned to greet another shopper.

By five, the party was beginning to wind down. Most of the villagers were still there, but they were murmuring about needing to go home and put dinner on the table, check on the children, and, for those with farms, complete evening chores.

I said good-bye to people as they left and foisted baked goods on them as they went. As I expected, Presha had provided way more cookies and pastries than anyone could eat.

I was handing another villager my business card when Craig walked out of the workroom holding the note from the minister in his hand. He looked at me, his dark eyes wrinkled with concern.

My heart went into my throat. I was about to ask what he thought he was doing reading a personal note addressed to me when the front door slammed opened. It hit the wall with such force that the windows rattled, and one of the vases would have fallen off its stand and crashed to the floor if Presha hadn't caught it in time.

Volunteer village police chief Kipling stood in the doorway, panting. He wore his usual uniform, a navy-blue outfit covered with shiny pins and metals, which likely meant nothing at all.

Craig stepped forward. "Kipling," he said, a little sharper than normal. "What's wrong?"

Kipling's eyes were wide as he searched all the dumbstruck faces in the room.

Craig was not struck dumb. "Get ahold of yourself. What happened?"

Kipling held his right fist up in the air and cried, "Murder! Murder!" And then he fainted.

Chapter Six

The chief inspector knelt by the fallen Kipling and checked the prostrate man's pulse.

I fell to my knees next to Craig. "Is he dead?"

Craig glanced at me. "No. He fainted. He's been known to do that time and again when he becomes overly excited."

"He's like one of those fainting goats," one of the bystanders in the shop said. "The ones that can drop to the ground at the slightest provocation."

"Not nearly as cute when it happens to Kipling as when it happens to a goat."

"Agreed," the first bystander said.

"He's going to be really embarrassed when he wakes up."

Several people inside the flower shop snickered at that.

"As long as he's not dead," I whispered to Craig. "And what did he mean when he yelled 'Murder'?"

"I plan to ask him just as soon as he comes to. You can count on that." Craig raised his voice, "Can someone hand me a glass a water for Kipling?"

Almost immediately, Presha appeared at Craig's side. Instead of handing him the cup of water, she dipped her fingers in the paper cup and flicked water on Kipling's pasty face.

The volunteer police officer groaned and rolled his head back and forth. His eyes moved up and down behind his eyelids.

Craig snorted. "Come on, Kip. Stop faking and open your eyes."

I couldn't help but feel that Craig was right and Kipling was much more awake than he was letting on because he was enjoying being the center of attention.

Presha leaned over and smacked Kipling on the cheek. "Wake up already!"

Kipling's eyes popped open and he rubbed his cheek. "What did you have to go and do that for?"

"Someone had to knock some sense into you," Presha said. "What are you doing coming into Fiona's opening and yelling about murder? Is that any way to treat a newcomer to the village?"

Kipling blinked at her a few times, as if he was trying to remember something important. "Murder? Who said anything about murder?"

"That's what you said." Presha stood over him with her arms folded.

I glanced at Craig to see if he was going to stop Presha from taking the lead in the questioning, but he seemed perfectly happy to let her do it. The chief inspector watched Kipling closely, as if looking for clues as to how reliable a witness the man was.

A light dawned on Kipling's face. "Oh! Yes, there was a

murder! I have discovered a murder." He held out his arm, and Craig helped him to his feet. Kipling wobbled for a moment.

Craig dropped the other man's arm. "What are you talking about?"

I scrambled to my feet as well.

Kipling's eyes went wide. "A body. I found a body, and with my expert eye I could tell right away that the sorry man died at the hands of foul play."

The villagers who were still in the shop created a circle around Craig and Kipling. If it wouldn't have been too obvious, I wouldn't have been the least bit surprised if they had leaned in and cupped their ears.

Craig held his arms out and said in his official cop voice, "Please, everyone, step back. Kipling just had quite a shock and he needs space. Let the man breathe."

Kipling put a hand to his throat. "I am feeling rather parched from the experience. I don't think that I can go on with my story until I have something to drink. Ale would the most helpful, I daresay. I know I'm on duty and all, but these are strange times we live in."

Presha returned a moment later with a fresh cup of water.

Kipling took a sip and wrinkled his nose. Clearly he had truly been hoping for the ale he had requested. He should have been happy with the water. Presha could have given him some of her extra-strong chai. That would have woken him right up.

Craig folded his arms. "You found a body? Where?"

Kipling pressed his paper cup to his forehead. "On the beach, just south of the harbor. I was doing my daily rounds." He puffed out his chest. "You know I keep a close watch on everything that goes on in the village, a very close watch, indeed. There is a reason that we have a very low crime rate here. My diligence has paid off."

The reason there was a low crime rate in Bellewick was actually because it was a tiny Scottish village that few outsiders visited; and if he *was* responsible for the crime rate, he wasn't doing a super job. In the two months I had been in Scotland, this would be the second murder, if what Kipling was saying was in fact true. I wasn't completely certain it was, or if he was just enjoying having a captive audience listen to one of his adventures.

"Are you sure it wasn't a harbor seal that washed up on the shore?" Presha asked. "It would be terrible if it was, but those can look suspiciously like a man at a distance."

Kipling shook his head like a defiant toddler. "No, no, it was a dead body." He paused. "It was a human dead body. I am sure of it. When I saw the form off in the distance, I walked right up to it to investigate. I was only two feet from him. There is no doubt it was a man."

"Who?" Craig asked. His patience was growing thin. "Whose body was it?"

Kipling took a deep breath and looked around the room. He seemed to take time to stare into the faces of each villager in turn. "It was the minister." He paused as that sunk into the group. "The body of Minister Quaid MacCullen has washed up ashore. He's dead."

I felt like Kipling had donkey-kicked me in the chest, and I stumbled backward. Presha pressed a warm and calming hand to my back, but it did nothing to soothe my nerves. The minister was dead? He had been in this very shop just last evening.

A rush of cold dread filled me. No, there had been no love lost between the minister and me, but he was someone I had known. Someone the villagers loved and relied upon. He was a man of God. And I knew, in his own way, he'd only tried to ostracize me because he truly cared about his parishioners and wanted to ensure their spiritual well-being. I felt terrible. That he should die—that any person should—before their due time . . .

Another thought hit me. Was I the last person to have seen him alive? I shook my head. That couldn't be possible because of the note on the front door that the minister had left. I knew it had not been there when Isla and I had locked up for the night yesterday. He must have come to the shop at some point, and then what? Gone to the harbor and drowned in the storm? That didn't make any sense at all. And if Kipling was right, why would anyone kill him? Who had a motive to do that other than . . . other than me? My heart pounded in my chest. The minister had been harassing me since the moment I set foot in the village, and it was widely known among the villagers. If anyone was going to look for someone with a motive, I would be at the top of the list. If it was indeed murder.

Craig removed his cell phone from his tweed sport coat pocket. I knew that he was calling the station in Aberdeen for reinforcements. The county's capital city was a half hour away. It would take Craig's team some time to gather up what they needed and drive to the Bellewick harbor.

Craig walked to the corner of the room to a place where he was less likely to be overheard.

I remained standing next to Kipling with Presha's hand on

my back, and villagers crowded around us. Many of them asking questions like a Greek chorus ringing inside my head.

"How did he die?"

"The poor man."

"What will the church do now?"

"Are you sure he's dead?"

"Was there much blood?"

"Was his head smashed in?"

"Do you think it was an accident and he just drowned in the storm? It was a terrible squall."

"Aye, maybe he lost his way. 'Twas an awful, awful storm, the worst we have had in two years, I'd say."

"Nay, I would say it was the worst we have had in four years, at least. The lightning was so bright, and the wind was so fierce. It shook me to my core."

"Aye."

My throat felt tight as the villagers moved closer in, and I had to escape their curious circle.

Presha shooed the villagers away from Kipling and me. "Now, it's after five and the flower shop is closed for the night. Why don't you all take your talk next door to my brother's pub? There you can gossip about this to your heart's content."

"Aye," a man said.

"Kipling can tell us everything that happened from the beginning," another man said.

Craig lowered his mobile phone from his ear. "No, Kipling is coming with me."

Chapter Seven

The volunteer police officer paled at Craig's announcement. "I don't know why I have to go with you, Chief Inspector Craig. I told you exactly where the body is located. What more do you want from me?"

"A lot more, Kipling. A lot." Craig put the phone back up to his ear. "Meet me at the harbor as quickly as you can," Craig said and hung up.

I pushed through the crowd, which was finally taking Presha's advice and making their way out the front door in the direction of the Twisted Fox.

"You're going to the harbor?" I asked Craig when I was finally standing next to him.

He looked down at me. "Yes. Kipling has done a lot of dumb things as a so-called police officer in his day, but he's never made up a story about a dead body before. I have to check into it."

"I'm coming with you," I said as the last villager left. Only Craig, Kipling, Presha, Isla, and I remained in the shop.

Craig slid his mobile back into his coat pocket. "Fiona,

stay here and mind your shop. This had nothing to do with you."

"If Kipling is right and it *is* Minister MacCullen who washed up on shore, it has a lot to do with me. I know you read that note."

His face reddened slightly. "I shouldn't have. I'm sorry."

"It's too late now." I lowered my voice. "You can't take back what you know."

He frowned. "It may not be the minister. When a body washes up on shore, it can be difficult to identify. I don't doubt that Kipling saw a body, but it does not mean it was MacCullen. There's no reason for you to see what surely promises to be a gruesome scene."

I started to make my case again, but the chief inspector put his hand on my arm. "Fiona, I don't have time to argue with you about this. I have to get to the scene before my constables do."

I took a step back. "Of course. I'm sorry. Good luck."

He dropped his hand from my arm. "Kipling, let's go."

Kipling blinked at him. "Go where?"

"To the beach. I already told you that you were coming with me."

"But I thought you said that to make the villagers leave. You really want to me to go back there?" the younger man asked in a shaky voice. "I don't want to do that again."

Craig folded his arms. "You have to show me where you found the body. Time is of the essence."

Kipling appeared a little green but nodded and straightened his shoulders. "All right, let's go."

Craig gave me one final nod and headed toward the door with Kipling on his heels.

"Well, that was a complete buzzkill," my sister said as she floated around the shop picking up empty plates and cups scattered around the room. "I mean, the only time you want to talk about death in a flower shop is when you are putting together arrangements for a funeral."

"Isla," I cried. "Don't be so crass. If Kipling is right, a man is dead, and he mostly likely came to a terrible end. We should not joke about that."

She snorted. "After the way the minister has been treating you, I don't know why you are the least bit upset that he's the one who might be dead."

"Isla!"

Presha stepped between us. "Girls! This is not a time to argue. Let us clean up the shop so that it will be neat and tidy for tomorrow. Neil Craig will take care of whoever the poor soul is. Any loss of life is terrible, but I hate to think it was the minister. He is a harsh man, but in his heart, I know he does the things he does because he believes it is the right thing to do for his congregation. The church will be reeling from the loss." Presha touched my arm. "And despite those last few minutes, you had a lovely opening, Fiona. You should be very proud of what you have accomplished in a short time."

"Thanks, Presha. I couldn't have done it without you. Everyone loved your refreshments." I bit my lip. "And you were a great help too, Isla."

My sister dropped her gaze to her feet. "Thanks, Sis."

Presha picked up her basket of dishes from the counter and

set them onto the rolling cart she had used to transport everything from her tea shop to the Climbing Rose. She turned to head out. "It was my absolute pleasure. Now I should be getting back to my own shop. I doubt my staff was very busy, since everyone in the village was here for your opening. Do not worry, Fiona, if there are any unkind murmurings about you and the minister, Raj will put a stop to it."

My face flushed slightly. How did Presha know I was worried about that already? She didn't know about my encounter with Minister MacCullen the day before or the unkind note I had found on my front door that morning. She wasn't a member of St. Thomas's, so I didn't even know if she knew about the uncomfortable encounter I had had with the minister the week before. However, someone at the pub would know, and it wouldn't be long before rumors began to fly around the village about the minister and me.

She squeezed my arm. "Take heart that the opening was a great success. Don't let this ugliness pollute your day. I'll be in tomorrow to check on you girls."

After Presha had gone, I said to my sister, "We can clean up later. I want to head over to the harbor."

Isla blinked at me. "But that's where they found the dead guy. Why would you want to go there?"

"That's why I *have* to go. I have to see for myself if it is Minister MacCullen."

"See, you are happy that it was him."

I shook my head. "No, Isla, no, I am not happy if it's him. I'm not happy when anyone is killed."

"But the minister—"

I squeezed her hand. "I know you are trying to defend me, but it doesn't help to be relieved someone is dead, and there is another reason I'm worried."

"What's that?"

"It won't be long before Chief Inspector Craig will be talking to me in an official capacity about the case . . ." I trailed off.

She covered her mouth for a second. Then she whispered, "The note. Do you think that the police will think you killed the minister over that stupid note?"

I picked up a daisy petal that had floated to the floor. "They might."

"Well, the police don't know about it. Just burn the note. It was like it never happened."

"That's the problem," I said. "Craig found it in the workroom and took it with him."

Her mouth fell open. "I think you might be in trouble, big sister."

"I know I'm in trouble, little sister," I said. "There is no 'think' about it."

Chapter Eight

The closer I came to the harbor, the more powerfully the scent of fish and salt water perfumed the air. Even though the heavy odor of dead fish was unpleasant, it reminded me of my childhood visits to Scotland and time spent by the sea with my family and my godfather, Uncle Ian.

The masts of large fishing boats came into view first, and then the weathered harbor shacks that housed the two food stands, bait shops, and scuba gear rentals along with the dock revealed themselves. A group of old men sat on weathered oil barrels at the front of the dock, just like they always did. It was as if they were the gatekeepers of the boats.

Thankfully, I didn't have to face their scrutiny today. Instead, I turned north in the direction of the beach. If I hadn't already known that was the place where Kipling had found the body, the large number of official-looking vehicles parked at the edge of the beach would have been a dead giveaway. Above, black cliffs that had once been in danger of development over-looked the harbor. That land dispute had resulted in the cliffs being named a national park, but that designation had come on the heels of the premature demise of a villager. It was a shame that Bellewick might be tainted by another untimely death so soon.

No one stopped me as I wove through the emergency vehicles and county police cars to reach the beach. I took care when I stepped down from the wooden dock's edge. On this part of the coast, the beach wasn't made up of smooth sand but of rocks that ranged from pebbles the size of a pencil eraser to smooth stones the size of my fist. The rocks were slick, as they had been under water at high tide, made higher than normal because of the storm.

The soles of my boots slipped on one of the stones. Not that I had known I would need rock-appropriate footwear when I dressed that morning. I almost took a tumble but righted myself before I fell. I froze in place with my arms out, like a gymnast on a balance beam trying to find her center. I was more concerned about drawing attention to myself than falling on my backend on the stones. Although that would hurt, I had fallen in the same spot before when Isla and I had played on the beach as children.

Once I'd gathered my footing, I started to walk down the beach. A cluster of emergency personnel was about thirty yards away from me.

The fickle North Sea, which had been so violent the night before, lapped gently against the coastline as if it could do nothing more than rock a baby to sleep. I remembered the storm, and I knew the story of the storm that had spit Baird MacCallister from the sea to Duncreigan, a mile inland from the waves. I knew better than to trust the gentle caress of the waves on the rocks.

The closer I came to the group of men and women, the more I could hear. Craig's voice rang clear above the others. "Step back!"

As the circle widened, I could finally see that everyone had been clustered around the body.

"Keep moving!" Craig ordered again. "We need room to work."

An EMT stepped on my foot. "Sorry," he muttered and then blinked. "Aren't you the American?"

I could see Craig now. He and two other men, one I thought I recognized as the county coroner, were leaning over the body. All I could make out was a dark pant leg and a bare foot.

"You are the American," the EMT said. "The one who is living at Duncreigan. I remember you."

Craig's head snapped up when the EMT said that, and he stared at me. I gave him a half smile, and he narrowed his eyes before turning back to his work. I was grateful he didn't kick me off the beach.

"Do you know who died?" I asked the EMT quietly. I suspected he wouldn't answer my question, but it was worth a shot.

To my surprise, he said, "It's Minister MacCullen from the village."

It was the answer I'd expected, but it was still unwelcome. I also knew I was now a murder suspect. How could it be that I had been in Scotland only two months and would already be a murder suspect twice? I guessed that had to be some kind of record, but certainly not one that I wanted. My first day in Scotland, I had discovered the body of my godfather's attorney behind the menhir in Uncle Ian's garden. Because of my unexpected inheritance and the location of the body on my newly acquired property, I had been an immediate suspect. Without knowing a soul in Scotland, I had been forced to clear my own name. Would I have to do that again?

"He must have gotten caught in the storm and fallen off the dock or a boat into the sea. It happens to the most seaworthy men, and I wouldn't say that the minister had much in the way of sea legs," the chatty EMT said.

I hadn't lived near Bellewick long, but I couldn't remember the minister making any reference to boats at all. That might not mean much, though; I had done my best to avoid him at every turn. I would have to ask Presha about the minister's relationship with the sea, if there even was one.

"It's a clear drowning," the coroner said. "You can tell by the way his face is bloated."

My stomach turned at that comment, because even though I couldn't see the minister's face, it didn't take much to envision what he described.

Craig stood up, and as he moved, his knees cracked. "We've done all we can do here. My men will keep searching the coast for evidence, but you can take the body back to your lab in Aberdeen now."

The coroner nodded. "Will do, Chief Inspector."

"What do you want me to do?" Kipling asked.

I hadn't even known that Kipling was still on the scene

until he spoke. He stood off to the side and held a white handkerchief to the corner of his mouth. He was as green as the kelp
that had washed up on the rocks and was doing his best not to
look at the body. I couldn't say I blamed him. I wasn't looking
either.

"You've done well, Kipling," Craig said, giving the other
man rare praise. "I'm sure I'll want to speak to you again before
this is all over, but until then, go home and get some rest.
You've earned it."

The coroner spoke softly to two crime scene techs, and the
two brawny men rolled the minister into a body bag and began
to zip it closed. The zipper stopped about halfway, which was
just enough time for me to lose my resolve and take a peek. The
swollen face of Minister Quaid MacCullen stared blankly back
at me. I knew he hadn't liked me from the moment he'd laid
eyes on me, but I didn't want to see him like this. For all his
criticism of the MacCallisters and of me, he didn't deserve this.
No one did.

Finally, the crime scene techs were able to yank the zipper
loose from its snag and zip the bag up the rest of the way.

Craig placed a hand on my shoulder and gently turned me
away from the body bag. My gaze had been so fixed on the
minister, I hadn't even known that the chief inspector was
standing next to me. "It's better if you don't look."

My stomach rolled over. "Too late."

He pursed his lips, and they disappeared into his full dark
beard. "What are you doing down here, Fiona? I thought I told
you to stay at the flower shop."

"You did, but after you left and the shop closed, I had to see for myself if it really was him." I frowned and felt tears gather in the back of my eyes. "It's so hard to believe that such an outspoken, strong personality could be ended like this. He shouldn't have died like this."

He nodded. "No one should."

I blinked away the tears. I didn't know if I felt weepy over the minister's death for his sake or selfishly for mine. I didn't want to be the focus of a murder investigation again so soon. Maybe my sister was right; maybe I was worried about his death because of how it would affect me. I didn't want to be so cold. "Presha said he did a lot of good for his congregation."

"He did," Craig said. "He was strict, but no one could question his dedication to his flock." He squeezed my shoulder once and then let go. "Go home, Fiona. You're tired, and you shouldn't be here."

"I do have business here," I corrected him. "You know why—it's in your pocket."

"The note, you mean."

I glanced around to make sure no one had overheard him. "Yes," I lowered my voice. "You had no right to take the note from my shop. I didn't give you permission to take it, and you didn't have a warrant when you did."

"When did he give it to you?"

I frowned. "It was tucked into the front door of the Climbing Rose this morning when Isla and I arrived at the shop a little before eight." I held out my hand. "I think you should return it."

He stared at my outstretched hand. "I'm not giving you the note back. It may have been the very last message Minister MacCullen ever wrote. If I know when he placed it on your door, I might be able to follow his trail until the moment he was murdered."

I sucked in a breath. "Are you sure it was murder?"

He stared down at me with his dark-blue eyes. Again, I marveled at how tall he was. I wasn't a short woman by any measure, but next to the chief inspector, I felt almost dainty. I was much more used to looking down at others and being in control over my own physical space. I couldn't seem to accomplish that when Craig was near, and it felt like a disadvantage.

"I'm sure," he said.

I scanned the beach and was happy to see that none of the people on the scene—the EMTs, crime scene techs, the coroner, or even Kipling—were paying us the least bit of attention. I was surprised to see Kipling still there—I would have thought he'd have bolted back to the village the moment Craig released him to spread the news of his great discovery and how he had single-handedly secured the scene and dragged Minister Mac-Cullen's body ashore or some such long tale. Instead, the volunteer officer was looking at the stony beach and kicking at the smaller rocks with the toe of his boot.

"How can you be sure?" I asked. "He could have just been out on a boat and been caught in the storm. He could have caught his foot in a line or hit his head and fallen overboard. He could have been wandering the dock, tripped over a seagull, and fallen into the sea."

His thick eyebrows came together. "Tripped over a seagull?"

"I'm just saying there are *many* possible scenarios that could explain how Minister MacCullen came to drown in the North Sea, and not one of them has to do with murder."

He scrubbed the side of his face. "That's true, but it wouldn't explain the hand marks on the back of his neck." He touched the back of his neck. "They were right here."

I blinked at the chief inspector, surprised he was so forthcoming with this vital bit of information.

"The bruises," he went on to say, "are clear indications that someone was holding him in place. My guess is that someone was holding his head under water until he drowned."

I shivered and couldn't help but wonder *why* Craig was telling me all this. I wasn't a police officer. I wasn't even sure if we were really friends. At the same time, I didn't stop him. I wanted to know. "At sea in that storm we had that seems crazy."

"Usually the sanest murderer makes the decision to kill in a moment of crazy. Very few murders are planned in detail for weeks and months. Most violent deaths happen in an instant, when the killer is too angry or distraught to think clearly. Without clear thinking, murder can seem like a viable option to remove a problem."

I shivered.

Craig put a hand on my shoulder and squeezed it again. "Go home, Fiona. There is nothing more you can do here."

I looked around and realized he was right. I was just in the way of his team trying to gather what little evidence hadn't been washed away in the storm. I nodded. "All right."

His straight white teeth appeared out from behind his dark beard. "I knew it would happen someday. I'm pleased to see it did sooner rather than later."

I narrowed my eyes. "What?"

"That you would finally agree with me on something. You

finally said I was right. I knew we couldn't be at odds forever." Another flash of white came out from behind the thick beard.

Before I could think of a smart comeback, he said, "Go. You need to rest. The minister's death isn't going to go away overnight. You will need strength for what's coming."

I was too worn out to ask him what he meant by that riddle. After saying good-bye to the chief inspector, I made my way to the wooden boardwalk, which was connected to the dock. I was eager to return to my flower shop and clean up from the party. Cleaning would distract me.

I hurried past the dock, but a voice stopped me before I could head back to town. "You've only been here a short while and there's another dead body popping up. If I believed in the magic ye are supposed to have, I would say that it was all yer fault."

I turned my head to see that the voice belonged to the old fisherman sitting on an oil barrel at the mouth of the dock. Two other retired salty seamen were at his side, snickering at his comments.

I kept walking.

"You can't run away from the mess you made," the old fisherman called after me.

I didn't slow down in my retreat, but the words dug into my heart all the same.

Chapter Nine

Rather than going straight to the flower shop after leaving the docks, I texted my friend Cally Beckleberry and asked if she was available to meet. She was, and I made a beeline for the Beckleberry law office. I knew Isla would be frustrated over how long I had been gone, especially since the Astra's keys were in my pocket, which meant she was stuck in the village until I got back to the flower shop, but that couldn't be helped.

Cally's practice was on Queen Street in a townhouse that dated back to the time of Jane Austen. After a rocky start, wherein I thought Cally was a murderess and she thought I was as well, Cally and I had become friends. We were both unmarried career women in our thirties and outsiders to the village. I was from Nashville, but Cally was from London, and to some of the townsfolk in the tiny Scottish village, London was just as foreign as Music City, USA.

I stepped through the outer door of her building that was always unlocked. I trudged up the stairs, and every step felt like my foot was weighed down with a pound of lead.

I knocked on the inner door to the law office.

"Coming!" Cally's refined English voice called out.

A moment later, she threw open the door. She was wearing a black skirt, a bright-yellow blouse that had puffed sleeves, and no shoes. The blouse was half untucked from her skirt, and the shorter side of her asymmetrically cut hair stood on end. Behind her I could see her black pumps lying on their side by the couch. Even slightly disheveled, she was beautiful. Had I worn the same outfit, I would have looked like an overgrown bumblebee that had recently been electrocuted, but on Cally it worked.

She ran her hands through her hair. "I just got back from Aberdeen from a meeting with a new client. I'm so sorry I missed your flower shop opening today. You do know I wanted to be there. I just have to take all the business I can get right now to establish myself." She didn't wait for me to answer. "I have a lot of clients whom I need to impress, so I will be placing a big flower order soon to make up for missing the party. Sending them flowers will be just the right level of sucking up."

I smiled. I also had to take all the business I could get. "I'll happily take your orders, but you don't have to make up for missing the party. You told me weeks ago you had to work."

She nodded. "Ever since Alastair died, I have to work even harder to keep the law office afloat." She dropped her gaze and turned around. "He did a lot around here. I didn't agree with everything he did, but he was very good at business."

Alastair Croft had been Cally's law partner and my godfather's attorney, the one I'd found dead in Uncle Ian's garden. Cally and I had bonded during the investigation into Alastair's death, as we both had been prime but ultimately innocent suspects in his murder.

I closed the door behind me and gave her a minute to compose herself. Cally was still dealing with the unexpected death of her law partner. To make matters worse, she had been in love with him.

She picked up her shoes and set them upright neatly in front of the end table at the far end of the couch. "What brings you here? I thought you'd still be at the shop working all hours. You have really been throwing everything into that place."

"I have to. If I'm going to stay in Aberdeenshire permanently, I need my shop to succeed. My godfather's money won't sustain me forever."

She nodded. Cally knew the financial situation I was in because she had been the executor of my godfather's estate after Alastair's death. I was comfortable for the moment, maybe more than comfortable by most standards, but I still had to make a living, and the best way I knew how to do that was with flowers. "And the opening went well. I might have gotten a wedding gig out of it."

She grinned. "That's great. And you were worried that the opening wouldn't be a success."

I rubbed the back of my neck, just as Craig had when he'd told me about the hand marks on the minister's body. I immediately dropped my hand. "I don't know that I would call it a success."

She raised one eyebrow at me. "Uh-oh. Will I need a drink to listen to this?"

I fell into the armchair across from the sofa. "I feel like you need a drink to listen to most stories I tell, so yes."

She grimaced. "Scotch it is. And one for you, too. I can tell you need it. I haven't seen you this worn out since you came to talk to me about Alastair's death."

I looked away from her. It was best to wait to tell her about the murder until after she had a Scotch in her hand. "Oh, no, I'm fine. No Scotch for me, thanks."

"I won't let you make me drink alone, Fiona."

"Fine. Just water it down a lot. My throat is still recovering from the last time you served me Scotch."

"You know, you should be able to handle it. You're the one with Scottish blood running through your veins. I'm pure English. I should be sipping tea and occasionally taking a nip of brandy for medicinal reasons."

"Tea sounds a lot more appealing to me, even with the brandy."

She shook her head. "Tea isn't going to cut it after the meetings I had today."

I sighed, resigned to my fate. I would have to start carrying antacids in my shoulder bag for the times I unexpectedly decided to drop in on Cally and she offered me a drink. Nothing I had ever drunk back in Nashville had been nearly as strong as what my barrister friend served.

Cally padded over to the bar cart on the far wall in her bare feet. She wasn't a conventional, buttoned-up attorney, and I was learning that more and more as our friendship grew. I thought that might be why I wanted her to be my friend so much. Most of my friends back in Nashville had been of the society set with perfect French manicures and 2.5 children, husbands, and dogs, usually Labs.

I had never quite felt like I fit in with them. I was the business-owner half of a couple in a long-term engagement that ended on horrible terms. My toad of a fiancé left me for our wedding cake decorator. None of my old friends would ever have allowed that to happen to them. One even told me that if I had paid more attention to my ex instead of my failing flower shop, his eyes would not have strayed. I didn't count her among my friends any longer.

Cally had her own sob stories when it came to love lost, and we could both drink to starting over on our own. We were two single ladies with no prospects for men in our lives and felt just fine about that. As soon as the thought struck me, an image of a certain large, bearded chief inspector came to my mind. I pushed the image away.

Cally handed me a tumbler half full of Scotch. I guessed she hadn't added more than a splash of water on top. "I can't stay too long. Isla is back at the shop, and I'm sure she is wondering what's become of me." I knew I would barely touch the drink. I had to drive back to Duncreigan, after all, but I held it in my hands for Cally's sake to make like I was at least considering taking a sip.

She held up her tumbler. "Then go ahead with your story."

"Minister MacCullen is dead. Looks like he was murdered." My announcement came out in an unpremeditated rush.

Cally was midsip when I spoke and choked on her drink.

She grabbed a tissue from the box on the side table and wiped her mouth.

I grimaced. "I should work on my delivery."

She sputtered. "For the sake of my esophagus, yes, I'd say you need to work on it. Now, tell me that again from the beginning."

"It was near the end of the opening party for the shop. Kipling stormed in saying he discovered a body on the beach. Craig jumped right into action and followed him out of the shop."

She held up her hand. "Wait, Neil was at your flower shop opening?"

"He was." I tried to answer disinterestedly.

She examined me, and I felt like a witness on the stand under her crisp interrogation. It wasn't a comfortable spot. "And don't you think it means something that the chief inspector was there?" she asked. "I'm sure that he had a million tasks he could have been doing on a Monday afternoon, especially after that terrible storm Sunday night, but he came to *your* flower shop opening."

"It might mean he's interested in flowers. I think more men should be. Some of the best gardeners I have known are men. It's not just a woman's job. I believe equal opportunity should go both ways."

She snorted. "It means that he's interested in flower shop *owners*, I think."

I frowned. "Do you want to hear about the minister or not? I tell you a man is dead, and you are more interested that the chief inspector popped into my flower shop opening than the poor man who lost his life."

She sipped her Scotch. "I don't think anyone has ever called the minister a poor man, but yes, please do go on. My apologies. How do you know it was the minister?"

"Kipling said the body belonged to Minister MacCullen, and I—I saw him. Dead, I mean."

"How?"

I told her about my field trip to the rocky beach.

She ran her cold tumbler back and forth over her forehead. "As your legal counsel, I would advise against going to crime scenes in the future. It's poor form, Fi." Before I could respond, she asked, "Had there been an accident? That was a nasty storm last night. Did he fall off the dock and drown?"

"That's what I thought, but Craig said no, it was definitely murder."

"Why's that?"

I squirmed, unsure if I could say anything more. Craig had trusted me with this information, and I had immediately run to Cally and repeated it. However, Cally wasn't only my friend; she was also my lawyer, and if I was in some sort of trouble, she needed to know about it so she could help me get out of it.

Cally arched her brow. "Are you holding information back from me, Fiona?"

I took a breath. "There were finger marks on the back of the minister's neck where he had been held under water."

"Neil told you that?" The skeptical look was back her in eyes.

I nodded.

"It just seems odd to me that Neil would tell you something so critical to a homicide case. He really shouldn't be sharing that information with a civilian."

"I thought the same thing," I admitted. "But I think he shared it with me because he knew I had a reason to be concerned." I went on to tell her about the threatening note I'd discovered that morning, the one that was still in the chief inspector's possession. I knew I didn't have any hope of getting that note back. I was kicking myself for leaving it out on my work table; had I just hidden it or burned it, I wouldn't be in this situation. I also told her about the minister's visit to the shop the night before. "I'm sure someone must have seen him leave in a huff. It won't be long before Craig learns about that too."

Cally shook her head. "Verbal and written threats? This is not good, Fi. The minister hates you, he's murdered, you are the prime suspect for the murder."

I nodded. "That's the gist of it. There's something else, too."

She pressed her Scotch tumbler to her forehead. "What is it?"

I told her about the incident outside St. Thomas's the week before.

She leaned back in her seat. "Did anyone else see this?"

"Half of the church, I would guess, and I would be willing to bet the other half heard about it by now. Emer Boyd said that the church elders instructed the minister to apologize to me."

"Do you think that was the reason he came to your shop the other night?" she asked.

"If it was, he really needs to work on his apologies."

Cally pressed her lips together for a moment. "In any case,

this isn't good news for you. It's more proof that you and the minister were in a dispute and that you would have reason enough to dislike him."

"Dislike him, sure," I said. "But kill him? That's a stretch."

She shook her head. "Add in the minister's threats, and one could argue that you killed him out of fear."

"That's ridiculous."

"You and I both know that, but people will talk. Also, I still don't think it was professional of Neil to tell you how the minister died." She frowned. "He must have had a reason for doing that, but I don't have any idea what it might be."

I frowned. "Neither do I."

"In any case, Fi, if you need an attorney, I'll be at your side."

"Thanks," I said. "But I would really rather it not come to that. I'll do whatever it takes so it won't."

She narrowed her eyes. "You're planning to play detective again just like you did when Alastair died, aren't you?"

"I wasn't playing. I had to get involved."

Cally pursed her lips again, as if she wasn't sure about that. "All right, fine. Your best defense is a good alibi. What do you have?"

"It depends when he died. Yes, I was at the cottage last night with Isla, but most of the night, I was at the Climbing Rose getting ready for today. I wanted everything to be perfect. I didn't leave the shop until close to eight, and the storm hit about nine and lasted the rest of the night. Isla was with me most of the time. She's my alibi, but I'm afraid the police will think she's lying because she's my sister."

She shook her head. "Neil won't say that. Was she with you every moment?"

"She wandered off in the late afternoon, close to four. She said she needed to go for a walk. She was gone a couple hours, but she was there when the minister stormed into the shop, and we left together."

"Where did she go for a walk?"

I swallowed, remembering that Isla had disappeared in the middle of the opening too and hadn't said where she'd gone. I didn't think Cally needed to know—it was most likely nothing, and she had just gone for a walk. "I don't know. Does it matter?"

"It might. I think the more the two of you corroborate your stories, the better. Did you ask her where she went?" Cally stared at her empty tumbler with a slightly disappointed expression on her lovely face.

"No, she showed up at the flower shop, and the weather was starting to turn bad. We were in a hurry to finish what we could before the storm broke. You and everyone else in the area know what happened after that."

She nodded. "It was quite a storm. One of the worst since I moved up here. I wouldn't have wanted to be by the shore during that. There were reports that some of the waves were twenty feet high."

I shivered. "But Minister MacCullen was out in that. The question is, when did he die? And what was he doing near the docks during such a terrible storm?"

"Not that I'm condoning your sleuthing, but if you can answer that first question, I think you could rest a little bit easier. Did you notice the note on your door when you closed up the shop for the night?"

I shook my head. "But I can't say with one hundred percent certainty that it wasn't there. We were in such a rush to return to Duncreigan before the storm hit. I wanted to make sure the garden and the cottage were secure."

"Did you see anyone as you were leaving the flower shop? Was anyone standing around?"

I thought back to the night before. My hands had been full of files and items that I wanted to take back from the shop. Isla hadn't been carrying a thing, and I'd been mildly annoyed with her over it. But I hadn't pressed her because she had seemed preoccupied. I knew she was fearful of the oncoming storm. My younger sister had been afraid of storms ever since she was a little girl. She had always climbed up on and hidden in my bed during foul weather. When she was given the choice, she always ran to me, her big sister, and not our parents. It had been no surprise that she opted to come live with me in Scotland when her other choice had been to move back home to the farm after college graduation.

I tried to remember if there had been anyone else on the street as we were leaving. It had been mostly empty. By that hour, everyone had holed up in their homes.

But one face came to mind. "I saw Seth MacGregor."

She cocked her head. "Hamish's nephew?"

"The very one," I said.

Chapter Ten

J ust before I left Cally's office, she advised me, as my attorney, to tell Craig about seeing Seth the night of the storm and then to butt out of the investigation. I didn't plan to do either. At least, I wasn't going to tell Craig about Seth until I had a chance to talk to Hamish about it. Hamish had a right to know his great-nephew was back in the village when he should be attending medical school in Aberdeen.

As I walked back to the Climbing Rose, I wondered why I'd been so upset over Seth being there. As far as I knew, he'd had a great reason for being in the village the night of the storm. Seth, a native of Bellewick, lived in Aberdeen, where he was studying to be a doctor. There was no reason for him not to be in the village; Aberdeen was a thirty-minute drive away. Still, it was the first time I'd seen him since the land deal over the cliffs was settled.

Seth had been one of the ardent environmentalists who protested the development of the cliffs. Raj had been too, and with the help of Cally, they had been able to save the cliffs.

Since Raj had been the ringleader of the protest group, my

guess was that he was the most likely person to know why Seth was back in Bellewick. Other than Hamish, of course.

I decided I would ask Raj about it the next time I visited the Twisted Fox. With my mind made up, I pushed open the door to the Climbing Rose to find my sister leaning against the counter and tapping on her phone's screen with an irritated expression.

"You know, it's going to cost you a fortune to text, since you have an American phone," I said.

She rolled her eyes. "I'm using the shop's Wi-Fi. Sometimes you still treat me like a child, Fi."

I grimaced because I knew this was true. To my surprise, as I scanned the shop, I found everything was neat and tidy. I'd half expected to come back to a mess, which was usually the case when I left my sister with cleaning to be done. "This place looks amazing. Did you clean up after the party?" I was ashamed to hear a little wonder in my voice.

Isla must have caught it too, because she asked, "What else was I going to do after you left me here alone? There really isn't much to do in the village."

"Thank you for doing it," I said. "I didn't expect it, but I'm glad to see it. I'm tired to the bone, as Mom would say, and I wasn't ready to face cleaning up this mess. It looks to me like everything is in order and we can lock up for the night."

She paused. "And Presha helped. She popped back in about an hour after you left."

"Ah," I said.

"I'm starving," my sister complained. "Where have you been?

I would have headed back to the cottage, but you have the car keys."

I winced. I hadn't even thought of the keys being in my pocket when I'd raced out of the shop earlier that evening. "Sorry about that. I didn't know I was going to be gone that long."

She frowned. "I couldn't lock up, because you haven't given me a key to this place either."

"I'm sorry, Isla," I said. "Today didn't go as planned for any of us."

"Especially not for the dead guy," Isla replied. "Are you going to be arrested over the note?"

I could a feel a headache developing behind my eyes. "No," I said, even though I wasn't positive that was true. I wrapped my arm around her shoulders. "Thanks for watching the shop while I was gone. Can I make it up to you by buying you dinner at the Twisted Fox?"

Her face cleared. "I guess you can do that. It will make up for it some, but I'm going to need a drink."

"I expected as much." My sister was twenty-two, and being able to walk into a bar and order a drink was still new to her. However, she became majorly offended if the server or bartender had the audacity to ask for her ID. I was waiting for the day that she would be flattered to be asked, not that there was any risk of that happening at the Twisted Fox. The drinking age in the United Kingdom was eighteen, so it was unlikely she would be carded at any pub in the country.

Isla and I left my flower shop, and I locked the door behind me. As I turned, I paused as my eyes fell on the spot where I had seen Seth standing across the street from my shop.

I knew he had been in that very spot, but had I been right in thinking he was walking across Duncreigan that morning? If he had, what connection did that have with the minister's death, if any? Typically, I wouldn't think there was any connection at all, but seeing Seth twice after he had been away for so long this close to the minister's death had me questioning his presence. I hoped Hamish could clear it up for me when I had a chance to ask him.

"Are you coming?" Isla asked. "What are you looking at?"

I blinked. "Sorry. I just have a lot on my mind."

"I have a lot on my mind, too," she said. "At least you have a job and a place to live. I'm in limbo." With that, she marched toward the Twisted Fox.

I sighed and trailed after her. I didn't want to break it to her, but no one had their life figured out at twenty-two. I didn't have it figured out at thirty, and I wasn't expecting fifty to be much better.

Isla threw open the heavy wooden door to the pub and flounced inside. Not waiting for me to enter, she made a beeline for the bar. The door thudded closed behind me, and it sounded like the lid being lowered on a coffin. I shook away that morbid thought. Clearly, the minister's death had affected me more than I'd realized.

My eyes adjusted to the pub's dim light and the coolness of the room. The Twisted Fox was in a well-insulated stone building that had been sitting in the same spot for over four hundred years. It was built like a fortified castle, and there was no chance a storm like the one from the night before could penetrate its thick wall.

Raj Kapoor had purchased the pub after the last owner had had to leave unexpectedly under very uncomfortable circumstances. Raj, who'd made his money through the laundromat, had told me he'd decided to buy the pub not for the liquor but for the history the building held. He was a historian by trade, and planned to write a history of the pub in between serving his personal mix of traditional Scottish pub fare and Indian cuisine. He had already discovered through his research that the building had once been a clan garrison.

"There you are, Fiona!" Raj called from his spot at the bar. "I am so glad you are here. You will not believe the good news I have!" Raj was a lean Indian man in his early sixties. In the last several weeks, Raj had been growing a mustache, so he looked less like his twin sister than ever before.

I made my way through the busy pub. It was close to eight, and the late dinner crowd was filing in. Laughter and voices filled the place as Indian spices permeated the air. I couldn't decipher one spice from another. I had been raised on my mother's southern cooking, which ranged from fried chicken to biscuits the size of my head. There hadn't been that many spices growing up on the farm. Even so, it all smelled lovely to me, and it wasn't until I inhaled the intoxicating scents that I realized how hungry I was.

Isla was already at the bar with a pint of Indian beer. Her goal was to try all Raj's beers, both British and Indian, before she returned to the United States.

"Wow! That's different. It's like drinking a chai with alcohol!" she exclaimed.

Raj grinned behind his black mustache and set a glass of water on the bar in front of me. "A little spicier than you are accustomed to, I would guess."

She took a smaller sip. "It is. I can't decide if I like it or not."

Raj threw back his head and laughed. "You American girls aren't afraid to say exactly what you think."

I sipped my water. "I don't think it's all American girls, but Isla certainly speaks her mind."

"You do too, Fiona. That was something I noticed about you the moment you entered the village. It was something Minister MacCullen recognized too. Maybe that's why he took such a dislike to you." He shook his head. "It is a shame the minister's death had to ruin your opening, Fiona. If I didn't know better, I would have said he planned it that way. Everyone in the village knew he had a strong dislike for you and Duncreigan."

My appetite vanished. "I am sorry the minister died. Any small impact that it might have had on my shop opening is minor in comparison to that."

Raj nodded and leaned over the counter to me. "'Course, there will be talk. I have already heard murmurs and the sun hasn't set yet."

My stomach twisted. "What kind of murmurs?"

Raj rocked away from me and made an apologetic face. "That you might have had something to do with his death. Everyone in the village knows that he singled you out as a troublemaker."

"I can't be the only one Minister MacCullen didn't get along with."

"Goodness no. The minister had been in the parish for over twenty years. I'm sure he butted heads with all sorts of people over the years, but I can't think of anyone who would want to kill him. He was a fixture here—Bellewick just isn't the same with him gone." He paused. "If you want to know more about the minister, you should ask Malcolm Wilson. If anyone knows anything about the minister's life, it's him. I'm guessing you want to find out more about the minister's life?"

"You guessed right," I said.

"Who's Malcolm Wilson?" Isla asked.

"He's the church sexton," Raj said. "He knows everything you need to know about the minister and the parish. He lives in a little cottage on the church grounds. Malcolm has been the sexton at the parish church for at least as long as I have lived in Bellewick, so that would be over forty years."

"If I had to put money on it, I would say that Malcolm was the one who did MacCullen in," said an elderly man, a regular at the Twisted Fox, who now stood at the end of the bar holding his empty pint out to Raj. The man had a perpetual squint and always seemed to have a pipe in his hand, so I'd nicknamed him Popeye when I first arrived in Bellewick. I didn't know his real name. I had never asked what it was, and now, after all this time, it seemed rude to ask for it. "No one could have worked for that man so long without finally snapping," he continued.

Raj took the empty glass from the old fisherman. "I don't see it. Malcolm is a gentle giant. I don't think he even bothers the mice that live in the church basement."

Popeye snorted.

Whether Raj was right or Popeye was, I knew that Malcolm Wilson was someone I would have to talk to. "Maybe I will stop by the church tonight to see him."

Raj refilled Popeye's pint and handed it back to him. "This would not be a good night."

"Why not?" I asked. "Because of the murder?"

"Nay, because of the ghosts," Popeye said, before shuffling back to his friends around the fireplace.

"Ghosts?" I asked.

Raj rolled his eyes. "Pay him no mind. There aren't any ghosts around the old church. But wait until the daytime to pay Malcolm a visit. He's had a shock with the minister's death. He might not look kindly on an evening visit from a stranger."

I wondered why Raj called Malcolm a gentle giant but then advised me to talk to him only during the day.

Raj shook his head. "I don't attend St. Thomas's, so I don't really know what the congregation might think of him. That's why you should talk to Malcolm. He will know. I do know drowning is a horrible way for anyone to die. The poor man is in my prayers."

I shivered as the image of Minister MacCullen's face in the body bag returned. I wished I'd never looked at the body. I would have preferred not to have that image to carry around for the rest of my life.

"You're cold." Raj clucked his tongue and sounded like the cafeteria lady back in my middle school lunchroom who always went out of her way to tell me I was too skinny. She had clucked her tongue just like that and then tried to foist food on me, as

I knew Raj was about to do. "You need a hot meal. That will make everything much easier to face." He placed a hand on his clean-shaven chin and rubbed it back and forth. "You need my chicken marsala. It will warm you through. That's what I'm prescribing for you. And I have news!"

Chapter Eleven

Raj grinned. "You will like my news because it does not involve the minister or his death."

I slid into the empty barstool next to my sister. "I'll take that kind of news. What's up, Raj?"

He clasped his hands together in front of his chest. "Carver Finley has agreed to come here and examine my foundation. Isn't that wonderful?"

I blinked at him. Twice. "Are you speaking in code?"

"Oh, you are as silly as Presha. Carver Finley!"

"Sorry, I'm still not following." I looked to Isla for help, but she merely shrugged and sipped from her pint.

Raj threw up his hands. "Fiona, Carver Finley is the foremost authority on Aberdeenshire history. He knows all that there is to know about the county."

I pictured an elderly man with reading glasses at the tip of his nose and a tweed jacket with elbow patches. Not that I had ever seen an authority on Aberdeenshire history before.

"He has been here for the last week assessing the chapel. You do know that St. Thomas's is raising money to save it? He's been in the pub a number of times for his meals while he's been working on his assessment, and when he was here, I just happened to mention my history of the pub."

"You just *happened* to mention your project?" I smiled, even though the mention of St. Thomas's brought the minister and his death to mind again.

"I could not let this opportunity pass me by. He wrote *Aberdeen, Then and Now.* I am sure you have heard of that title."

"Sorry," I said. "It wasn't on the recommended reads list at high school in Nashville."

"Oh, I do appreciate your American sarcasm."

I laughed. "I'm glad to hear that he will be looking at your project."

"My sister told me all about your opening. I am very sorry that I was not able to be there with you." He waved his hands in the air. "As you can see, the Twisted Fox keeps me very busy." Raj set another glass of water in front of me without asking. I thanked him. "I gave you the water, but surely you need a beer after the day you have had," he said.

"He has a point," Isla said. "I'll have the marsala too, Raj. I'm starving."

"I'll have the cook start on your meals right way." He turned and went into the kitchen.

The door swung closed after him.

After he was gone, I glanced around the pub. I was on the lookout for Seth MacGregor. For some reason, I felt it was important that I speak to him for Hamish's sake. I needed to know if he was just visiting the village or was there on a more permanent basis. Because if he was back in the village permanently, what did that mean for medical school or the money Hamish had sent to Seth for his schooling? I scanned the room for Seth a second time. As far as I could tell, he wasn't anywhere in the room. He might already be back in Aberdeen.

"What's gotten into you?" Isla asked.

I glanced at her. "What do you mean?"

"Ever since you got back to the flower shop this afternoon, you have been looking around like you are being followed or something."

Before I could answer her, Raj reappeared with two plates of steaming chicken marsala in his hands. He set them in front of Isla and me. The steam coming from my dish clouded my vision for a moment as the strong spice pushed away any other scent in the crowded pub.

I smiled, grateful that I didn't have to answer my sister's question. "Raj, have you seen Seth MacGregor lately?" I took a sip of water.

Isla jumped off her barstool and made a *yip* sound like a small dog whose paw had been caught in a door.

I sprang to my feet. "What's wrong? Are you all right?"

Isla's blue eyes were twice their normal size. "Um, I—I thought I saw a spider."

"A spider?" I asked in disbelief. "You sounded like someone pinched you."

She shook her head. "No, it was a spider. A big one, close to the size of a hamster."

Raj grabbed a newspaper from the end of the bar and rolled it into a cone. "I can't have hamster-sized spiders running around my pub." He came around the bar with the paper cone in strike position.

"You're going to scare the spider away if you stomp around like that, Raj. Then you will never catch him," Popeye said from his post by the fireplace.

Popeye's pals, who were always with him, it seemed, laughed.

Isla looked at her feet, and I did too. There was no spider of any size to be seen.

"Um," my sister stammered, and made a show of looking under the bar a bit longer. "I guess he got away."

I felt my eyes narrow. For as girly and delicate as my sister portrayed herself to be, she wasn't afraid of spiders. She'd grown up on the same farm in Tennessee I had, she'd done the same chores, and she'd walked through spider webs with as much regularity as I had. She'd never once freaked out over a spider, whatever the size, and there had been some doozies back on the farm. In fact, if I remembered correctly, her favorite book as a child had been *Charlotte's Web*.

"What's going on with you?" I whispered to my sister

She blinked at me with her big blue eyes. When she did that, I knew she was doing her best to mimic a Disney princess and I *knew* she was up to something. "What are you talking about, Sis?" she whispered back. All the while, Raj walked up and down the bar with his rolled newspaper.

I waved my hand under the bar. "The spider thing. You and I both know you aren't afraid of spiders."

"I am afraid of spiders. Is that a crime?"

I rolled my eyes. "You never were before."

"Well, this one was different. It was the size of a hamster, Fi," she hissed. "I think even the toughest person on earth would have been afraid of that. *You* would have been afraid of a hamster-sized spider. He looked me dead in the eye. He wanted to take me out. I could tell!"

Raj lowered his makeshift weapon with a disappointed sigh. "You see him again, you tell me."

Isla nodded, and her smooth blonde locks fell over her face. "I will." She glanced around the bar. "I'm so sorry to have made such a fuss." Her voice came out in a southern-sounding purr. It was so like our mother's when she was trying to convince our father to do something he didn't want to do that alarm bells went off in my mind.

Raj still had his head under the bar in search of the spider when a rich male voice said, "If you are trying to determine the age of the bar, it is not nearly as old as the rest of the building."

Raj jerked backward and whacked the back of his head on the underside of the bar. He dropped the rolled newspaper onto the floor.

As I jumped off my seat to avoid knocking into Raj, my back pressed up against the firm chest of a man. Strong arms spun me around, and discerning green eyes looked me up and down.

Chapter Twelve

I stepped out of the man's grasp and bumped into my sister, feeling like the ball in the middle of a pinball game.

Raj placed a hand on his cheek. "Mr. Finley, I wasn't expecting you so early. You said you were coming to look at the pub's foundation tomorrow. I did not expect to see you today, but I'm quite pleased that you are here."

This was Carver Finley? He was nothing like the elderly, elbow patch–wearing historian I'd conjured up in my head when Raj first spoke of him. This historian was handsome in a contrived way that I suspected took a good amount of work to maintain. He had sparkling white teeth, a thick swath of blond hair that was brushed back from his forehead in precise waves, and just enough scruff on his face to look like he didn't care about his appearance, though I presumed he cared quite a bit.

I peeked at Isla. "Close your mouth," I whispered out of the corner of mine to my sister.

She snapped her mouth closed and wiped away a bit of drool that had gathered at the corner.

Carver gave Raj a winning smile. "I'm here for a meeting

on another matter, but I am looking forward to my visit tomorrow. From what I can tell, this is a fascinating building." He cocked his head to peer under the bar. "I wonder what was so fascinating under there to gather your attention and the attention from these two beautiful ladies?"

Raj's face turned a deep shade of red. "Isla thought she saw a spider."

"He was the size of a hamster," Isla said, somewhat breathlessly.

The smile widened across the historian's face. "A spider. Well, we can't have that in a place where people eat, can we?"

Raj and my sister shook their heads mutely. I stopped myself from rolling my eyes at their reactions to Carver Finley.

"Raj was just telling us about you." I said, holding out my hand. "I'm Fiona Knox of Duncreigan, and this is my sister Isla."

He took my hand and gave it a professional shake before letting go. "It's a pleasure to meet you both. I've heard of Duncreigan—the garden there is supposed to be magnificent. I would love to see it before I leave the area."

I smiled but made no promises. There weren't many people I let inside my garden. However, I would keep a visit with him in mind. It would be interesting to hear a historical authority's take on the menhir. As far as I knew, the menhir hadn't been dated. Maybe if I could pinpoint exactly how old the stone was, it might tell me from where the magic had originated.

"What meeting brings you to the Twisted Fox?" Raj asked.

"Minister MacCullen," Carver said as he brushed a piece of imaginary lint off his sleeve.

I leaned back against the bar for support. I hadn't expected him to say that.

"What a tragedy that was!" Raj pressed his hands together as if in prayer.

"Indeed," Carver agreed. "I imagine that everyone in the village is wondering what brought the minister to his end."

"I'm sure the police are doing everything they can to find out. I don't know if you know Chief Inspector Neil Craig, but he is a good man and will get to the heart of what happened to the minister in no time at all."

"I've met him," Carver said with a slight curl to his lip.

Clearly Craig had spoken to Carver, and I would hazard a guess that it had not been a pleasant encounter.

"Yes, the minister's death is a tragedy for the village," Carver went on. "I was very sorry to hear about it. He was the driving force in favor of the chapel restoration project."

"Will the project go on now that the minister is dead?" Raj asked. I leaned forward, desperate to hear the answer to the question I'd been dying to ask.

Carver smoothed an imaginary wrinkle in his sleeve. "It's hard to tell. I'm uncertain that the congregation would have pursued it without his persistence, and what a shame that would have been. It is a lovely structure, or at least what is left of it. It will do wonders in telling us what religious faith looked like in Aberdeenshire back in the twelfth century. It is important that history like that be preserved for future generations."

He said all of this like it was a well-practiced speech on the campaign trail. And perhaps it was. Carver Finley was campaigning to save Aberdeenshire's rich history before it was completely pushed aside by the modern world. He deserved credit for that.

The front door of the Twisted Fox opened, and golden light from the setting sun poured into the large room.

"There you are, Carver!" Emer Boyd smiled broadly and hurried toward us. "Thank you so much for meeting here to talk over next steps."

Her husband, Douglas, followed a few paces behind her. He dragged his feet as if he'd rather be anywhere else.

"I hope we didn't keep you waiting very long," Emer said. "We were over at the church checking on everything. The sexton has done a good job of keeping the show running, and we found a pulpit supply minister to fill in for Sunday services until the presbytery sends us an interim minister. And of course, there is the minister's funeral to plan. It must be befitting of such a great man. As you can imagine, it's been quite a scramble. Both Douglas and I are exhausted."

I peered around her at Douglas, who was staring at the top of his shoe and obsessively scratching at his right arm. The man had either a terrible case of poison ivy or a nervous tick.

"When will the funeral be?" Raj asked.

She glanced at him. "We don't know yet. We can't set a date until the police release the body." She grimaced when she said this, but then brightened. "That's why we have to do all the planning that we can now. I have several leaders in the presbytery set to preach and serve communion. I think it all will be well."

I nodded thoughtfully. I wasn't sure yet if I would attend the minister's funeral. It seemed hypocritical in a way, after the many rocky encounters he and I had had.

She smiled at Isla and then me. "I see you've met Carver Finley, Fiona. I'm very glad to see that."

I smiled in return, unsure why she was so happy that Carver and I had met.

Emer seemed to read my thoughts by what she said next. "I'm glad that you have met because we will all be working at the church together soon, of course. Just as soon as we make arrangements for you to provide the flowers, Fiona."

Before I could respond to that, Carver said, "And I was very happy to meet Fiona, since I hear she is from Duncreigan, which I have heard so much about."

She tightened her grip on the handle of her designer handbag. "I'm sure Duncreigan is fascinating, but as you know, the chapel ruins are really the historical wonder in Bellewick."

I raised my eyebrow. I hadn't realized we were in a competition.

Emer cleared her throat. "I know you have much work to do on your assessment of the ruins, so Douglas and I don't want to keep you. Shall we begin our meeting?" She pointed across the pub at a couple who were leaving a table by the window.

"I'll send one of my waitstaff over right away to clear the table and take your orders," Raj promised them both.

"Thank you." She blushed. "I know it might seem crass to be getting on with the restoration, but this project is what Minister MacCullen cared about most. Saving this church will be his legacy. The church has already changed the name of the chapel restoration fund to the Reverend Quaid MacCullen Chapel Fund in his memory."

Before anyone could comment on that, Emer looked to Raj. "Coffees please, Raj, to start. Mr. Finley, will you follow me?"

Carver nodded, then smiled at Raj. "I am looking forward to assessing the pub. It will be an interesting project for me, and I do enjoy interesting projects. I hope you remember that, Miss Knox."

I frowned.

Raj puffed up his chest and beamed from ear to ear. There was nothing else in the world that the famous historian could have said to make the pub owner any prouder. "Those coffees will be right up."

Carver nodded as he and Emer wove around the table in the crowded pub with Douglas following in their wake.

I wanted to ask Raj about the odd couple, but the cook appeared from the kitchen with two steaming plates of chicken marsala, and I was immediately distracted by my growling stomach.

Raj personally took the tray of coffees to Carver's table. When he returned, he was grinning from ear to ear. "He said the pub has history," he said dreamily.

I glanced at Isla, who was blatantly staring at the handsome man across the room. I was on the lookout for more drool on her lips. Thankfully, there was none to be seen.

I smiled. "You've already discovered a lot of it, Raj. I'm excited to see what Carver will be able to add to your research."

"Me too." Raj began putting away a tray of clean beer steins. "Now what was your question again, Fiona, before the spider sighting and Mr. Finley's arrival?"

I sipped on my glass of water. "Seth MacGregor. When was the last time you saw him?"

My sister spun back around in her seat and began digging into her dinner as if it was the last meal she might ever eat. Maybe I hadn't been doing a great job of feeding her since she came to Scotland.

He cocked his head. "It's been over a month since I've seen Seth. As soon as the coastline was saved from that developer, he left. As far as I know, he's living in Aberdeen."

I frowned. "Are you two still in contact?"

"Somewhat. We are like-minded when it comes to environmental issues, so we move in the same circles online, if you count that. But I haven't been personally in touch with him since he left for Aberdeen. Why do you ask?"

"I thought I saw him in the village yesterday across the street from your pub. It was in the evening right before the storm hit. I assumed he was in the village to see you."

Raj placed two more glasses under the bar. "He never came in, and I was here all night. I kept the pub open after hours so that those who were here during the storm didn't have to venture out into that mess of weather."

"That was nice of you," I said absently. I had been positive Seth was back in the village to see Raj, and I couldn't think of another reason for him to be here. "Are there any environmental causes in the village that Seth would be interested in participating in now? Anything that would draw him back?"

Raj smoothed the right side of his mustache and then the left. "No. There are always causes to fight for, but in the village of Bellewick, all is calm in the fight for the green cause, at least for the moment."

I bit my lip. Perhaps I was overreacting about seeing Seth in the village, but I didn't want Hamish to be hurt again.

"Oh!" Raj said. "Emer is waving me over. I should go see what they want. I would love to share some of my Indian dishes with Carver."

I laughed. "Go. I'm glad that Carver is so impressed with the pub."

He beamed. "Me too." He hurried to their table with a fresh pot of coffee and a small plate of lavender lemon cookies that I recognized from Presha's teashop.

All the while, my sister kept her head down and her face hidden under her hair.

Chapter Thirteen

The next day, Isla and I spent the entire day working in the shop and worked well after closing. Throughout the day, I did my best to push thoughts about the minister and murder from my head, but to be honest, I wasn't having much luck at that. Instead my mind was plagued with memories of the time the minister and I had clashed. Would those times convince the village and police that I was guilty of the minister's murder? I couldn't see the chief inspector arresting me without a lot of evidence. He would want to be sure, or at least I hoped.

It was midafternoon before a single customer entered the shop. When the front door did finally open, I leapt up from a chair in the back room, nearly tripping over myself to make a sale.

"Keep you cool, Fi," my sister said as I hurried by her.

"Hello!" a round middle-aged woman with bright pink cheeks greeted me in the front room of the shop. "You must be Fiona. I'm so sorry I haven't stopped by your shop sooner than this. It's just—" Her words were cut off by a string of sneezes. When the sneezing finally subsided, she removed a handkerchief from her red patent-leather purse. "I'm so sorry. I was just telling you that I haven't stopped by because I'm allergic to flowers." She sneezed.

My brows knit together as I glanced around the front room of the shop. If someone was allergic to flowers, this was the last place they should really be.

She held out her hand to me. "I'm Bernice Brennan. I own the jewelry store in the village."

I nodded. I had passed the store many times when walking to the flower shop and had always been tempted to stop. They had a whole array of beautiful pieces in the front windows, so much so that I couldn't help but wonder what they might have in the back. "It's nice to meet a fellow shopkeeper in the village." I shook her hand and released it.

She smiled. "It is, but that's not really why I've come here. I'm an elder at St. Thomas's."

"Oh," I said, and my face fell. Was she about to accuse me of killing her minister? I licked my lips. "I'm so very sorry for your loss. The church must be reeling from what has happened."

"It is. The entire congregation is in shock, and I accept your condolences on behalf of the church, but I wanted to share our sincerest apologies over what happened the Sunday that you tried to visit to our church. All the church elders were horrified to see how Minister MacCullen treated you. He should never have turned you away like that."

I blinked, surprised that she would bring this up at all. "There's no point in rehashing it now . . ." I trailed off, thinking *now that the minister is dead.*

"Perhaps not, but I wanted to personally tell you we were ashamed of the minister's behavior. I don't believe he ever came to you and apologized himself."

The minister had come to see me at the shop, of course, but he most certainly had never apologized.

"I appreciate that. Emer Boyd apologized as well."

Bernice wrinkled her nose at the mention of Emer. "When did she do that?"

"It was at my opening. She mentioned that she would talk to the church elders about me providing the chancel flowers as well."

"She's not a church elder. She shouldn't be going around pretending to be one."

"I didn't think that she was," I said, surprised by Bernice's reaction. "She was only trying to be nice."

"Emer is always trying to be nice," Bernice grumbled. "I know she is the church treasurer, but if you ask me, she should spend less time meddling in church business and focus on her own affairs."

I wondered what those affairs were that needed Emer's attention. But I stopped myself from asking. I didn't want to know, and the last thing I wanted to do was get caught up in church politics when I was already involved in a murder. It seemed to me that there was a power struggle of some sort at the church now that the minister's death had left a void.

Bernice sneezed.

"It was so nice for you to stop by and tell me this. It really does mean a lot to me, but I don't want to keep you much longer. I would hate to cause you another sneezing fit."

She rubbed the handkerchief under her nose. "It really is a shame, because I do love flowers. I think they are so beautiful, and the ones that you have here are the prettiest that I have ever seen."

I beamed. "Thank you."

She tucked her handkerchief back into her purse. "I should be off. Please come visit our church again. We would love to have you. We won't turn you away."

I promised her that I would.

"And if Emer stops by again to tell you something about the church, tell me, would you?" she asked.

I raised my brows. She wanted me to snitch on another member of the church. "I don't know that that's my place."

"It won't take you but a moment." She smiled and squeezed my hand. "You come stop by my jewelry store whenever you like. I would love to show you around. The shopkeepers in Bellewick need to stick together. That's what I always say."

I promised her that I would.

Isla walked over to me after Bernice was gone. "Is it just me, or do you think something weird is going on over at that church?"

I glanced at my sister. "I don't think it's just you at all. Let's get back to work."

She nodded and went to the back room.

At the end of the work day, Isla ran out of the back room. "I have some news."

I arched my brow. "That sounds serious."

"I got a job!"

"A job?" I blinked.

She nodded. "Raj gave me a job waitressing at the Twisted Fox! I'm going to be a waitress there."

"But you work here," I said.

She rolled her eyes. "I know that, but I can work here days and there nights. It's perfect."

I blinked again, surprised by my sister's initiative. "Isla, I think that's great!"

She grinned. "Those student loans aren't going to pay themselves. I start tomorrow, so I'd just like to go home tonight and chill."

I wasn't ready to go home just yet. "That's a good plan. You head back. There are a few things I want to check out before heading home." It was the height of the summer in County Aberdeen, and the sun wouldn't set until long after ten. I handed her the car keys.

She narrowed her eyes. "You're not going to mess around in the minister's murder, are you?"

"What?" I gave her a shocked face. "Me? Why would I do that?"

She placed her hands on her curvy hips. "Because you're a meddler, Fi. You heard Raj. He said that you shouldn't go talk to that saxton guy."

"Sexton," I said. "And he said I shouldn't go talk to him last night. A full day has passed."

"Whatever. And I don't like that name. It sounds dirty."

"I think it's the British version of a caretaker or janitor."

She threw up her hands. "Then why don't they just say that? Brits are so weird. I seriously have no idea what they are saying half of the time."

I didn't want to start a conversation about dialects with her. There was a place I wanted to be that might give me better insight into how the minister died. "You can come with me if you want. I wouldn't mind the company."

She checked her phone. "I'll go back to the cottage. Ivanhoe has been trapped inside all day. I'm sure he can't wait to get out." A blush crept up her neck and onto her pale cheeks. One problem of having the British complexion was that everyone on earth knew when you were embarrassed. The same happened to me. But what was Isla embarrassed about?

"All right," I said. I wasn't ready yet to press her into telling me what was really going on. "I'll see you back at the cottage."

She hesitated. "Are you sure you want to walk?"

"It's only three miles," I said. "And I could use the exercise. I have been crammed inside the flower shop for weeks."

She frowned. "Well, text me when you're heading home just so I know, and if you want me to come get you, I can."

I hugged her. "Thank you, Isla." She nodded, then spun on her heel heading in the direction of the car.

Her blonde hair bounced on her back and her black boots clicked on the cobblestones as she walked away. She thought she was too curvy, but by anyone else's interpretation she was a stunning girl—woman, I corrected myself. Isla Knox was no longer a child. It was something that I had to keep reminding myself.

When Isla disappeared from sight, I went in the opposite direction toward the sea. I followed the same path I had taken early that morning along the cobblestone streets until I came to the harbor. The briny scent of the ocean welcomed me back.

Chapter Fourteen

The harbor faced east, so the sun was to my back, and vibrant colors played across the boats' ropes and masts and across the sea itself. It was eight o'clock in the evening and boats were coming into the safe harbor for the night. In summer, the fishermen tried to stay out as long as they could when the fishing was good, and even in the hustle and bustle of the end of the day at a busy harbor, it was peaceful. It was hard to believe there had been such a violent storm two nights before.

After such a bad storm, the fishing would be very good, as the waters and the wildlife would have been churned up from the bottom of the sea. I knew this because I remembered visiting Florida's eastern coast a few weeks after a hurricane almost hit when I was a child. Even from the near miss, shells and sea life had washed up on the shore for weeks. I had been on the beach with Isla, who was small at the time, when a huge conch washed ashore. It was bigger than my head. I'd run to it and added it to my collection.

That shell currently sat in one of the many boxes my mother had shipped to Scotland. I just hadn't found it yet.

I stood by an old diving shed at the edge of the dock. There was a collection of oil barrels there, and the three old sailors who always seemed to be in the same spot were still there. I knew that if the minister had been near the docks the day of the murder, they were the ones who would know about it.

"Aye, it's a beautiful night, is it not?" one of the old seamen called out to me.

I smiled to myself. I'd known that if I just stood there long enough, they would talk to me.

"The sea, she's being nice today," he said. "That is usually her way. She throws a tantrum, and then after she is all but a beauty. It's how she makes us forget, and it is how she makes us risk our lives to have the pleasure of being rocked by her again."

I couldn't help but agree. At the height of the storm, it had felt like there would never be a clear night again, but now the sea was calm with only a few whitecaps out in the middle, adding more tranquility to the scene than any real danger.

"Ewan, you be a poet worthy of Robert Louis Stevenson himself," said one of the other men, who was missing an eye.

Part of me wanted to ask the old seaman how he lost his eye, but I knew it would be a long and involved tale, and I had much more important questions that needed to be answered at the moment.

"It is a beautiful night," I said as I walked over to the men on their barrels. I couldn't understand how they could sit on them day in and day out. The oil barrels, even when turned onto their side, like one of them was, didn't look all that comfortable to me. "It's much different than Sunday night," I went on to say. "That was my first storm since I moved here. It was a doozy."

"*Doozy*," Ewan said, looking me over. "I don't know what this means. It must be one of those American phrases; no one ever knows what they mean. Like *Internet*."

I didn't think *Internet* was an American word, but I didn't want to argue with Ewan when I needed information.

"My father never liked my American expressions," I said.

"You mean Ian MacCallister," Ewan said.

I blinked. "No, Ian was a good friend. My father is Steven Knox. He is from Aberdeenshire, but the city, not the village of Bellewick. He and Uncle Ian, who was my godfather, were like brothers when they met in school."

Ewan looked confused for a moment, but his face cleared. "My mistake. You just have the black hair of a MacCallister, and I know that you inherited Duncreigan. I put two and two together."

"You put two and two together, Ewan," the fisherman without the eye said. "And you came up with five like you always do."

"She should be glad I thought she was a MacCallister." Ewan sniffed. "That's quite an honor in this community."

"Uncle Ian never had any children," I said, becoming increasingly uncomfortable with this conversation.

The two old seamen sitting with Ewan shared a look that I couldn't quite interpret. I shook my head. "In any case, it was quite a storm, and what a tragedy to come right after, to lose such an important person in the community."

"Aye, you must be talking about Minister Quaid MacCullen," said Ewan, clearly the ringleader of the trio.

The sailor with one eye pointed in the direction of the rocky beach. "I heard that MacCullen washed up on the beach. Seemed strange to me. He's not a man I had ever seen this close to the water. I always thought he was afraid of it or couldn't swim."

"I thought the same," Ewan said.

"Aye," the other fisherman, who sat in a wheelchair and was missing a leg said. "But I saw him by the docks just before the storm. The old minister stuck out like a sore thumb around the harbor. It was clear he didn't know where he was going. I offered my help, but he either didn't hear me or he pretended he didn't, because he wouldn't look my way. If he was going to pay me no mind, then I would do the same to him."

He must have seen me staring at his leg because he added, "Aye, a shark took it, lass."

The other two men laughed.

"Don't let him pull *your* leg, miss. Old Milton lost his leg in a car accident," Ewan said.

Old Milton glared at him. "It is my leg that was lost. Let me have my story about the shark."

"Very well. I won't correct you every time you tell a lie to a passerby about your battle with the shark, but if you are going tell such a yarn, make it a great white."

Old Milton nodded. "Only a great white is worthy enough to take my leg."

"What was the minister doing at the docks?" I asked.

Old Milton thought about this for a moment. "He looked

like he was waiting for someone. There would be no other reason for him to be down at the docks. He had never been here before."

"Did you see anyone?" I tried to keep my impatience out of my voice. I knew these old sailors wanted to draw their stories out and tell them in their own good time. If I wanted to hear the whole tale, I had to be patient. Not my strong suit at all.

"He was talking to a young dock worker. I recognized him right away." Old Milton wrinkled his nose as if he smelled something foul.

"Who was it?"

"Remy Kenner."

Ewan clicked his tongue. "Remy Kenner, you say. Why, there isn't a worse sort of man who took in a breath of life."

"Why do you say that?" I asked.

"Remy Kenner is sour to his very core," Old Milton said. "A cruel man, never got any higher up than a helping hand around the dock and doing hard labor. No one would want to be stuck on a boat with that man."

"They would throw him over the side for sure," the one-eyed sailor said.

"Aye," Ewan said. "But truth be told, he would take at least three men with him, so a boat captain knows it's better to play it close to the vest as far as Remy Kenner is concerned."

Remy Kenner was sounding more and more like a viable murder suspect, which was something I needed now.

"And the minister was meeting with this unsavory person," I mused. What could Minister MacCullen have to do with Remy Kenner, an unkind dock worker whom these seamen, who I knew must have seen all sorts of terrible things in their day, seemed almost afraid of? "Where can I find Remy Kenner?" I asked.

Ewan's mouth fell open. "He's not a man you want to find, lass. You would be very sorry if you did. I know that his poor wife is."

"You can be certain of that," Old Milton agreed.

It seemed to me that Remy Kenner certainly could drown someone as old as the minister, since he was a strongly built dock worker and had access to boats to toss the minister into the North Sea. Remy might just be the person I needed to hand over to Craig as a viable suspect.

Which made me ask my next question. "Have you told Chief Inspector Craig or the police about seeing the minister with Remy Kenner?"

"Old Milton who had the tale to tell was not here when the police came."

"I had a wee nip the night of the storm." Old Milton's craggy face reddened. "And it had gone to my head a little too far."

The one-eyed seaman laughed. "You had a bit more than a wee nip." He looked at me with his one good eye. "Take it from me, lass, he had enough to drink to put a whale under the table."

"Were you drinking when you saw the minister with Remy?" I asked. If Old Milton had been the last one to see the minister alive, other than the killer, he'd need to be able to say he'd been sober when he saw the two men if it went to trial. But why was I thinking about a trial? I was getting way ahead of myself. All I had to go on from what these men had said was a lead. It was a good lead, but still only a lead.

"Looks like we have company," Ewan said.

"Ah," Old Milton replied. "It's Seth MacGregor."

I spun around at that, and sure enough, Seth was standing at the edge of the harbor. He was a long and lean man, just a year or two younger than me. He'd fashioned his hair differently than I remembered it a couple of months ago. His head was turned in profile, so I could see that the hair at the sides of his head was short and the top was brushed back into a fauxhawk.

Ewan scratched the day-old growth of stubble on his chin. "What's he doing here? I thought the boy had left us for life in the big city. I never thought he'd be one of the children to stay. Always can tell the ones who will stay and who have the big eyes for the city. Seth was one of the big-eye boys, I can promise you that."

Seth was still looking north, toward the rocky beach where Minister MacCullen had washed up that morning. Was he looking that way because of the murder?

Old Milton clicked his tongue. "Smart as a whip, Seth MacGregor is, but not a whit of what you Americans call 'street smarts.' Maybe he came back because Aberdeen was too much for him."

"Now that I see him, that stirred a memory," the one-eyed man said.

I turned to him. "Oh?"

"He was here at the harbor the night of the storm as well." He turned to his friend. "That must have been about the time you saw the minister with Remy, Old Milton. Because I had seen Seth, and then came straight here. That's when you told me about seeing Remy and the minister."

Old Milton nodded. "That sounds right, but you didn't say anything about seeing the MacGregor boy."

The one-eyed man shrugged. "I hadn't thought anything of it. There was no reason why I would be suspicious of Seth Mac-Gregor walking around the docks. He was born and raised in this village."

My pulse quickened. Seth had been at the docks the same time the minister was? Was he somehow connected to the minister's death? Had he seen something? Had he spoken to the minister before he died? I turned and stared at Seth, who seemed deep in thought.

"But you have probably seen him the most out of any of us, lass," Old Milton said.

I tore my eyes away from Seth and looked down at Old Milton. "Me? Why do you say that?"

Old Milton shifted in his wheelchair. "Why, I would have thought that the boy was staying with his great uncle Hamish, and if he is staying with Hamish, you should know about it, since Hamish's cottage is on your land."

I didn't say anything. For some reason, I didn't want the old sailors to know Seth hadn't been to Duncreigan. But did I really know he *hadn't* been there? In all actuality, he could have been staying with Hamish in his cottage and I would never have known it. In all the time I had been living in Scotland, I had never visited the garden caretaker's cottage.

When I turned back to Seth, he was staring at me. Shock registered on his handsome face, and he turned and fast-walked away from the harbor back toward the cobblestone streets and into the heart of the village.

It was time to get to the bottom of why he was in Belle-wick. I started after him. "Seth?"

He started to jog.

Was he really running away from me?

"Seth, stop!" I shouted.

Seth glanced back at me and then bolted.

I took off after him at a dead run.

"Is that girl an Olympic sprinter?" I heard Ewan ask as I ran.

Chapter Fifteen

I came around the side of one of the large fisherman's boats, expecting to see Seth on the other side, but he was gone. There were so many alleyways and streets that led out of the harbor area into the village, it was impossible for me to know which way he'd gone.

I gasped for breath and held my sides as if my burning lungs might come bursting out of my ribcage. I was not an Olympic sprinter, not even close, and now, because I'd told my sister to take the car, I'd have to limp the three miles home.

I texted my sister as promised and told her I was leaving the village and planned to be home in an hour. I guessed it would take me at least that long to walk to the cottage at a leisurely pace.

As I walked on the cobblestone streets, I kept my eye out for Seth, but there was no sign of him. If I hadn't thought he was up to something before, I definitely did now.

I walked down Prince Street, where my shop and the Twisted Fox were located, and double-checked the door to the Climbing Rose. It was locked up tight, and I was happy to see there were no threatening notes taped to the door. I walked by the Twisted Fox and could hear Celtic music playing inside the pub. Raj must have hired a band for the night. I was almost tempted to go inside and tap my toes with the rest of them, but I knew I had to be getting home. Isla would be worried if I wasn't back within the hour as promised.

I quickened my pace and headed down Prince Street, out of the shopping district, over the troll bridge, and past the round-about with the unicorn statue in the middle. I was about half-way to the cottage when I realized I was in no condition to make the trek. I was exhausted and cranky. I looked westward toward the setting sun.

Sheep with spray-painted marks of pink, green, blue, and orange stood a few feet away, nibbling on the short grasses that grew along the green foothills of the mountains. Behind those foothills were the mountains themselves. There, heather-covered bases grew into sharp peaks with mounds of snow on the tops of them like whipped cream on a sundae. Above those mountains, the red-gold sun that was outlined in magenta waited to make its final descent for the night. Even more reason to give up walking back to the cottage.

I took my phone out of my pocket and was about to text my sister to pick me up when a set of headlights blinded me. I held up my arm to protect my face and jumped to the side of the road.

I stood on the shoulder of the road waiting for the car to pass, but it never did. The bright lights remained trained on me. The driver's side door of the jeep opened, and my heart sank as the large form of a man exited the jeep. I felt a mingle of relief and dread when I recognized the man walking toward me. I knew I was in for it.

Chief Inspector Neil Craig stood in the beam of his jeep's headlights and crossed his arms over his broad chest. "What are you doing out in the middle of the road? Where's your car? Did you have an accident? Are you all right?"

I blinked as my brain processed his rapid-fire questions. I ticked my answers off on my fingers as I spoke. "I'm walking home from the village. My car is fine. My sister drove it home a couple of hours ago. And I'm also fine." I smiled, feeling quite pleased with myself that I could easily answer all his questions, and in order, too.

He threw up his large hands. "Bloody hell, Fiona, a man was murdered and dumped in the sea, and you're walking along a country road in the dark like you're on a Sunday afternoon stroll through a garden. How naïve can you be?"

Apparently, the chief inspector wasn't as satisfied with my answers as I had been. "I'm not naïve," I said.

He folded his arms again. "Oh really?"

"It's not completely dark yet." Just as I said that, the sun dropped below the mountains.

"You were saying?" Craig asked.

"Did you plan that?"

He shook his head and rubbed the back of his neck. "Can you please get in the car? I'll give you a lift home."

I had half a mind to turn down his offer, but I thought better of it. It went from twilight to pitch black rapidly in the mountains.

I walked over to the jeep, but before I could open the door

for myself, Craig opened it for me. I told myself that didn't mean anything. I had seen him open car doors for criminals before. Of course, in those cases the criminal was usually in handcuffs and being shoved into the back seat of the jeep, but I wasn't one for splitting hairs.

I climbed in, and Craig closed the door after me without a word. He got into the driver seat and started the engine.

I was quiet for a long minute. "Okay, maybe walking home at night wasn't the best idea I've ever had."

He glanced at me. "Maybe?"

"Hey, I'm trying to admit I was foolish here."

"And you are doing a bang-up job of it." The side of his mouth twitched.

I narrowed my eyes at him until I saw the slight upward turn of the corner of his mouth. "Chief Inspector Craig, are you teasing me?"

"I never tease." There was a full-on smile on his bearded face now.

Now I was certain that he was teasing me.

"Why did you walk home when you could have gone with your sister?" His tone was serious.

"I wanted to take a walk around the harbor."

He glanced at me with his dark eyebrows raised. "You just happened to want to go for a walk around the harbor, a place that is mere feet away from where a dead body washed up yesterday morning." He returned his attention to the road.

"I did. The harbor is beautiful in the evening."

"I won't argue with you on that point, but I know you went there to meddle in the investigation. It would save us both a lot of time if you just came out with it and told me what you learned."

I was quiet for a minute, and then I said, "Since you asked so nicely, I spoke to the old men at the docks."

"I spoke with them too."

"Not Old Milton, you didn't."

"Old Milton?"

"He was one of the three men at the docks tonight, and he wasn't there when you interviewed the others. He's missing a leg; a shark took it." I saw no reason to ruin the old fisherman's tale. "Old Milton said he saw the minister and a man by the name of Remy Kenner arguing at the entrance to the dock before the storm. They told me to stay away from him. Have you heard of Remy Kenner?"

Craig took a deep breath. "Rembrandt Kenner. Yes, I know him. He's trouble with a capital T. I've arrested him countless times on charges of possession, assault, and domestic violence. Those old codgers were right to warn you away from him. Please promise me you won't approach him."

I ignored his request. "Rembrandt Kenner? That seems quite a name to live up to."

"It does, doesn't it? Maybe that's why everyone calls him Remy. Everyone knows he won't amount to anything."

I raised my eyebrows. "That seems like a harsh statement."

"After you see Remy, which I'm sure you will at some point in a village as small as Bellewick, tell me if the statement isn't harsh enough."

"You said he's been arrested for domestic violence. Does he have a family?"

"Yes, a wife and a son. Claudia Kenner, his wife, is one of the sweetest women you will ever meet. It is a complete mystery to everyone as to why she stays with him. I wish I could say I think she will leave him someday, but I have seen bad relationships like theirs too many times before. Some of them end very badly. The little boy is about two, and his name is Byron. I have appealed to Claudia many times to leave Remy for the boy's sake."

I shivered. "So do you think Remy is the type to drown the minister?"

"If he had a reason to, yes," he said, as if he had no doubt in his mind. "I don't think it would be completely random, but if Remy became angry enough, there is no limit to what he might do."

It seemed to me that Remy Kenner was becoming more and more like a viable suspect. "I wonder what he was arguing with the minister about, then."

"I plan to find out just as soon as I drop you off safely at Duncreigan, watch you go into the cottage, and lock the door behind you." He tightened his grip on the steering wheel.

I shifted in my seat. "I could come with you. An extra set of ears and eyes might pick up on something, and if he really is that awful, you might need backup. The only police—or sort of police—in the village right now is Kipling, and he isn't much help for anything."

"Fiona, no. Remy Kenner is not a man to trifle with. As far as I'm concerned, I would much rather he never knew that you existed. It's safer for you that way."

"You sound almost afraid of him." I studied his profile.

"I'm not afraid of him for myself, but I do fear what he could do to people who aren't prepared to deal with a man like him. He could hurt you. He *would* hurt you." He turned and looked at me with worry in his eyes. "I would never forgive myself if that happened."

"It wouldn't be your fault," I said.

"If you were hurt by him," he said, "it would be my fault because I didn't make it clear enough how foolhardy speaking to him actually was."

As much as I hated the chief inspector telling me not to talk to another citizen of the village, a small part of me was touched by his concern. I told myself he would be concerned about all the citizens under his care in the same way. I was nothing special to him. It was something that I was starting to repeat to myself more and more often.

"In any case, I don't believe the minister was killed at the harbor."

I looked at him. "Oh?"

"From his preliminary investigation, the coroner said there was fresh water in the minister's lungs. My guess he was drowned somewhere else in fresh water and then dumped into the sea with the hope that the storm would take care of his remains."

I shivered at the thought as we came up the long-graveled road that led to the cottage at Duncreigan. The jeep's headlights fell on the cottage, and its bright beams outlined my sister, standing in the front doorway and hugging a distressed-looking Ivanhoe to her chest. I didn't know if Ivanhoe was distressed because he wondered what had become of me or because Isla was hugging the life out of him.

My sister dropped the cat inside the cottage and closed the door. "Fi! Where have you been? You said you would be home an hour ago. I've been texting you and you haven't answered. I thought you were dead!"

I pulled my phone out of the back pocket of my jeans. Sure enough, there were ten text messages from my sister. "I'm sorry, Isla," I said. "I must have had the phone on silent and didn't hear it. But I'm fine. I left the village later than expected, and Chief Inspector Craig was kind enough to give me a ride home."

Isla brushed her silky blonde hair over her shoulder and looked up at the six-five police officer. "Thank you so much for taking care of my sister. It's nice to know that the police in Aberdeenshire are conscientious of the welfare of their citizens."

I stood behind the chief inspector and just stopped myself from making a gagging gesture at my sister. I might have, too, if I hadn't been afraid that Craig would see me out of the corner of his eye.

"It was no trouble," Craig said gallantly.

I stepped between them. "Thank you again for the ride, Chief Inspector, but we won't keep you. I know that you have much work to do."

A smile widened across his face as if he knew exactly what I was up to. That was saying something, because I had no idea.

"I'll walk you to your jeep," I said.

Craig said good-bye to Isla and followed me back to his car. He opened the door to the jeep and held it. "So that information about Remy Kenner was the only thing you learned at the harbor tonight? There's nothing else?" He searched my face.

Biting my lip, I looked away. I wanted to tell him my

suspicions about Seth MacGregor, but I didn't feel I could do that until I spoke to Hamish. He had a right to know his great-nephew was back in the village and possibly tangled up in trouble again before the police knew about it. I would have to tell Craig in time, just not yet.

"He's the only person Old Milton said he saw with the minister," I said, technically telling the truth.

He nodded and looked back at the house. "How long is your sister staying here?"

My heart dropped, and I glanced over my shoulder. Isla had gone inside, but she and Ivanhoe were watching from the window by the dining room table. Her pretty face was clearly visible, and I bit the inside of my lip. I should have expected something like this. Isla was young, beautiful, and full of energy. It was little wonder that a man like the chief inspector was interested in her. It made sense. Then why did it make me so upset?

I shook the cobwebs from my head. "I'm not sure. It might be longer than I first thought. She got a job waitressing at the Twisted Fox today. She just graduated college and is trying to find her footing in the real world."

He smiled. "They why on earth did she come to Bellewick? This is nothing close to the real world."

I shrugged, knowing that the chief inspector was trying to be funny, but I couldn't muster a laugh.

"Yes, well." Craig frowned. "You might want to consider another form of transportation to travel to and from the village if she plans to be here long. You can't be walking home on the road at night, and certainly not in the winter. There are many twists and turns, and add snow and ice, it becomes quite dangerous."

I shivered. "I can't imagine Isla staying here all the way to the winter, so it will be a nonissue then."

"You never can be certain. She might find a reason to stay," he said.

My heart sank a little bit more, but the chief inspector didn't seem to notice, since he went on to say, "This place takes a hold of you, and it doesn't let go. Many people who grew up and swore they'd leave the village, never to return, come back in the end. It has a way of doing that. Look at yourself; you're here."

"I'm here because it's what Uncle Ian wished. It didn't have anything to do with a pull of the land."

"It's the garden that pulled you here," he said.

"Maybe," I murmured. "That's what my godfather would have wanted me to believe."

"I should go," he said with some reluctance. "I want to pay Remy Kenner a visit before I return to Aberdeen for the night."

I couldn't stop myself from saying, "If he is as awful as you say he is, be careful. Please."

He studied me. "I will. Tell your sister that I said good-bye."

"I will," I whispered, and watched with a fallen heart as his jeep drove away.

Chapter Sixteen

The next morning, I awoke before dawn. I wanted to catch Hamish before he headed to the garden for the day. I knew he would be up, as he was an early riser.

But if I was being completely honest, I wanted to visit his cottage to make sure Seth wasn't staying there. It wasn't that I expected Hamish to tell me everything about his life, but if another person was living at Duncreigan, I should at least be aware of it.

Part of me was afraid that the reason Seth had run away from me at the docks was because Hamish knew he was in the village. What I didn't understand was why Hamish would keep that secret from me.

In my head, I practiced what I would say in case I found Seth at Hamish's cottage. I didn't want to upset Hamish, but I also wanted to know why he had kept this secret from me, assuming he had a secret.

While I prepared for my visit to Hamish's home, my sister and Ivanhoe slept on my bed. I had again spent the night on the couch by the hearth in the main room of the cottage amidst all the shipping boxes from back home. I really would have to find some time to deal with them. I felt like the room was closing in on me and I couldn't find anything.

My back ached as I tied the laces of my hiking boots. If Isla was going to stay in Scotland on a more permanent basis, the sleeping arrangements had to change. In this case, age did matter. At twenty-two, she could sleep on a log and be perfectly refreshed the next morning. I was eight years older than her. If I slept on a log, I would look like I got hit by a double-decker bus.

The air outside the cottage was damp and chilly like most mornings in Duncreigan. I guessed it was sixty degrees Fahrenheit. I hadn't made the mental leap to think in Celsius yet.

After growing up in Nashville, where the summers went from hot to hotter to too hot to think, the cool Scottish summer was welcome. It was nice to live in a place where I wasn't trapped inside with air-conditioning because the outdoors was too miserable.

The path to Hamish's cottage was well worn from the thousands of times he had faithfully made the half-mile trek from his cottage to the garden at Duncreigan. I followed the mossy path, taking care not to slip on any of the granite rocks that poked up out of the ground. Hamish's cottage was higher in elevation than mine, and I quickly found the incline was steeper than I'd expected it to be, so I was happy I'd worn my hiking boots. The boots weren't from back home, where cowboy boots were more commonly seen on the streets of Nashville. I'd purchased the boots on a day trip to Edinburgh when I finally made the decision to stay in Scotland for good.

As I crested the steep hill, Hamish's cottage came into view, and it took my breath away. If I'd been Gretel from Hansel and Gretel, I would have run to this place; it looked just as adorable as the cottage did in that story. Thankfully, there was no witch inside who planned to feed me sweets before throwing me in her stew pot.

The cottage was smaller than mine, but also made out of granite. That wasn't a surprise. Aberdeen was called the Granite City, and most of the buildings there and in the surrounding area were made of the local stone. The cottage had once been a bothy, a small Scottish cottage or building in the mountains that was left unlocked as a place where travelers could take refuge from the Scottish weather.

Uncle Ian had converted the bothy into Hamish's cottage when it was clear that Hamish couldn't make the daily three-mile walk from the village any longer. It had taken Hamish some time to accept the gift, but I thought he now loved living out in the foothills away from the hubbub of village life.

I stood a few feet away from the old building and admired it. The old bothy had one chimney on the back of the building, and a bright-yellow front door. Hamish had continued the yellow theme by surrounding the house with yellow roses and daisies. It was charming and breathtaking. I wasn't surprised that his place was so well cared for. Hamish took pride in everything he did. He would also take pride in his home.

I couldn't help but wonder if he'd decided on the yellow roses because that was the color of the climbing rose in the middle of Duncreigan's garden. I suspected that he had. Hamish wouldn't plant a flower by accident. Each seed, bulb, and plant was thoughtfully considered and gently settled into the ground with care.

I stepped up to the front door as dawn was just breaking over the pasture. I knew that beyond the pasture, it was breaking over the sea. Even a mile away from the coast, I felt the stiff breeze coming off the water.

There was no knocker on Hamish's front door, so I rapped my knuckles in the middle of it.

There was a crash on the inside of the cottage, and I heard Hamish yelp, "Duncan, you be careful with that!" A moment later, the front door flung open.

Hamish blinked at me over his bulbous nose. He had his work trousers on for the day, and he wore brown suspenders over a white button-down. His feet were bare, and Duncan the squirrel perched on his shoulder.

"Miss Fiona, I didn't expect to see you here. Is everything all right?" His eyes were wide. "Is it the garden?" he asked, alarmed. "Is something wrong?"

"No," I said soothingly. "As far as I know, the garden is fine. I haven't visited it yet this morning."

He frowned. "Then what brings you to my bothy, Miss Fiona? I'll be at the garden within the hour. You didn't have to come all this way so early."

I smiled brightly. "I hadn't visited your cottage yet. I thought it was time I dropped by. You walk to the garden several times a day. The least I could do is make the short walk to come see you."

"I—I have meant to invite you over, Miss Fiona. You have

been very busy in the garden yourself and opening your shop, and I . . ." He trailed off.

I wrinkled my nose. I hadn't done a great job of creating a cover story as to why I'd decided to walk to his bothy so early in the morning. Any hopes of being an international spy fell by the wayside at that moment. "I'm so sorry to intrude, Hamish." I took another step back. "We can talk when you come to the garden later this morning."

He gripped the door handle. "Don't run off, Miss Fiona. You're welcome here. All of this land and this cottage is yours. You don't need my permission to come here. You can go wherever you like at Duncreigan."

I shook my head. "Even so, I should have warned you or let you know that I planned to stop by sometime. I am sorry. We can talk later." I turned to go.

"Wait! Don't run off. Why don't you come inside for a spot of tea? I have just finished my breakfast, or I would offer you some of that too. I can make you scrambled eggs on toast if you like. I have a bite of it every morning."

I gave a sigh of relief. "Just tea would be lovely. There is no need for you to trouble yourself."

"It's no trouble, and tea it is." He opened the door wide to let me in, and I wasn't prepared for what I saw. Books, dozens, no hundreds, no thousands of books covered every surface of the room. There were so many in the small room that they ran up every wall. They outlined the fireplace and the windows. So many books. There were paperback books and hardcover books. Some were very old with peeling leather spines, and other were brightly colored new paperbacks. Big books, small books, giant books, and tiny books.

Not only were there books along the walls, but they were in the middle of the room, too. They sat in intricately designed piles that came up to my waist. The only reason I knew the location of the kitchen was because there weren't any books on the stovetop or in the sink. I stood in the doorway of the cottage and my mouth hung open.

"Let me make the tea, Miss Fiona." He patted my arm so that I would let him through.

I stumbled to the right and bounced off a stack of books that came up to my elbow, but thankfully the stack didn't topple to the floor.

Hamish went to the kitchen and put the kettle on. "It shouldn't take long for the water to heat up. It was already warm when I put it in the kettle."

"Hamish." It was all I could say.

His typically red cheeks turned an even deeper shade. "This is why I don't have people over so often. They would not view my books like I do. They see my books as nothing more than sheets of paper bound together, but Miss Fiona, they are much more than that. They are my friends."

I managed to stop gaping at the room. "How many are here?"

He shook his head. "Don't know. I've never had a reason to count them. As you might guess, it is hard for me to walk by a bookshop and not buy a volume or two."

As my eyes traveled around the small and cramped space,

I realized there was no way Seth or anyone else could be hiding in Hamish's bothy. There was nowhere to put him.

The cottage was a one-room setup, other than the tiny bathroom in the back corner. I was willing to bet there were books in the bathroom too.

Hamish removed two mugs from the cupboard next to the stove. As he did, I caught sight of a stack of paperback novels in the cupboard next to a handful of glasses and mugs. He closed the cupboard door. "Master Ian knew of my collection, of course, and he never judged me about it. Many times, he would come here to borrow a book. He said it was like having his own public library on Duncreigan. You can borrow a book whenever you like too, Miss Fiona."

My eyes traveled around the room and over the countless spines. The cottage was like a library, but a disorganized library. A librarian would have had a heart attack at first sight of Hamish's collection of books.

"Other than the garden, all I have are these books. They bring me comfort on the long and cold Scottish nights."

"I can see that, and I will certainly want to borrow a volume or two when winter hits," I said.

He smiled and carried two empty mugs and a basket of tea to the table. He also had a sugar bowl of brown sugar and cream.

There were two chairs at a small round table tucked in the corner. One of the chairs was empty. I assumed that was Hamish's chair, since it was the one that could actually be sat on.

At the table, there were two place settings side by side. A normally sized one with silverware like what would be found at any home, and a miniature one with a tiny placemat, an even smaller towel, and a hollowed-out acorn that I assumed was used as a cup. I smiled at the setting that was clearly for the squirrel.

The caretaker cleared the other chair of books and set them on another pile in the opposite corner of the room. He pushed the stack of books in the middle of the table to one side, which left me about five square inches for my teacup, but it was all I needed.

The kettle whistled. Hamish bustled over to the kitchenette again and poured the hot water into a plain white teapot. "What kind of tea would you like?" he asked as he picked up the meshed tea ball and was ready to add the tea from one of the square canisters on the table.

"I'll have whatever you're having." I sat at the table.

"Earl Gray is my favorite, but I usually have that in the afternoon when I need a little more spunk. I like to start the day with Scottish Breakfast tea."

"That sounds perfect." I folded my hands in my lap and waited to be served, like my mother had taught me when she had thought Isla and I could use some manners training as children. None of the training had stuck other than the ability to quietly wait for tea.

Humming to himself, Hamish filled the tea ball with leaves. He reminded me of an old woman fussing over her tea set.

Duncan sat at his place at the table as well, as if he was waiting for his own cup of tea. If Hamish had filled the acorn with tea, I wouldn't have been the least bit surprised.

He set the tea ball into the teapot and closed the lid. "I am sorry I haven't asked you to visit sooner, Miss Fiona. I suppose I was embarrassed by my home."

"You never had to worry about me judging you. This is your home. The home that Uncle Ian gave you. You may do with it as you please."

"But I do not own it, Miss Fiona. You do."

"In name only," I said.

He nodded. "Even so, I know that you didn't march over to my cottage this early in the morning just to see it. There must be something else on your mind."

"The morning after the storm, you left before my sister or I woke up."

He nodded. "I did. As soon as the weather cleared, I made my way up here. I wanted the comfort of home after a terrible storm."

"I understand," I said. "Did you go to the village at all yesterday?"

"Nay, you know I don't go to the village unless I absolutely must. Neither Duncan nor I like the big crowds."

I shook my head. If Hamish didn't like crowds of people and thought tiny Bellewick had crowds, he would not do well in Nashville, or in Aberdeen, for that matter. It made more and more sense why Uncle Ian had given him this bothy to live out his days at Duncreigan. I was so glad that he had.

"How was your opening of the flower shop? I did want to come . . ." He trailed off. "I just don't go to the village much . . ."

"Hamish, it's fine. You told me weeks ago that it would be difficult for you to be there. I respect that. I'm actually here to talk to you about the opening."

"Oh, did something happen?" His thick eyebrows knit together in concern.

"You could say that." I went on to tell him about Kipling running into the shop and discovering the minister's body.

"The minister, dead? How awful."

"Did you know him?" I asked.

"'Course I knew him. I've lived in Bellewick all my life. I wasn't a churchgoer like Master Ian was, but I would go with him to services from time to time. Minister MacCullen was a powerful speaker. I could tell that he touched the people he spoke to with his words."

I raised my eyebrows. This was another side of the minister that I hadn't known about. I realized that I hadn't really known anything about him at all, when it came down to it, except how he felt about Duncreigan and the MacCallister family. Even so, Uncle Ian had faithfully attended St. Thomas's whenever he was in Scotland. There had to have been something about the minister as a man of God that he liked and respected.

"The congregation will have quite a time replacing him after all these years. He was a fixture in the church."

It was the second time I had heard the minister being referred to as a fixture.

"How did he die?" Hamish asked.

I held my empty teacup by its delicate handle. "Chief Inspector Craig said that he was murdered."

Hamish stared at me. "Minister MacCullen was murdered. I can't believe it. Murder doesn't happen in our little village."

I didn't bother to remind him about the body he and I had found together in the garden the day I arrived at Duncreigan.

"Chief Inspector Craig says it's murder, and I'm a suspect. Again."

He smacked the top of his table, and my teacup would have bounced off and shattered on the floor if I hadn't caught it.

"Neil Craig has no right to think such an awful thing about you." Hamish's voice shook. "That boy has been trouble since he was young. I have seen no change in him."

Chief Inspector Craig was in his late thirties, and at six five and over two hundred pounds, I didn't think anyone would consider him a boy apart from Hamish MacGregor. Hamish and the chief inspector had a bad history. When Craig had been a teenager, he and a friend had broken into my godfather's garden with the intention of stealing the menhir. Hamish had caught them in the act and never forgiven the attempted theft.

I found myself defending the chief inspector. "If you look at me on paper, I am the best suspect for the crime. The minister had been harassing me from the moment I arrived. The police could argue that he finally pushed me too far, and I killed him. I didn't, of course, but that's what they could argue."

Hamish snorted. "Bollocks!" He pressed his lips together as he picked up the teapot and refilled my cup.

I cupped my hands around the mug and soaked the warmth in through my fingertips. "When was the last time you saw Seth?"

Hamish's bushy eyebrows disappeared into his hairline. "My great-nephew? I haven't seen him for weeks."

I raised my eyebrows. I could have sworn the hiker I'd seen making his way across Duncreigan on Monday morning was

Seth MacGregor, and if he had been there, I'd assumed he was there to see Hamish. Could I have been wrong?

"What is this about?"

"I've seen him a couple of times in the village over the last few days, and . . ." I trailed off. I opted not to mention seeing Seth at Duncreigan now that I was doubting myself, but there had been no doubt that I saw him outside the Climbing Rose the night of the storm or that he had run away from me at the docks.

Hamish poured tea first into my cup and then into his own. "And?"

I took a deep breath. "I think he might be involved in the minister's death."

He dropped the teapot.

Chapter Seventeen

I caught the teapot before it hit the floor, but not before hot tea splashed my wrists. I deposited the hot ceramic pot on the table. It teetered back and forth but thankfully stayed upright.

Hamish jumped up from his seat. "Miss Fiona, are you hurt?"

I examined the red spots on my wrists. "I should be all right."

"Nay, you need to put those under cold water." He pulled me to my feet and walked me over to the porcelain sink. Turning on the faucet, he shoved my wrists under the stream of cold water.

I shivered from the cold, but it did soothe the burn. "That helps. Thank you, Hamish."

Hamish let go of my hands and turned off the water. "Seth doesn't have anything to do with the minster's death. He doesn't live in the village anymore."

"But he was here," I said. "I saw him." I didn't add that he had run away from me when I'd tried to confront him.

"He grew up in the village. There is no rule that says he cannot return." Hamish returned to the table and started to mop up what little tea had spilled with a paper napkin.

"I know that," I said quietly. "But his behavior has been suspicious . . ."

"Neil Craig thinks he did this?"

"As far as I know, Chief Inspector Craig isn't aware Seth is in the village."

"That is good." He slid into his chair. "Tell me what you believe Seth has done."

I sat back down as well. "I don't know if he has. He just seems to be at the wrong places at the wrong time. Last night, I spoke with the old fishermen who sit at the entrance to the docks. One of them told me he saw Seth near the minister while the minister was arguing with another man."

"Who was the other man?" Hamish asked.

"Remy Kenner," I said, and watched his face, waiting for a reaction. I wasn't disappointed.

Hamish grimaced. "Wretched man. I cannot believe that Seth would be tangled up with him. There must be some sort of mistake."

I wasn't so sure. If what everyone had told me was true and Remy Kenner was tangled up in just about every kind of crime, it stood to reason that Seth might know him because of his gambling problem.

"I doubt you will meet anyone who cares for Remy, including his own wife." Hamish sighed, looking ten years older than he had a moment ago.

"Do you know his wife?"

"I know Claudia like you know everyone in a small village. I don't think I have ever spoken to her any more than to say hello."

Duncan jumped back on the table. He had fled when the teapot fell. Hamish stroked the squirrel's head.

"Did you know that Seth was in the village or planning to come here?"

Hamish removed his hand from the squirrel's head, and Duncan gave Hamish's hand an irritated swipe with his tiny paw. Hamish resumed petting the small animal. "Nay."

"Has he tried to contact you at all?"

He clenched his jaw for the briefest of moments. "Nay, he hasn't."

I leaned back in my chair. "I'm sorry, Hamish. I know it's difficult for you to talk about Seth."

"The boy means well," Hamish said, barely above a whisper. "He does." He dropped his hand from the squirrel's head a second time and stared at the tabletop. "If he comes to the village, I do not expect to hear from him. He is a grown man. He is too busy to come and see his great-uncle. He doesn't owe me a visit."

"But you were helping put him through medical school," I said.

"That was a gift. There was no obligation that he had to come see me, and I did it more for his grandfather, my brother, to fulfill the promise I made to him. I have told you this." He wouldn't meet my eyes.

I stood up from the table. "Can you think of anyone who would want to kill the minister?"

Hamish seemed to take my abrupt change of subject in stride. "The minister was not well liked, and he did not care for the MacCallister family or for the garden. I'm sorry that he's dead, but I am not sorry that I won't have to see him again. I would think there were many in the village who didn't care for him. He was a strict man, but I don't know who disliked him so much that they would do such a terrible thing."

"And Seth? Did he have a reason?"

Hamish dropped his eyes to the table again.

"Hamish," I said in a pleading voice. "The police will eventually find out whatever you don't want me to know about Seth and Minister MacCullen. Don't you think it would be better if you just come out with it?"

"Seth wouldn't hurt anyone. It should not matter what his past with the minister is."

I thought about this for a moment. Did I think Seth could murder someone? With the right motivation, yes, I did. He had said as much to me about a land developer who had threatened his environmental causes in May. But I could not say this to Hamish. "If I know, it will be easier for me to help him when the chief inspector finds out. Because trust me, he will."

"You can't tell the chief inspector this. It would shine a poor light on Seth."

I bit my lip. I was torn. I should tell Craig, because not telling him could impede the investigation, and I didn't trust Seth. He had run away from me. Why would he run away from me? Was he feeling guilty about something? He was a known liar, as he had lied to Hamish repeatedly about his gambling problem and going to medical school when he had dropped out. Hamish was still desperately holding on to that lie because he had given Seth so much money and supported him since Hamish's brother died.

I had never heard the story of what had happened to Seth's parents, but I knew Hamish's brother had raised Seth and had made Hamish promise he would look after Seth after he died. Hamish had taken the promise to heart, perhaps too much.

"Tell me. I won't tell Chief Inspector Craig," I said, thinking it would be better if at least I knew Seth's history with the minister, even if Craig did not. If Craig ever learned that I had withheld information from him about the investigation, he would never agree with this rationale.

Hamish nodded as if he had come to some sort of decision. "Many years ago, when Seth was applying to university, he wanted to go to school at St. Andrews very badly. St. Andrews was Minister MacCullen's alma mater. He went there for university and seminary after that. My brother, who was very active in the parish, asked the minister to write a recommendation letter to the university on Seth's behalf. He thought it was the best way to give his grandson a chance of being accepted."

I didn't like where this story was going. "What happened?"

"The minister agreed to write a letter, and he did. He mailed it directly to the university. Neither my brother nor Seth read the letter before it was sent."

I nodded. This was not an uncommon practice with college recommendation letters.

"When my nephew went to the university for a visitation day," Hamish went on, "he was enthralled with the place. He went through all the day's activities, believing he would attend there at the start of the fall term. Sadly, at the end of the day he was told that he needn't finish his application because he would not be accepted."

"Because of the letter," I said.

He nodded. "The minister wrote a letter, but it was not a recommendation. It was the complete opposite. He ruined my great-nephew's chances of ever getting into the university. The school officials didn't even tell him that he wasn't accepted to the university until the very end of the day because somehow there had been a mix-up with his paperwork. They didn't know he was visiting the university on that day." Hamish took a shuddering breath. "My brother was so heartbroken when he heard that he left the church. He said he couldn't look at that man any longer on Sunday mornings knowing what he had done to Seth. The incident caused my brother great stress, and he already had a weak heart to begin with."

I *really* didn't like where this story was going.

Hamish stared me in the eye. "One night, not long after this, he had a heart attack. He died because of it, Miss Fiona. He thought he had ruined Seth's future by making the request to Minister MacCullen, and his heart could not handle the burden. Seth was the one who found him."

I shivered. "You can't know that was the reason he had the heart attack."

"I do know. I was with him when he died. He asked me to help Seth, and I have." Tears gathered in his eyes.

"How long ago did all of this happen?" I asked.

"Ten years ago. Seth was only eighteen at the time. He and his grandfather were close. I don't think he ever recovered from my brother's death, and he blamed the minister for it."

"And now the minister is dead . . ." I whispered. "But surely Seth would not have waited an entire decade before he did something. If he wanted to hurt the minister, why wait so long?"

"The police won't care about the time that's gone by, Miss Fiona. You can't tell them this."

"Hamish, Chief Inspector Craig is a smart man. He will find out. Someone in the village is bound to remember Seth's history with the minister. Someone will make the connection and tell Craig." I took a breath. "And you must realize that your brother's death, as loosely related to the minister as it may be, makes you just as likely a suspect as Seth because you and your brother were so close."

He stared at the table again. "I suppose it does. Which is why, Miss Fiona, you must find out what really happened. I do not fear for myself, but you have to protect Seth. If the boy has done something wrong, you are the only one who can help him to set it right." He took a breath. "If he is back in the village, it must be for a reason, and I don't know what the reason could be if he didn't want me to know he was here. My only guess would be he is up to something that I would not approve of. That is worrisome, Miss Fiona, very worrisome."

"I don't think Chief Inspector Craig wants me to get involved in a murder investigation again. It would be wiser to stay out of it."

"You can't, lass. I need your help. I would do it myself, but . . ." He looked around his cottage. "The only place I go these day is here and the garden." He appeared shaken at the very idea of going to the village.

I remembered how upset Hamish had been when I had first moved to Scotland and unfortunately discovered a dead body in my godfather's garden. Now I wondered if he had been more upset because so many people had descended on Duncreigan. Maybe it had more to do with that and less to do with the actual murder.

As if he could read my mind, Hamish said, "I'm not one for crowds, Miss Fiona. I'd much rather be here in my own home surrounded by my books or alone working in the garden at Duncreigan. I would not be happy at the docks."

I stood up. "It's all right, Hamish. I can go alone, and I promise that I will find Seth and figure out what's going on. Craig might not like my involvement, but I will do it for your sake."

He nodded. "Thank you, Miss Fiona. I don't know how I will repay you."

"Hamish, you take care of my godfather's beloved garden. You don't need to repay me at all. We're friends, and this is what friendship is." I walked to the door.

Tears gathered in the old man's eyes, and he said in a low voice, "I have not done right by my brother. He would not be pleased with the state Seth is in now. That is my fault."

"No, Hamish," I said, shaking my head. "Seth is a grown man and should take responsibility for his own problems. Maybe the minister was cruel in what he did, but Seth still landed on his feet. He got into medical school at the University of Aberdeen."

His face fell. "But I don't know if he is still going to that school, Miss Fiona."

I placed my hand on the handle to the tiny cottage's door, but I turned back to Hamish before opening it. "Hamish, do you think Seth could have killed the minister if he was angry enough over what happen ten years ago? If he blames the minister for his grandfather's death?"

"Miss Fiona, I don't feel like I know my grandnephew well enough anymore to be able to answer that. I don't know what he is capable of." A tear rolled down his wrinkled cheek.

Chapter Eighteen

It was still early when I left Hamish's bothy. The sun was just breaking through the clouds. Isla would be sleeping for at least another hour, so I saw no reason to go straight back to the cottage. Instead, I followed the path to the garden from Hamish's home, which went right by my cottage. Ivanhoe stood in the front window. He pressed his two front paws flat against the glass pane and showed me his belly. Even though I couldn't hear him, he meowed, baring his teeth.

I had been in such a rush to leave that morning to talk to Hamish that I hadn't fed the cat, and it appeared that Ivanhoe was staging a protest because of my oversight. I waved to the Scottish Fold as I hurried by, and he arched his back and hissed. There would be payback when I returned to the cottage. Even so, I wanted to reach the garden before Hamish arrived. There was something that I had to do, and it would be best if I were alone when it happened.

The topography sloped down as I neared the garden. As always, the ivy-covered walls came into view first. The ivy's waxy green leaves and thin tangled vines crossed every which way over the stone surface. It was good to see the garden wall flourishing. When I'd first arrived at Duncreigan two months ago, the ivy and everything in the garden except the climbing rose that wrapped around the menhir had been dead. What I hadn't known at the time was that the garden had died when my godfather, the Keeper of the Garden, died. The garden would not bloom again until the new Keeper, me, arrived at Duncreigan. When Baird had bargained with the sea, he had tied the Keeper closely to the garden. Not for the first time, I wished that my godfather had left me more instructions as to how to control and use the magical gift he had left me.

I was still getting used to my magical tie to the garden, but slowly, as I had watched the flowers and other plants flourish under my care, I had begun to believe. Hamish might physically take care of the plants by watering, pruning, and weeding with my help, but I was the one with the mystical connection to the garden.

I removed the skeleton key from my jacket pocket. Pushing the ivy aside with my left hand, I fitted the key into the lock with my right hand and turned my wrist.

The heavy curved wooden door opened inward, and I fought my way through the tangled vines and through the doorway.

I blinked on the other side of the wall. Now that the sun was up, its light reflected off every petal and every leaf in the garden.

Bright white and pink peonies and roses of every shade, from almost-black purple to the purest white, glistened. I made a mental note to cut some of the peonies while they were still at their peak. They would sell well in the shop, I thought.

Lavender and coleus flourished in large bunches, and butterfly bushes were adorned with orange, teal, and pale-yellow butterflies and round bumblebees with their hairy legs covered in pollen.

As much as I wanted to wander around the garden to prune and weed and inhale the sweet scent of every flower, I knew I didn't have time. If I wanted to do what I had come there to do, I had to do it before Hamish arrived.

Hamish knew I was connected to the garden. He knew that the garden would not bloom without a living Keeper. What he didn't know was how physically connected to the garden I was. He didn't know that if I touched the menhir, the action could lead to visions. Uncle Ian had told me about the visions in a letter, but it wasn't until I had experienced them myself that I truly believed it.

Only two people knew about my connection to the standing stone in this way: my sister and Chief Inspector Craig. My sister because she had read the letter that Uncle Ian left me, and the chief inspector because he had witnessed my connection with the stone firsthand. He had been in the garden when I touched the stone and received a vision. After that incident, neither he nor I had ever mentioned it again, but I knew it wasn't something Craig would soon forget.

I took a deep breath and walked beyond the willow tree with its delicate leaves and around the hedgerow. When I came around the large bush, I wasn't the least bit surprised to see the fox, my godfather, on the other side.

The red fox sat beside the menhir as if he had been waiting for me for quite some time. I nodded at him, and before I could change my mind, I placed my hand between the rose's thorns on the worn rock.

I closed my eyes and waited. Nothing happened. I frowned and opened my eyes. Perhaps what had happened before when I'd touched the stone had been a fluke or tricks of my mind. I began to pull my hand away from the stone, but before I could, I was transported outside the garden.

The rain pelted my back and I was wet and cold. It was dark, somewhere between night and day. I lay on my stomach in the mud. Painfully, I reached my hand over my head and my knuckles scraped against rough stone.

"There you are. Have you decided to choose your own grave? That was thoughtful of you." The voice came from above me, but I could not distinguish if it was male or female. I wanted desperately to turn onto my back so I could see who was speaking. I tried to roll over, but pain shot through my right side. I wondered how I had gotten that deep bruise. What had I been doing to get where I was now? And more importantly, how did I get out of it?

"I would prefer if you not move. It will make this much easier for both of us."

I felt the sharp pressure of a knee in my back. Fear coursed through my body, and even though I didn't know what exactly was happening in the vision, I knew I had good reason to be afraid. A very good reason.

Hands, strong hands, were around my throat. They were squeezing tighter and tighter. I gasped for air.

I flew back from the standing stone and landed on my butt just short of the hedgerow. My hand flew to my throat. It wasn't tender. I touched my side and didn't find a bruise. Breath whooshed in and out of my lungs. I was fine . . . for the moment.

The fox stared at me, and I stared back at him, panting. Tears sprang to my eyes as the memory of the knee on my back and the hands around my throat rushed back. Was this going to happen to me?

The vision before this one had been a glimpse into the future. Everything in that vision had come to pass. Did that mean that someone was going to try to strangle me in the mud and rain? I would do just about anything to avoid that.

The final words from my godfather's rules came to mind. *You will see things that you may not want to see.*

The red fox walked over to me and placed a black paw on my knee. He stared at me with bright blue eyes. My gasping breath began to calm and my thoughts to clear. If the vision was a glimpse of the future, that meant it was still to come, and just maybe I could change it.

Tentatively, I reached my hand out to the fox and scratched him between the ears. He closed his eyes, much like Ivanhoe did when I scratched him in the same spot. Then he backed away, one step at a time. I struggled to my feet. My legs were still a little wobbly from being thrown back from the stone.

Standing next to the stone, the fox cocked his head.

I brushed leaves and grass off the back of my jeans. For the moment, I would put the vision behind me. "Thank you," I murmured to the fox.

The fox cocked his head in the opposite direction.

I sighed. "I wish you could tell me what really is going on."

The fox stared down at his black paws, and I knew he wished the same.

Chapter Nineteen

"It's like he was born to ride," Isla said from the front seat of my Astra. Ivanhoe had his back paws braced on her lap, and his two front paws were pressed up against the dashboard. After my unforgivable mistake of not feeding the cat the moment I awoke this morning, I had decided to try—try being the operative word—to make it up to the cat by taking him to work that day.

I glanced over at the cat from my spot on the driver's side of the car. There was a slight smile on his round face. "Maybe he likes riding in cars. I really don't know how often his old owner would take him out and about."

Isla pet the cat on the back, and he didn't react to her caress. He continued staring hard out the window. "You might want to promote him to shop security," she said. "He is quite a vigilant cat."

"I noticed," I said. "I hope I won't need shop security in the future."

"You can never be too careful," she said seriously.

I raised my eyebrows. It wasn't often that Isla sounded so serious. "Are you worried about it?"

"Of course I'm worried. A man has died, and I know that you plan to poke your nose in the case. You shouldn't, and I'm not the only one who thinks so. The chief inspector would agree with me."

"I know he would." I parked the car in the lot just on the other side of the troll bridge as I always did. "The minister is dead. I'm not worried about anyone else wanting to break inside my shop."

"If you say so," my sister muttered.

Isla opted to carry the cat to the shop. He rested against her shoulder as I fitted my key into the lock and opened the front door. She set him on the floor, and the feline began inspecting the showroom.

"I think he likes it here," Isla said, flipping her ponytail over her shoulder.

"Looks like it." I smiled and adjusted the cat's bed, a tote bag of Ivanhoe's food and toys, and my shoulder bag in my arms. I knew he would not be happy if he didn't have his favorite bed to sleep in. It had been a present to him from Alastair Croft, his previous owner, whom he'd loved. Sometimes I thought he only tolerated me and really loved the old owner.

My smile widened as I watched Ivanhoe move around the room. I had always wanted to have a shop cat, but back in Tennessee, that had never been an option. The landlord of my old building there hadn't allowed it. However, things were different in Scotland, and I could make my own rules because I'd bought the flower shop's building outright, which meant Ivanhoe was being promoted to shop cat. Although I would take him home to Duncreigan every night. I didn't think the cat would do well if left alone very long. He was a very social animal.

Ivanhoe pressed his flat Scottish Fold face into the flowers that were at his height. He shoved his nose into a purple cluster of hyacinths and inhaled deeply.

"Hyacinths smell lovely, don't they?" I asked the cat. "It's one of my favorite scents."

The cat looked at me over his shoulder with an irritated glance. If he had been able to pull his folded ears further back on his round head, he would have.

I held up my free hand. "Sorry to interrupt. You go ahead and inspect the place."

Isla laughed.

I tucked the bed under my arm and walked to the sales counter. Everything was neat and tidy, just how I'd left it the night before. It was an old habit of mine—I never left a mess behind for the next day, no matter how late that kept me at the store. To me it was important to start each day fresh, like a new blossom.

Ivanhoe sniffed several more flowers and then stood in a beam of light that came through the front window in front of a cluster of white daisies with bright-yellow middles.

"Here you go." I set the bed in the place he'd clearly chosen.

I could have been mistaken, but I thought the cat slightly

bowed his head to me, like a royal honoring a favorite subject, and a subject to Ivanhoe I was. I shook my head and walked over to the sales counter.

"I think the cat has you trained." Isla laughed.

"Since day one. Could you run over to Presha's and pick up coffee and scones for both of us?"

"You know Presha is never going to give up coffee to go. I'll be coming back with two chais."

"I guess that will have to do until I get around to ordering a coffee maker for the shop."

"Or find yours in the hundreds of boxes Mom had shipped over here. That must have cost her and Dad a fortune."

"Please don't remind me." I walked over to the driftwood counter and picked up the to-do list I had left myself the night before.

When I'd had my flower shop in Nashville, I'd had the habit of leaving myself extremely detailed notes about everything I had to do the next day.

Isla fiddled with her phone. "I might be gone for a bit. I always like visiting with Presha."

"Okay, that's fine," I said vaguely as I stared at the note.

"And," she went on to say, "Raj said that he wanted me at the pub at four o'clock. He wanted to do some training before the dinner rush."

"That's fine," I murmured as I read the list.

1. *New arrangements*
2. *Write press release for Aberdeen newspaper.*

3. *Contact the mother of the bride who seemed interested—a short hello email about the store will suffice, don't be pushy!*
4. *Organize the molding and flower wires in the workroom.*

All the tasks sounded very mundane, and I remembered writing them, but at the very bottom of the list there was another note not in my hand. It was written in block letters.

Stay out of the murder!

The paper drifted from my hand and floated to the worn hardwood floor, writing side up so that I could clearly read the last reminder, the only reminder on the list that I hadn't written.

The only thing that I could think to do was call Neil Craig and tell him to get the heck over here. I went so far as to take the phone out of my shoulder bag, and my fingers hovered over the screen, but then I set it on the counter. If I called Craig, he would know that I have been investigating the murder on my own and would order me to stop. I couldn't stop now, after I had promised Hamish that I would see how Seth might be involved.

Isla scooped up the note, and I didn't move to stop her. I was too consumed with wondering if I should or shouldn't call Craig. If I called him, he would come stomping into my shop, read the note, and lock me in Duncreigan, maybe forever. How would I keep my promise to Hamish about helping Seth if he did that?

In truth, I didn't know that Craig would keep me under

house arrest, but it was a small chance, and a chance that I wasn't willing to take.

Isla stared at the piece of paper. "Fi, are you in trouble?"

I took the note, folded it, and stuck it in my pocket. I wasn't going to make the same mistake twice and leave it lying around. "Of course not."

"Don't treat me like a child like you always do. It says *Stay out of the murder* on that list, and I know that's not your handwriting. Who wrote it?"

"I don't know," I said.

I was really tired of getting threatening notes at my shop. This didn't bode well for my business.

"When did they write it?" my sister asked.

"I don't know that either."

Her brows knit together.

"Isla, please don't worry. I'm sure it is just some kind of prank. There's nothing you have to worry about."

"You're my sister. If someone is threatening you, I worry."

"You shouldn't."

"You would do the same for me."

I frowned. I couldn't argue with her there. If I felt that my little sister was being threatened, I would defend her to the end. I sighed. "I don't know what is going on. It seems like I opened my shop and everything went topsy-turvy."

"You should tell the chief inspector. Neil will take care of whoever did this."

"Neil?" I asked, and blinked at her. *I* didn't even call the chief inspector by his first name. The fact that my sister did only confirmed that there was something between them. I shook off the uneasy feeling. Craig was far too old for her. I told myself that was why I was uncomfortable with the idea. I cleared my throat. "I'm not going to tell *Neil* anything about this, and neither will you."

"Fi, that's ridiculous. Someone is threatening you." She put her hands on her hips.

"We don't know that. It could be a prank."

"Still, someone came in here and wrote on your note. That's creepy."

I had to admit she was right. It was a little bit creepy. Okay, a lot creepy. "All right, all right, I'll tell him. Just not right now. The shop is about to open, and we have a lot of work to do. Let's just take a look around to make sure everything is all right. If it is, I can tell Craig later. How does that sound?"

"It sounds like you are trying to think up ways to avoid telling the chief inspector about the note."

I didn't bother to respond. When we'd arrived, I had put my key in the lock before testing the door because I had assumed it had been locked. I knew I had locked it; I had checked on the walk home from the docks before I'd left the village for the night.

I went to the back door at the end of the workroom. That door was locked tight. The windows were nailed shut. It was something I planned to have fixed when I had time. But someone had gotten in here after Isla and I left. A knot formed in my stomach at the very thought of the intrusion. I wanted to feel safe here, but first Minister MacCullen's death and now the note writer had robbed me of that. "Let's just make sure no one is still here."

Isla shivered. 'Do you think they still could be?"

I shook my head. "No, but I will feel a lot better knowing no one is here. I'll look in the workroom. You check here and the bathroom."

She chewed on her bottom lip. "Okay. If you hear me screaming, come running."

I went into the workroom. The only places someone could hide would be in one of the two upright storage cabinets or under the large island that I used as my worktable. I checked all spots and found nothing.

No screams came from the showroom or the bathroom, so I assumed that Isla had also found nothing. I went back through the doorway into the front of the shop. She held her hands aloft and shrugged.

At least I knew that whoever had broken into the Climbing Rose was no longer there because Isla and I had searched all the possible hiding places with Ivanhoe softly snoring in his cat bed. I knew the cat would not have been able to sleep if he sensed someone menacing was there.

"Fi?" my sister asked in a small voice.

I turned in her direction.

She had her arms wrapped around her body. "Are you scared?"

I had two choices in that moment. They were the two choices a person has in every moment of their life: to lie or tell the truth. I opted for the truth. "Yes, Isla, I'm scared."

Chapter Twenty

I decided that I wouldn't tell Chief Inspector Craig about the presumed break-in at the Climbing Rose until the end of the day. There were a few people I wanted to talk to today about the murder, and I knew if I told him this early, he wouldn't let me out of his sight for the rest of the day.

At noon I walked to the Twisted Fox to pick up lunch, armed with an arrangement of red-and-gold sunflowers for Raj. He and Presha had helped me so much with the flower shop that I wanted to say thank you, and it was the least I could do because he refused to take any money from me for the meals I ate at the pub.

Raj was setting plates of tandoori chicken in front of a couple sitting by one of the pub's narrow windows when I walked in. "Enjoy your meals." He bowed to them before backing away. He smiled when he saw me standing at the bar. "Fiona, what a pleasure. How is the Climbing Rose?"

"Much quieter than opening day," I said. The truth was I hadn't had a single customer all morning. I reminded myself that we were a new business and it was the first week, but it didn't make it any easier to swallow. I would never be able to survive another flower shop going under. "I stopped by to pick up lunch for Isla and me."

He grinned from ear to ear. "It is good to hear that Isla is with you at your shop. It means that she is a hard worker. She will fit into the job here as a waitress very well."

"She said she was working for you this evening."

"She is. It is one of our slowest nights, so it's a good night to begin her training." He pointed at the flowers in my hands. "Who are these for?"

"You." I set them on the bar in front of him. "It's just a little thank you for everything that you have done in helping me get the Climbing Rose up and running."

He beamed. "I will cherish them. Men love getting flowers too, whether they are secure enough to admit it or not."

I smiled. "That's good to know."

"I saw you eyeing the tandoori, so I will have my cook whip up some of that for you and Isla to go."

"Thanks, Raj. I really should get back to my shop. I need to drum up some business."

"Business will come, Fiona. You must be patient."

Patience wasn't one of my best characteristics.

He went back into the kitchen as the door of the pub flew open. A round, short woman walked into the pub with a small boy on her hip. "Where is Raj?" she demanded. "I have to speak with him now!" Her dirty-blonde hair fell out of the haphazard knot at the top of her head.

"He—"

Before I could finish, Raj appeared with a takeaway

package in hand. "Claudia, is everything all right at the laundromat?"

"Raj, thank goodness you are here. I have terrible news."

"Whatever for?" Raj asked. "What happened?"

Tears sprang to her eyes. "It's Remy. The police came and took him to Aberdeen for questioning." She placed her free hand over her heart. "They think he killed Minister MacCullen."

I felt all the blood drain from my face. This must be Remy's wife, Claudia, and their son.

"What am I going to do?" Claudia wailed.

"Go," Raj said. "Do not worry about the laundromat. Your place is with your husband right now. I will find someone else to watch your shift. Don't you worry, Claudia. That should be the least of your worries." He reached under the counter and came up with a basket of chocolate candy bars. He unwrapped one and handed it to the little boy. "Would you like a candy, Byron?"

She shook her head. "No, I have work. I need the money." She paused. "And Remy told me that he doesn't want me with him when he's questioned."

The child grabbed the sweet from Raj's hand.

Raj pressed his lips together as if he was holding back a comment about Claudia's husband.

Claudia put Byron on the floor, and he wobbled back and forth for a moment on pudgy legs but found his balance. He wobbled to the far end of the bar, gripping the barstools for support with his free hand as he went. In his other hand, the chocolate was already beginning to melt. It wouldn't be long before the boy was covered from head to toe in chocolate.

"If you need to work, you are more than welcome to," Raj said. "If you have to leave for any reason, just let me know, and I will handle the laundromat."

A tear rolled down her round cheek. "Thank you, Raj. Thank you. I don't know what I would do without your understanding. You have been so kind to me, so many times . . ." She trailed off and seemed to take notice of me for the first time. A red flush ran up her neck and onto her full cheeks. "I am sorry to have disturbed your lunch."

I shook my head. "It's fine. I'm sorry to hear about your troubles."

The woman's eyes narrowed, and she studied me. "Who are you?"

"Claudia," Raj said. "This is Fiona Knox. She just opened the Climbing Rose Flower Shop next door." He pointed to the vase of sunflowers on the bar. "Those are from her shop. Aren't they lovely?"

Her eyes narrowed, and she placed her hand on her hips. "You!"

I blinked at her. "Me what?"

"You're the reason my Remy was taken to the Aberdeen police station today. You are the reason that he's in this trouble." She shook her finger at me.

"I—I—"

"I spoke to the old men on the docks, and they told me that they didn't talk to the police about Remy until after they told *you* they had seen him there with the minister. They wouldn't turn on one of their own, but since they told you, you got Neil

Craig involved, and now look what has happened to my husband." She jabbed her finger into my chest.

I jumped off the barstool and rubbed the place where she'd poked me. "Hey, that hurt."

"You're lucky I don't cause you more pain for what you have put my family through."

"I only told the police what I knew. Old Milton at the docks is the one who saw Remy with Minister MacCullen the day he died, not me. If you want to blame anyone, you should blame your husband for getting into an argument with the minister in the first place. And what exactly was the argument about, Claudia? Do you know anything about it?"

"How dare you!" She grabbed the vase of sunflowers from the bar and threw them on the hardwood floor. The vase shattered on the floor as water, shards of glass, and bright-yellow petals scattered every which way.

A hand flew to Claudia's mouth, and Byron, who thankfully was at the far end of the bar and safe from shattered glass, began to cry.

"I'm sorry. I'm so sorry." Claudia ran to the end of the bar and scooped up her child. Without another word, she ran out of the pub.

The pub was silent for a full minute after she left. Even Popeye and his cronies by the fireplace didn't utter a word. But slowly, conversation and laughter resumed as if nothing odd had transpired.

I stared at Raj with my mouth hanging open. He shook his head and went back into the kitchen. A moment later he came out with the broom and a dustpan and started to sweep.

I took the broom from his hand. "Let me, Raj. It's my fault this happened."

He didn't release his hold on the broom. "She was the one who chose to throw that vase, not you. Do not take responsibility for things you have not done, Fiona. It may get you into trouble in the future."

"All right," I muttered, unsure what he meant. "But at least let me sweep. It will make me feel better to be helpful."

One of the old men held up his empty pint glass, indicating that he was ready for another. Raj relented. "All right." He let go of the broom and walked over to Popeye and his cronies to get their next round of drink orders.

By the time Raj finished serving the men, I had the mess cleaned up. I squatted on the floor, cleaning up the last of the water with a paper towel I had found behind the bar. My knees cracked as I stood.

Raj shook his head. "Poor Claudia. The woman is a tortured soul. I wish I could help her more than I already have, but I don't know what more I can do as long as she remains married to Remy. There isn't much anyone can do until she leaves him."

I threw the paper towel away in the wastebasket behind the bar. "From what I've heard, Remy is not a nice guy. He's not kind to anyone, even to his wife and family. Why is she defending him?"

Raj shook his head sadly. "Why does anyone defend someone who hurts them? Because they're scared. Scared to be alone. Scared to be without the person they love, no matter how awful that person might be. Scared of the unknown. It's very sad. I have seen glimpses of Claudia, what she could be. I know she could stand on her own two feet if she was just willing to trust herself and try." He shook his head again. "But until she trusts herself enough to do so, she never will."

I frowned. My previous relationship had not been abusive, but I had been taken for granted by my ex-fiancé. Just like Claudia, I had been too afraid to leave the man I loved. How could I judge her, when in a way I had been doing the same thing for years? My sympathy for the woman grew despite the fact that she had ruined a bouquet of my most beautiful sunflowers. Flowers could be replaced; people could not.

"Please do not take to heart what Claudia has done. She was upset and overwhelmed. I know that she is a good person despite who her husband is. That's why I gave her a job at the laundromat when I bought the Twisted Fox and I needed more help at my old business. It's a good situation for her because I let her bring Byron with her to work."

"That's very kind of you, Raj." I picked up the takeaway bag of food. "I should take this to my sister. She must be starving now and will be wondering what happened to me." Looking back at Raj, I asked, "What do you think Remy and Minister MacCullen were fighting about down by the docks that day, Raj?"

He shook his head. "I don't have the faintest clue, Fiona. Not the faintest."

Chapter Twenty-One

I decided to the close the flower shop at four when Isla left for her waitress training. We hadn't had a single customer all day, and it seemed pointless to sit around feeling depressed about what a sad beginning my new business was having when I could be asking questions about the minister's death.

The more I thought about how the minister had died, the more I thought it was related to the church. It was the central part of the minister's life. It had to be related somehow. The church itself was probably the best place for me to learn more, but before I walked to the church, I decided to drop in on Bernice Brennan before she closed up for the day. She had said that I could come see her at her jewelry store anytime, and she might be able to shed more light on the minister before I headed over to the church.

The jewelry store was on a neighboring street just a few doors down from Raj's laundromat. The shop had a bright-purple front door with a bejeweled knocker. I'd never seen anything like it. The knocker looked like it was covered in diamonds. I knew it couldn't be the real thing or the knocker would have been stolen long ago.

There was an OPEN sign in the window, and I pushed the door inward. The inside of the showroom was bright. The walls were a soft gray color, and the floor was light-colored hardwood. There were half a dozen large waist-high cases throughout the room holding jewelry. Many of the pieces looked very old.

The front room was empty, but a voice called from the back. "I'll be right out!"

I wandered around the space while I waited. There was some lovely Celtic jewelry in many of the cases. This would be a good place to shop for the holidays for my mother and sister, I decided, assuming I could afford anything in the store.

A moment later, Bernice appeared from the back room. Her face was red and her eyes were puffy.

I took a step toward her. "Are you all right?"

She shook her head, and a tear appeared in the corner of her eye. "I'm not."

There was a box of tissues on top of one of the glass cases. I grabbed it and carried it over to her. She took it from my hand and plucked three tissues from the box before setting it aside. "Let's sit," she said. "I need to collect myself before any other customers wander in." She walked across the room to a set of armchairs tucked in the back corner.

I followed Bernice to the chair and sat opposite her. She touched the corner of the tissue to her eye. "I'm so sorry to be such a mess. These last few days have been very hard."

"Since the minister died?" I asked.

She nodded. "It's so awful."

This surprised me. She hadn't been the least broken up over the minister's death when she'd visited my shop. In fact, her lack of emotion over his death had surprised me.

"I am very sorry for your loss.'

She squeezed my hand. "I know you are, and I appreciate that."

I realized that she was the first one I had seen cry over the minister's passing, and that, more than anything, seemed impossibly sad—that no one was heartbroken over the loss of a fixture in the community.

She wiped tears from her eyes. "I am sorry. What can I help you with?"

I shifted my weight. "Actually, I'm here to talk to you about the minister, if that's all right. Do you know anyone that was upset with him before he died?"

She frowned. "Minister MacCullen had a strong personality and even stronger opinions. He wasn't afraid to share either of those with anyone. I think you can attest to that."

I nodded.

"I have already told you that the church elders were upset with him about the way that he treated you. We will not be the kind of church that turns people away at the door. It was unacceptable." She frowned. "It grew worse after you left."

"What do you mean?"

She pursed her lips. "From time to time, the minister has been vocal about his dislike for the MacCallisters and Duncreigan."

I nodded. I already knew this. It was something I had learned my first week in Scotland when the minister stopped me in the middle of the street and told me just what he thought about them both.

"But after he chased you away, he spoke unkindly about Duncreigan and you in the sermon. He said affiliating with you at all was wrong."

I placed a hand on my stomach. I felt like I had been punched in the gut. I knew the minister hadn't liked me, but to say that from the pulpit in the church that my godfather loved was too much.

"Of course, the congregation was aghast by what he said. We all thought very highly of your godfather Ian. He was a good man and loyal to the church, even when he knew that Minister MacCullen didn't care for him. He died serving his country. Several members of the congregation were so angry that they stood up and walked right out of the service. After the service, the church elders met for an emergency session. We had to decide how to handle it. It seemed to us that the minister had finally crossed the line."

"What did you decide to do?"

She folded her hands in her lap. "We called the presbytery. If anyone could straighten the minister out, it would be them."

I gasped. "The minister was at risk of losing his job because of me?"

She shook her head. "It was unlikely that he would lose it. It takes quite a bit to remove a minister from the pulpit. We just can't order him to leave, but several church elders, myself included, were so horrified that we called the presbytery, which oversees each parish within its judication within the Church of Scotland, to complain. The presbytery promised to send the minister a letter of warning, and on the next Sunday they would send one of their members to visit our church so that he could report back to the presbytery."

I winced. I knew the minister must have hated the idea of being watched by his superiors while preaching from the pulpit that he had held for the last twenty years. It must have felt like a terrible insult to him.

"When do you think he would have gotten this letter?"

"Just a few days before he died. The church elders received a copy as well. It was scathing. The presbytery reprimanded Minister MacCullen harshly."

It was making more and more sense to me why the minister would have stomped into my shop the evening before he died and left me that threatening note. He was blaming me for his dispute with the church elders. Part of me wished that I had never tried to go to the church that morning. If I hadn't tried, would the minister still be alive? Was that small action what had set all of this in motion? I pushed those thoughts aside.

Bernice must have read my mind, because she reached across the gap between us and squeezed my hand with her bejeweled one. "We at the church know this isn't your fault. No one there is blaming you for the minister's death, anyway."

I felt tears gather in the corners of my eyes. "Thank you," I whispered.

She let go of my hand. "Minister MacCullen had been our pastor for the last twenty-some years, and the truth is, there had been tension between him and the church for the last few years. It seemed that the minister wanted to go a different direction than the rest of the church."

"Why did the members stay?" I asked.

She smiled. "Loyalty. That church doesn't belong to the minister. Ministers come and go. It belongs to the people and the community of Bellewick." Her smile widened into a grin. "And Scots are stubborn people. When we make a decision, we dig our heels in hard."

I chuckled. "I've noticed that. What else was the church upset with the minister over?"

She pressed her lips together again. I thought she wouldn't answer me, but after a long pause, she finally said, "The chapel ruins."

"Doesn't the church want to save them?"

"Of course we do, but we just think that the money the minister was putting toward the ruins could be used for more pressing needs. There are many in our parish who need help. Wouldn't it be better to help others than put all that money toward the ruins? We wanted him to use half the chapel budget for other ministries. The minister refused. The chapel ruins had become his obsession."

"Emer Boyd mentioned the chapel project as well," I said.

Bernice wrinkled her nose at my mention of Emer. Just as quickly, her face cleared. She leaned forward and patted my knee. "I am glad that you came by. It gave me a chance to tell you what I wanted to say when I was in your shop but couldn't get out before all of that pollen."

I started to stand. "I should go and let you close up the shop." My mind was reeling from all that I had learned about the minister, and I want to leave the jeweler so that I had some time to think.

She snapped her fingers. "Don't leave just yet. I have something for you. I kept meaning to give it to you, and I have just remembered it. I'm so sorry for the delay."

"Something for me?" I asked. "What do you mean?"

"Wait here," she directed. "I'll just be a moment." She hopped out of her chair and bustled to the back of the shop.

While she was gone, I stood up and walked around the room. I felt agitated and a pressing need to get to the church and learn more about the minister. There was a piece that I was missing. Yes, he didn't like Duncreigan on the MacCallisters, but there had to be a reason why for him to feel that strongly. As of yet, no one had been able to give a good reason.

Bernice reappeared, holding a long, narrow jewelry box. She set it on the counter before me. "This is for you."

"For me? I didn't buy anything."

"It's a gift," she said. "One that I was meant to give you the moment you arrived in the village. I am so sorry that I forgot."

I stared at the box.

"Open it," she said.

After a moment of hesitation, I put my hand on the box lid and lifted it. Inside, on a bed of purple velvet, was a necklace. The charm on the end of the necklace was about the size of a British pound and in the shape of a triskele, just like the ones carved into the menhir in my godfather's garden.

"It's the finest white gold. When Ian brought it to me, I knew it was special. The craftsmanship is wonderful. I would guess that it's at least a century old. It's handmade." She pointed at the charm. "You can tell by the edges. I was more than happy to polish up this piece for you as he asked."

"He brought it to you?"

She nodded. "He said that it was to be a gift for his god-daughter." She paused. "For you. Put it on. Let's see how it looks."

With shaky hands, I took the necklace out of the box and opened the clasp. I slipped it around my throat.

Bernice slid a tabletop mirror in front of me. "Oh, it's the perfect length for you. It's perfect."

I stared in the mirror and touched the charm. It was perfect. "Thank you," I whispered.

She smiled. "Ian is the one who should be thanked."

"I'll thank him too," I said, thinking of the fox.

I left the jeweler with the triskele necklace around my neck and more questions in my head than I had answers.

Chapter
Twenty-Two

L ike most of the buildings in the village, St. Thomas Church
was made of solid granite. Its sharp steeple could be seen
from anywhere in the village except the docks, which were at
or below sea level, depending on the tide.

The parish church was located on Chapel Street, two blocks
over from my flower shop. On my way, I passed the village
school, which was just next to St. Thomas's. I realized it must
be the school where Emer Boyd's husband was head teacher. It
was a newer building with a more modern feel. It had a flat roof
and large windows, which peered into colorful classrooms. I
wondered how the village felt about the modern-looking
school. Was this an example of the changing times in the village that some of the villagers feared?

A handful of children played in the playground with an
adult looking on, who I assumed was a parent and not a teacher,
since school was out for the summer.

The cobblestone flagstones that led to the front door of the
church were flat and smooth after being trodden on for hundreds

of years. The roof of the church came to a point in an "A" shape just above a large rosette stained-glass window.

The cemetery, right next to the church itself, was beautiful. I could have wandered through the grave markers for hours marveling at how old they were, much older than any I could have come across back in Nashville. I knew that some found cemeteries unsettling, but I found them peaceful. And the one outside the parish church was certainly one of the loveliest I had ever seen. Beyond that, I could see the ruins of the centuries-old chapel. At first glance, it was just crumbling stone, but one remaining wall stood tall. Moss lined the top of it.

I was tempted to go back and explore the ruins, but I had come to the church for one purpose, and that was inside. Besides, I didn't want to leave Ivanhoe alone at the Climbing Rose for too long. I was still uneasy because someone, it seemed, had entered my shop the night before to leave that scribbled message on my to-do list. I needed to tell the chief inspector about that, but the more time was passing since I'd found the note, the more I didn't want to share that information with Craig, who would blow it way out of proportion.

I stopped at the church's front door. It was the very place where the minister had turned me away. I bit the inside of my lip and pushed open the heavy door. I found myself in a small vestibule the size of a walk-in closet. Another large wooden door stood in front of me. I opened that, and I was inside the sanctuary.

The cavernous room smelled like candle wax and decaying flowers. It would be a boon to my business if I got the church as a flower client. I mentally kicked myself. I knew that

I shouldn't be thinking about ways to expand my business when the minister of this great church was lying in the morgue in Aberdeen. How could I use his death as an opportunity to grow my business?

Dappled colored light from the rosette window behind me fell on the hard wooden pews. Unlike the padded chairs that made up the seating at my home church back in Nashville, these pews were not made for comfort; they were made for petition. In a church like this, I could understand how someone could believe in God or fear him.

I believed, but my faith was shaky and confused. Perhaps it was something I would need to spend some more time on. The problem was, it was much easier keeping busy with the everyday things, and even trying to solve murders, than it was deciding what I believed.

However, now that I was the Keeper of a magical garden and my godfather had returned to earth in the form of a fox, I was able to more readily accept things that I might have questioned in the past.

The pulpit from which I knew Minister MacCullen had preached from for the last twenty years was in front me, high off the ground and ornately carved with Christian symbols. I made out a chalice, a lamb, and a triangle. In my mind's eye, I could see him shooting fire and brimstone from that high perch onto the congregation.

The interior of the church was beautiful in a dark and foreboding way. I could see it as a place where I would want to confess my deepest and darkest misdeeds. Currently, one of those misdeeds that was nagging at the back of my brain was the knowledge that I'd withheld important information from the chief inspector.

I slipped into one of the front pews and knew that I needed to tell him about the note, but even more than that, I knew I needed to tell Craig about Seth MacGregor, no matter what I'd promised Hamish. With his history of gambling, Seth could have gotten desperate enough to kill the minister, but I didn't understand what that had to do with Minister MacCullen. Certainly, the minister would have known about Seth's gambling problem. The entire village knew, and it was difficult for me to believe that the straitlaced minister who had refused to drink alcohol would have approved of gambling. But Seth's gambling problem wasn't a secret, and Seth would have had no need to kill the minister over something that was common knowledge.

Then was Hamish right and was Seth's possible motive, or at least the motive the police would cite if they thought Seth was guilty, the decade-old recommendation letter to St. Andrews? Even if those events had caused the death of Hamish's brother, it seemed to me a very long time to hold a grudge.

It was time to call Craig. I was removing my cell phone from the pocket of my light jacket when a deep Scottish voice shook me from my thoughts. "The church is nothing without the people. The people make up the church, but I do love it when the building is empty like this. It feels more sacred, as if you can feel the very presence of God."

I looked up from my phone at a large man, as tall as Craig if not an inch or two taller. He had a full head of white hair and a pockmarked face that gave his complexion character more than disfigured it. He wore black slacks and a gray work shirt, and his hands were calloused and stained with dirt along the knuckles. Those large hands were wrapped around a broom that looked like one I would see the cleaning crew at my high school use when I was there late working on the school paper. The broom's business end was four feet across and could slide under the pews to grab the tiniest speck of dust.

I jumped out of my seat and knocked my knee on the edge of the pew. I winced and gripped my knee. There would be a bruise there come the next day. "I'm so sorry. I didn't mean to intrude."

"A prayerful person is always welcome in an open church. Please sit back down. You seem to have knocked yourself quite hard there on the edge. I've done that a time or two. It does ache ye." He smiled.

I did as I was told, not so much because he told me to do it but because my knee was killing me.

As if he could read my mind from earlier, he added, "The church is opened to less prayerful people as well. It is open to all."

I shifted on my seat.

"The pew isn't as comfortable as you would like?" he asked.

"It's not," I conceded. "It's not much like what I had back home."

He smiled. "I bet those seats are quite cushy. You might even want to take a nap in them."

I nodded. I didn't admit that I'd dozed off in the pews of my home church more times than I could count.

"In the Church of Scotland, the goal is not comfort. Old

John Knox was a proponent of repentance, and he thought the more uncomfortable you were in the pew, the quicker you'd repent. Do you have anything to repent, miss?"

"Don't we all?" I asked.

He grinned, and as he did, I noticed that a few of his teeth were missing. Hamish had a few teeth missing too. It seemed to be common in older Scottish men.

I slid out of the pew with as much grace as possible, but I banged my hip on the end. Another bruise to add to the collection. "I just was peeking at the sanctuary. I haven't been in here in a very long time. I'm Fiona Knox. My godfather, Ian Mac-Callister, was a member of this church for his entire life."

"Aye, Ian was a good man. I respected him for coming to services here when he wasn't being deployed to some godforsaken corner of the world. He and the old minister weren't chums, but I am sure that you already knew that."

I nodded.

He held his right hand out to me. My small hand disappeared into his giant fist, and his skin was just as calloused as I'd expected it to be.

"Malcolm Wilson, church sexton. And you have a fine name to be in the Church of Scotland with the name Knox. John Knox would be proud to know one of his relatives was in the church that he built."

"John Knox built this church?"

He smiled. "Not the brick and mortar, but he is the one who brought Calvin's teachings to Scotland and began our state church."

"I don't think I'm a direct descendent," I said.

"You should do your genealogy then and find out. I could help you. When I'm not caring for St. Thomas's, I spend most of my time on the computer finding all the historical figures who share my blood. I'm a direct descendent from William the Conqueror, for one. I don't talk about that much, though, since he's not a Scot."

I opened my mouth to ask a question, but he was faster.

"The minister didn't care for Duncreigan, as I'm sure you know. He warned against trusting in anything other than the power of God."

"I don't claim to have the power of God, and my godfather Ian MacCallister was a member of the Church of Scotland. He would never have argued against the power of God either."

"We have been hearing much about you from the pulpit," Malcolm said.

I grimaced. "Bernice Brennan told me that as well."

"Aye." He nodded. "Bernice is a good woman. She cares for this place and the people. I believe his last sermon said we should embrace the history of the church and not let new people in the village distract us. You're the only new member of the village, as far as I know. And you are a lovely lass with those bright blue eyes and raven-colored waves. I could see how some might be distracted by ye."

I blushed.

"It is difficult to lose a minister who has been at the helm of the parish for so long, but . . ." He stopped himself and said, "As you can imagine, everyone in the congregation was in a great shock."

I nodded. "I'm sure the congregation feels a great loss."

"The minister was not the easiest man to get along with, but you already knew that, didn't you?"

I raised my eyebrow.

"I saw that little scuffle between you at the church door."

My face felt hot.

"I would guess that everyone in the village has heard that story by now."

"Great," I muttered.

"Despite his temper, Minister MacCullen was a good shepherd. He kept people in the pews and money in the church coffers. That's more than a lot of pleasant ministers can accomplish."

I considered this in light of what Bernice had told me about the congregation's loyalty to the church and community.

"Now, lass, tell me why you are really here."

I blinked up at him. "What do you mean?"

"You aren't here merely to see the inside of the church and reminisce. I know you solved Alastair Croft's murder in May, or at least you helped the chief inspector solve it. Are you meddling again? Because I don't think that is wise."

I opened and closed my mouth. Was this another warning like the writing on the to-do list?

"I have already spoke to Chief Inspector Craig," Malcolm went on as I tried to decipher his last statement. "So I don't know what I can tell you that will help. I imagine he has told you everything."

I almost laughed but stopped myself in the nick of time. "Why would you think the chief inspector has told me anything about the case?"

"It is well known in the village that he cares for ye." He

started to sweep the aisle, dipping the broom under the pews as he went.

"That's ridiculous."

"Is it, lass?" he asked as he moved up the aisle. "When you really stop and think on it? Is it ridiculous?"

I followed him down the aisle. "What did you tell the chief inspector?"

"What did he say I told him?"

"Nothing. He didn't tell me anything. That would go against his training as a police officer, so it would be helpful to me if you could tell me everything that you told him. I am interested in the case." I didn't see any point in hiding it from him.

He nodded. "Verra well, but you will have to come with me to the garden if you would like to hear my tales about the minister. I have much weeding and watering to do."

"The garden?" I asked. As always, any mention of a garden perked me up.

He nodded. "The village has a community garden, and on a hot day like today, it could use some extra attention."

The temperature was supposed to reach twenty-three degrees Celsius that afternoon, which was about seventy-five degrees Fahrenheit. That would be downright cold at the height of summer in Tennessee, but in Scotland it was shorts weather. Well, at least to the Scots. Not to me.

"Follow me, lass." He carried his broom to the corner of the sanctuary and nestled it there before going through the door next to the corner.

After a moment's hesitation, I followed him. The doorway

led into a narrow corridor. If I'd held my hands out from my body, my palms would have been flat against the stone walls. There was an open door to my right, through which I could see the corner of the altar and the curved stairs that led to the pulpit platform.

Malcolm passed the doorway, walking deeper into the corridor. When my eyes adjusted to the darkness, I could see a crack of light around a door at the end of the hallway. Malcolm opened the door, and the abrupt bright sunlight flooded the space, blinding me for a moment. It was so severe, I thought I was being thrown back into a vision like the ones the garden had given me.

Chapter Twenty-Three

M uch to my relief, the vision I expected to overtake me never came. It was hard enough to receive them in my dreams or when I touched the menhir in the garden. I didn't want to get them at random as well.

I hurried out the door after the sexton. The church door closed with a thud behind me, and I found myself in a vegetable garden surrounded by a wooden fence that came up to my hip. In the back corner of the garden, there was a large shed with three rain barrels sitting on cinder blocks, and beyond the fence, I had my first clear glimpse of the chapel ruins.

The bright sunlight reflected off the moss crawling along the crumbing stones of the foundation and one standing wall.

I turned back to Malcolm and the garden, which was bursting with vegetables and herbs. "The garden seems to be doing very well."

"It is," he said proudly. "Villagers signed up to take care of the grounds and grow fresh produce for their family, because for the most part they don't have the land to do it around their own homes. I know you can understand the need to garden to reconnect with the earth."

"Nothing makes me calmer than gardening or working with flowers. I wouldn't say I am an artist, but it is definitely a medium I love."

"I suppose it's different in America. On all of the television shows, everyone has big houses with expansive yards."

"Not everyone lives like that, but I did grow up with a lot of green space on a Tennessee farm. My closest neighbor was a mile away."

He grinned, showing off his missing teeth again. "We have a real American farm girl here in our little village, then."

"I don't know if I qualify as a farm girl any longer. I've lived in an apartment in Nashville for the last six years."

He grinned. "Once a farm girl, always a farm girl."

I clicked my tongue. "Don't you let my sister Isla hear that. She's doing her very best to leave her farm girl image behind."

"Ah, I think she should be happy for it. Not many children grow up with so much space and freedom."

I didn't reply. He was right that the farm had had plenty of space, but freedom less so. There were always chores to be done, all day every day. It didn't matter if you didn't feel like it or were tired. It didn't matter if it was Easter or Christmas. Daily chores had to get done.

Malcolm walked over to the rain barrels and attached a hose to the first barrel. "The tomatoes, in particular, need lots of water. In the heat, I like to water them twice a day."

"I used to grow tomatoes in pots on my patio back in Nashville. They did well there. They like hot and humid weather."

"Maybe you can help. Tomatoes have always been a challenge for me. They aren't made for Scotland, I gather. Maybe you can give me some advice as to why my tomato plants grow so slowly."

"I can surely try." I glanced at his tomato plants, which were rather petite for this late in the growing season. "Can I help you water while we talk?"

He smiled at me. "I will never turn down an extra set of hands. Wait until you see how the barrels work. I made them myself. The water runs through the gutter on the shed and fills each barrel, and when I turn on the hose, the pressure inside the barrel pushes the water out. The barrels are up on cinder blocks because that increases the pressure inside."

He pumped water out the bottom of the rain barrel, and after a bit of gurgling, it came out of the hose. In no time at all, it watered the carrot and cabbage gardens.

"How much water does one of those rain barrels hold?" I asked.

"Sixty gallons each, and we have three of them, so we can collect one hundred and eighty gallons of water. Of course, the storm from two nights ago filled our barrels to the brim." He handed me the hose.

"Will there be more rain? Or are storms like that few and far between?" I asked as I pointed the hose on a bed of lettuce and kale.

He looked up at the crystal-clear blue sky. "If the conditions are any indication, I'm going to say yes. The sky is telling me yes, there will be more rain."

I bent my neck all the way back and looked at the sky too.

I wondered what in the bright blue sky told him that rain would come. To me, it looked like it might never rain again. I returned to my task of watering the garden. Just like when I watered at Duncreigan, the act soothed me. Gardening and working with flowers was the one place I could find my equilibrium. It was when I felt most in control over what I was doing and most like myself.

I moved the hose from the lettuce and kale to the broccoli and cauliflower, which were still in the early days of growing. "I like your rain barrel setup. Would you be interested in making a similar setup for Duncreigan? I'd love to take advantage of all the rain we get in Aberdeenshire."

He blushed ever so slightly, and the redness to his cheeks was made more pronounced by his striking white hair. "Why, I would be honored to do that for Duncreigan. I have never seen the garden and have always been curious about it. This community garden was my idea. I have been wanting to do it for years, but Minister MacCullen was always against it."

"Why?"

He shook his head. "It is hard to say why the minister took a stance against the issues he did. When I brought it up this year yet again, he said yes as if I hadn't asked for the same thing a half dozen times before."

I frowned. It was strange that the minister had had a sudden change of heart. "How much would you charge to set up rain barrels at Duncreigan?"

He pressed his lips together as if in deep thought. "How are you watering now?"

I turned the hose onto the next raised bed—this one was

beans. "There is a well in the garden with a water pump attached to a hose similar to this. We certainly get enough rain to fill the well, but by using your system, I can help the well last much longer."

He cupped his chin with his hand. "I can tell that you have given this a lot of thought."

I nodded. "Of course I have. Water is essential for a happy garden."

Malcolm nodded as if in approval. "I can see Ian made the right choice when he left Duncreigan to you. You do care about it and want to see it flourish. There were many who questioned Ian's decision when it came to be known in the village, but clearly, he knew what he was doing."

"Who did they think the garden should have gone to?"

He rubbed his chin. "Everyone agreed it should go to someone from the village and certainly not an American." He smiled. "No offense, I hope."

"None taken." I moved the spray to the next vegetable bed. This one, I believed, was carrots and radishes. It was hard to tell because the shoots were small and barely above the ground. "Did the minister ever share what he thought should happen to the garden? Was there someone he thought that it should go to?"

He shook his head. "If he'd had his way, Duncreigan would have been burned to the ground after Ian MacCallister's death."

I shivered. I didn't have any doubt that that was exactly was the minister would have wanted.

Malcolm cleared his throat as if he thought he had said something wrong. He hadn't; he had only spoken the truth illustrating the minister's hatred for Duncreigan. The only problem was, *why* had the minister felt so strongly about the garden and about the MacCallisters?

I was finishing watering the carrots when my stream of water stopped abruptly. "Are the barrels out of water?"

He frowned. "Nay, they shouldn't be, not with the amount of rain that we had." He took the hose from my hand and tested it. A pathetic trickle came out. "Something must be wrong." Malcolm examined the nozzle and then squatted in front of the barrel. He removed the hose from where it connected to the first rain barrel, and only a small drip of water came out of the opening.

With a frown, he said, "Something must be blocking the hole. I should be soaked by now. I wonder if a stone or leaves got in there." His frown deepened. "Any debris should have been stopped by the mesh top."

I squatted on the ground a few feet away from him and peered into the hole, but saw nothing but blackness.

He stuck his index finger into the hole. "There is definitely something blocking the hole, but I can't grab it. My fingers are too large. Maybe you will have better luck." He scooted back from the opening, and I crouched in front of it.

I prayed there weren't any creepy-crawlies, especially not hamster-sized spiders. I took a deep breath and stuck my fingers inside the hole. I felt something metal, and I was able to get my two fingers around it and turn it. When I did, I unblocked the hole and water came rushing out, soaking my shoes.

"You got it," Malcolm cried. "Now bring your hand out so we don't lose too much water. Quickly now!"

Death and Daisies

Several gallons of water had already gushed at my feet in the time that I had been trying to remove my fingers, which were still curled around the piece of metal. I could have dropped the metal piece to save more water and let it fall to the bottom of the barrel, but I wanted to see what I had in my hand. I pulled back inch by inch through the gushing water, and my hand came out and the piece of metal with it.

As soon as my hand was cleared, Malcolm jumped into action and replaced the hose so that no more water would escape. I hopped to my feet in the wet grass, which was now a slippery and muddy mess.

I stumbled a few feet away. Slowly, I uncurled my fingers.

In the palm of my hand was a simple gold medallion with a cross and three intersecting rings in the middle. As soon as I saw the medallion, I knew where I had seen it before.

Chapter Twenty-Four

I held the medallion out for Malcolm to see it.

He removed a white handkerchief from the back pocket of his trousers and wiped his brow. "That is the minister's medallion. He wore it every Sunday when he preached. He said it was important that the cross was big so that the congregation could see it, even those who sat in the back."

I felt my shoulders fall. Malcolm had come to the same conclusion that I had: it was Minister MacCullen's medallion. I had hoped that I was wrong.

"How would the medallion end up in the rain barrel?" I asked.

Malcolm shook his head. "I don't know, but I should take it inside for safekeeping." He held out his hand to me.

My fingers curled around the medallion. It was evidence. I had seen the minister wearing it the day he died. "If it was Minister MacCullen's, it might be important. I should give it to Chief Inspector Craig."

"I can give it to him." He continued to hold his hand out as if he expected me to drop the medallion on his palm.

"I'll probably see him first." I pressed my closed fist to my chest.

The church sexton studied me. "You do not trust me with it." It was a statement, not a question.

I shook my head. "No, that's not it. It's just . . ." I trailed off because I couldn't think of another believable excuse. I didn't trust Malcolm, not completely. I didn't know if I completely trusted anyone related to the minister's murder other than Chief Inspector Craig.

"Very well. You can give it to the police. It makes no difference to me." He backed away and turned on the hose again. This time the stream was powerful enough to reach the tomatoes on the opposite end of the garden.

I dropped the medallion in the pocket of my jacket. I should have left right then, but I wanted to find out what else Malcolm might know about the minister's death. "Malcolm, how did Minister MacCullen seem that day?" I asked.

He stared back at me. "What do you mean?"

"Did he appear nervous or upset? Did he have a lot on his mind?"

"The minister always looked like he had a lot on his mind." With the tomatoes watered, he turned off the hose. "He was the only minister in this parish, so he had many responsibilities. He did all the calls on the sick and the dying, and never for a moment complained about it. He was here every Sunday and made sure if he ever took any time off, it was another day of the week. I can count on one hand how many Sundays he'd missed in the last twenty years."

Malcolm painted the minister as a man dedicated to his

congregation. Had I misjudged him? "Do you know anyone who was upset with him? Who could have done this horrible act?"

"The minister was a hard man. I think you know that. There were many who weren't completely happy with the way he led the church. They would have preferred a more progressive pastor."

"Do you think someone would have killed him if he wasn't progressive enough?" I asked.

"Why bother if you could stop coming to church altogether? And some have opted to go to more progressive congregations in other parts of Aberdeenshire. It's much easier to choose a new religion than to kill someone over it."

"Was the minister upset when members left the congregation?"

"Yes and no, I think. He hated to lose the numbers, but I think on the whole he was happy not to work in a place where people would speak out against him. That has not always been the case. Lately, more members of the church have been voicing concerns with how the minister was running the parish."

"Concerns about what?"

"Concerns about the chapel behind the church. They didn't think it was a good way to spend church funds. There are many other needs in the parish, but the minister seemed to be fixated on the chapel restoration project." He wrinkled his nose. "If you ask me, Emer Boyd was the driving force behind it."

"It doesn't sound like you care much for her."

"Emer just reminds me of a woman I knew once . . ." He trailed off.

I waited to see if he would tell me more.

He shook his head. "I have been on this earth for many years and have seen all sort of things, good and bad. I don't know why either happen, but I do know that I cannot understand the ways of God. So, long ago, I made a promise to myself to accept the ways of God as they are. It was too painful for my mind to view them in any other way. I wondered how God would want to accomplish his miracles. It seemed to me that he could use whatever means that he wanted, even the magic from Duncreigan, to do his good."

I thought of my visions when I touched the menhir in the garden and had to agree with him. "Why did Minister Mac-Cullen always hate the MacCallisters? Is it the rumors of magic?"

He shook his head. "It's much more than the magic. Much, much more. When the minister was a young man, he was married, and he says Duncreigan stole his wife."

A shiver ran down my back. "Duncreigan stole his wife? How?"

"The minister and his young bride came to Bellewick twenty-some years ago to take over the parish. They were here only a year before his wife died."

"How did she die?"

"She got lost in a storm like we had the night the minister died. It was just as violent."

"Why did she go out in it?" I asked.

He clicked his tongue. "She had just lost a child. Stillbirth. And she was mad with grief, so she wandered out into the storm looking for relief."

"The poor woman. That's terrible." Hearing this, I felt a little compassion for the minister for the very first time. "Why hasn't anyone else told me this story? No one seemed to know why the minister hated Duncreigan. How do you?"

"Because I had to run and find the doctor to tend the minister's wife during the stillbirth, but the minister was a proud man and he made me promise not to tell a soul. I never have, until now. It doesn't seem like there is much use in keeping the secret any longer now that they are all dead. Even the doctor died ten years ago, if not more. He was well into his nineties when he died. I couldn't tell you if he remembered."

"This is an awful story, but I still don't know what this has to do with Duncreigan." I took a breath and asked the question that I suspected I already knew the answer to. "Where was she headed when she got lost in the storm?"

The sexton looked me straight in the eye. "Duncreigan."

It was the answer I'd expected but hadn't wanted to hear. "Why?"

"She had heard about the magic of the garden, and she hoped that something could be found there to give her comfort. She wasn't finding it in her husband or in his interpretation of God. Ian's father took care of the garden at that time. He claimed that he didn't know the minister's wife was on her way to Duncreigan to seek his counsel. It's very possible that he didn't. Back then, there were no cell phones, and there have never been phone lines going as far out from the village as Duncreigan. The MacCallisters didn't seem to mind that and liked to keep to themselves.

"But the minister didn't believe that. He was sick with grief and claimed that Ian's father lured his wife to Duncreigan with some promise that he could help her. The police were even involved, but it was no matter. There was no way to prove that Ian's father and the minister's wife were ever in communication, and Ian's father vehemently denied it. In truth, most at the time believed the grief-stricken mother got the idea in her own head to walk to Duncreigan and, as I have told you, got lost in the storm. It is not the first or the last time a person has gotten lost in a storm raging off the coast."

Even though it was a warm summer's day, a persistent chill ran down my back. I wrapped my arms around my body. I wished I had known the truth about the minister and his history with Duncreigan. I didn't believe that what had happened to the minister's wife had been either the garden's fault or Ian's father's fault, but had I known, I might have been more understanding and a little more reasonable when dealing with Minister MacCullen. I might have given him a bit more benefit of the doubt instead of writing him off in my head as some crackpot. It just reminded me that no one really knew the baggage another person was toting around behind him or her. It was impossible to know, but it was important to remember that everyone had a secret, like Malcolm had said. I had my own, but nothing as tragic as what the minister had faced.

Malcolm walked over to the rain barrels. "It seems that this one is empty. We lost of a lot of water when we were trying to get that necklace out of the barrel." He smiled. "No matter. This is Scotland. It will rain again in another day and refill our coffers."

He opened the barrel top and leaned over it. I could see

how someone wearing a necklace could lose it in the water. But why would the minister have been leaning over the rain barrel?

"Did Minister MacCullen work in the garden?"

Malcolm chuckled. "Nay, he had no interest in it."

"So, he would have no reason to peer into the rain barrel like you are right now?"

He straightened up. "Nay, no reason at all. Is that how you think his necklace got in there?"

"It's the only way that makes sense for the necklace to have fallen into the water."

Malcolm looked at the rain barrels, then at me, and back again.

I couldn't be sure if I was right. In my mind's eye, I saw the minister leaning over the rain barrel and someone pressing down on the back of his neck, keeping him in the water. That must have been what had caused the bruises on his neck. The minister must have struggled to fight back, but the killer had been too strong for him. It was all too awful to even think about. I took two large steps back from the rain barrel. Being that close to them was uncomfortable.

"Malcolm, when was the last time you saw the minister wearing the medallion?"

He was quiet for a long moment. Finally, he said, "It would have been in the afternoon of the day he passed on, the day of the storm. I was in a rush to complete my work at the church because I wanted to be home before the storm hit. The minister was in his study. I assumed he was working on his Sunday morning sermon. He often worked late into the night on his sermons."

"I need to call the chief inspector."

He blinked at me. "Why?"

"Because I think we're standing in a crime scene."

Chapter
Twenty-Five

Craig picked up on the first ring, and I didn't give him time to say a single word. "Chief Inspector Craig. It's Fiona. I think I found the place where the minister was murdered."

"Where are you?" His voice was sharp, all business.

"At St. Thomas's."

"Are you alone?" His sharp tone hadn't changed.

I glanced at Malcolm. "No, Malcolm Wilson, the church sexton, is with me."

Craig gave an exasperated sigh. "Where is this crime scene exactly?"

I turned away from Malcolm and went on to tell the chief inspector about the rain barrels and the community garden behind the church in a hushed voice.

"I'll be there in twenty minutes. Don't touch *anything*, and don't move an inch from where you are right now."

I promised I wouldn't.

"If anything happens or you feel uncomfortable, call me immediately. Do you understand?" Craig asked.

I lowered my voice so that Malcolm couldn't overhear me.

"Is there something going on with the sexton that you're not telling me?"

He didn't say anything.

"Why would I feel uncomfortable?" I asked. As I asked, I turned back around to take another look at the rain barrels, and Malcolm Wilson disappeared around the side of the shed.

"Please, Fiona, just stay put and keep your phone on you. Tell Malcolm to stay there too." He ended the call before I could tell him Malcolm had disappeared.

I bit my lower lip. Should I go after Malcolm and tell him that Craig wanted him to stay with me in the garden? I decided that I should at least see where he'd gone.

Behind the garden, the ruins stood. If I went to the ruins, I could keep an eye on the community garden. I would have a clean view between the two of them.

I opened the back gate that separated the community garden from the ruins, and a sense of stillness fell over me. Between the gate and the ruins was a field of wild daisies. Their white and yellow heads bobbed in the breeze. I hated to walk through them to reach the ruins out of fear that I might hurt them. To my left, I spotted a narrow trail through the daisies that led to the chapel ruins. I hurried over to it.

The chapel ruins were beautiful in a forlorn sort of way, and I could see why the minister had been so determined to save them. If no effort was made now, there would be nothing left in a few years. As I came closer to the ruins, I could see that the one remaining wall was held in place with a rickety-looking brace made from a four-by-four pounded into the earth. I wanted a closer look and stepped forward. As I did, my foot caught on the edge of the chapel's crumbling foundation, and I fell face first into the shallow pit.

I groaned as I rolled onto my back. Thankfully, I kept my face from making contact with the earth by throwing out my hands at the last second, but my right wrist was sore from the heel of my hand hitting the ground.

I looked up and could see the bright blue sky and the overhang of an elm tree. The pit was about the size of a grave, and the momentary comparison was eerie this close to the cemetery.

I had started to sit up when a smooth voice asked, "Are you quite all right?" The accent was English, the refined type of English that I imagined Prince William or Prince Harry would have.

I blinked as the face peering at me came into focus. It was the historian, Carver Finley.

"Would you like some help getting out of there?" He flashed his white smile at me again. If the archeology thing didn't work out, he could always work as a toothpaste commercial actor.

"I'm fine," I said, and tried to sit up. When I did, my palm slipped on the mud, and I fell on my back again with a splat. I groaned and squeezed my eyes shut. "Please tell me you didn't see that."

He laughed. "If I did, I would be lying, and a gentleman never lies."

I opened my eyes. "In this case, it would really be okay."

He grinned, nearly blinding me with his teeth. "Very well, I didn't see a thing. Now, may I offer you assistance so that you may escape from that ditch?"

I grabbed hold of his hand and let him pull me up. Although he was a thin man, he was surprisingly strong, and I popped out of the ground like a jack-in-the-box. He clasped me to him, and my cheek pressed up against his chest. I appreciated that he had helped me out of the hole, but this was a little more up close and personal than I wanted to be. As politely as I could, I tried to disengage myself from his hold.

"My apologies." He stepped back, allowing me to escape around him. I moved to a safe distance away from the hole. "Are you here visiting the site? I'm happy to see someone in the village is interested in archeology. Perhaps I could show you around. Not too many have come to see what I am doing here. It if weren't for Emer and the minister, I think there would be no interest at all. I must admit, on face value alone, the site does not have much going for it, but its historical value for the area is priceless."

"Why is there only one wall still standing?" I asked. I glanced around for the crumbling stone of the other walls that had once made up the chapel, but found none.

"Looters, I'm afraid. Over the centuries, many have come here and stolen the crumbling stones to make their own homes. It is much easier than pulling the granite from the earth." He shook his head. "It is a terrible shame, because from what I have learned, this was quite a chapel in its time, and it served the entire county. As much as I want to reconstruct the church to its former glory, the stones that were taken can never be returned. They are holding retaining walls and fireplaces together all over Bellewick and beyond."

"How old is the chapel?"

"Early twelfth century. This chapel was certainly constructed before the Reformation."

"I'm surprised to see you working here so soon after . . ." I trailed off.

"So soon after the minister was killed? I know it might appear callous, but this is the best way I can honor Minister MacCullen. He was very excited about this project and recognized how much value it added to his own church."

"What kind of value?"

He studied me for a moment. "Tourism, for one. Donations for another. If this church can be put on the national registry as a historical marker, the possibilities are endless. The church can apply for all sorts of historical and museum grants to restore and preserve it."

"Why doesn't the church just register for the historical marker now?"

"It would be easier to get on the registry if I can prove the site has some sort of historical significance to the area. That's what the minister hired me to do."

"The church is paying you to be here."

He laughed. "You think I'm doing this for free? I'm a poor academic. I can't just walk away from my own research if the price isn't right." He paused. "I have been meaning to talk to you—"

"Fiona!" A voice shouted my name. "Fiona!"

"Sounds to me like someone's father is calling her home for dinner," Carver said.

I frowned and backed away from the historian. There was

something calculated about the man that I didn't like. If what he said was true, he would have had no reason to kill Minister MacCullen, as far as I knew. That didn't mean I had to trust him, though.

"It was nice talking to you," I said, and headed back to the community garden.

"You too, Fiona, you too," Carver said.

As I walked back through the field of daisies, Craig saw me and threw up his hands. "I told you to stay by the community garden. What on earth were you doing?"

I frowned. "I was looking for Malcolm. I thought he wandered over to the chapel ruins. I knew you would have wanted to talk to him. You can see them from the garden."

"I couldn't see you!" he cried.

I folded my arms and studied him. "Chief Inspector, I think you need to calm down. You're going to give yourself a heart attack."

"The only person who is going to give me a heart attack is you, Fiona Knox," he muttered under his breath. "You don't know how I felt when I couldn't find you. Did you even think about that?"

"Chief Inspector, are you scared?" I let my arms drop to my sides.

He closed his eyes for a moment. "I'm scared for you, Fiona. I know you tend to run off and do stupid things like talk to murder suspects without me. Don't you understand that someone who has committed murder once is more likely to do it again?"

I clenched my teeth. "Of course I know that. That's why I'm here. I want to find out what happened!"

He took a step toward me. "That's not your job." He pointed at himself. "That's my job."

Before I could protest more, he went on to say, "You shouldn't be anywhere close to this church. You're making yourself a target again. Wasn't last time enough for you?"

I was about to snap back at the chief inspector when I studied his face a little bit closer. He was actually scared for me. This wasn't a territory thing for him. This wasn't me getting in the way of his job. He had actual concern on his face . . . for me. "I—I—" I was at a loss for words because I was genuinely touched by his concern, but at the same time, I wasn't going to promise him I would stay out of the investigation. I had to protect myself and my reputation, and I had promised Hamish I would look into Seth's involvement, if there was any at all.

Thankfully, the chief inspector saved me from making any false promises by gaping at my muddy coat as if he was seeing it for the first time. "What happened to you?" he asked.

My face turned bright red. "Ummm. I took a little spill in the chapel ruins. The ground is a bit uneven there."

He wiped a hand down the side of his face and closed his eyes. "I can see it will do me no good to continue to lecture you."

I smiled. "Finally, something we both agree on."

Craig rubbed the spot between his eyebrows. "Just show me what you found."

I walked him over to the rain barrel and explained my theory that the minister's head had been pushed into the water and held there until he drowned. "The water flow was interrupted, so Malcolm asked me to stick my hand in there and pull out whatever was stuck. His hand was too big to fit." I put my hand in my pocket and pulled out the medallion. The broken chain dangled between my fingers. "This was blocking the opening."

Craig took the jewelry from my hand. "This is the minister's. I recognize it. It was something he always wore."

"That's what Malcolm said, too."

"Malcolm knows you found this?" He weighed the large medallion in his hand as if his hand were a scale of some sort.

I nodded. "I told you he was the one who told me to stick my hand in the hole, and he saw me pull it out. He wanted to take it back to the church for safekeeping, but I didn't give it to him. I thought that I should give it to you, which is why I called you here."

"Thanks for that." He pulled a small plastic evidence bag out of his pocket. I had learned from the previous murder investigation that Chief Inspector Neil Craig had all sorts of odds and ends hidden in his coat. He was sort of like Inspector Gadget that way. The funniest part was that, by the way the coat hung on his body, you wouldn't know he was carrying so many things on his person. It was a baffling accomplishment in sport jacket engineering as far as I was concerned.

"Was he wearing it when you saw him outside the Climbing Rose just before the storm?"

I nodded. "He was."

"Well, this might be just what we need to pin down the time of death. It's been a little hard to determine. His body was badly bruised from being thrown this way and that in the sea, and all the salt water his body absorbed impacted the estimated time of death, too. This will be very helpful indeed."

I smiled.

He frowned. "I still don't think you should be involved in this."

"You wouldn't have found the medallion without me," I exclaimed.

"Malcolm would have found it when he tried to water the garden."

"He would have found it, but would he have known its importance? Would he have thought to give it to you?" I folded my arms. "I don't think so."

"Okay, I agree with you that it was lucky that you were here when the medallion was discovered, but I can solve this case without your help or luck."

Malcolm came out of the back of the church.

I blinked. I had seen him go out the garden gate. How had he circled back and gotten inside the church without me spotting him?

"Chief Inspector," he said. "I thought I saw your car. Fiona gave you the medallion, then?"

Craig left me standing in the middle of the community garden and walked over to the sexton. "She did." He tucked the evidence bag holding the medallion into one of the many interior pockets of his coat. I wondered if his sport jacket was standard issue for chief inspectors in Scottish police departments or if he had them specially made.

"She told me she would," Malcolm said. "She seems to think that it might have something to do with the minister's death, but I can't see how."

"I will take it back to the lab just in case, and I am calling in my crime scene techs to take in these water barrels. I want them thoroughly searched and the water tested."

Malcolm, who was an inch taller that Craig, glared down at the chief inspector. "I need the rain barrels, Chief Inspector. I need to be able to water the garden."

"You will have to use village water until the rain barrels have been examined." Craig's tone left no room for argument.

Malcolm folded his arms across his chest and appeared to be settling in for a good long pout.

I glanced back over my shoulder at the chapel ruins. Carver Finley leaned on the side of the shed, watching us with a small smile playing on his lips. It was clear he'd been listening to the conversation. How long had he been there? Had he heard the conversation I had had with Craig and my suspicions about the rain barrel too?

The historian wiggled his fingers at me and smiled. Goosebumps broke out on my arms.

Chapter
Twenty-Six

I was about to tell Chief Inspector Craig about seeing Carver, but when I turned back around to face the church, I saw a third person had joined him and Malcolm just outside the church's back door. Emer Boyd stood in front of Craig with her perfectly manicured hands on her narrow hips. She and Malcolm stared at Craig with the same frustrated expression.

The head of the village's welcome committee and church treasurer waved her arms in the air. "Chief Inspector Craig, you have to tell me what is going on. I represent the church now that the minister has passed."

"There has been a discovery related to the minister's death at the church."

She put her hand to her chest. "In the sanctuary? Who would defile a church in such a terrible way?"

"It was outside the actual building of the church."

"I thought the minister drowned in the ocean." She scowled.

"We know that he was dumped in the ocean. That's how he washed ashore, but the coroner is certain that he had fresh water in his lungs. Minister MacCullen didn't drown in the ocean."

She shook her head. "Even so, it can't have anything to do with the church or the chapel ruins."

"Who said anything about the ruins?" Craig asked.

Emer blushed. "I just assumed that's what you were going to say next. I believe that if you see what is going on with the chapel ruins and all the good that St. Thomas's is doing in the village and beyond, you will agree with me that no one related to the church could have had anything to do with the minister's tragic death. As you can imagine, the congregation is devastated by the news."

I felt my brow go up. Devastated by the news? Hadn't Malcolm told me that most of them weren't happy about the idea of spending so much money on the project? It seemed to me someone was lying. In this case, I was more inclined to believe the sexton. I had a feeling Emer was the sort to insist everything was fine when it so clearly was not.

"To thoroughly investigate the murder, I have to investigate *all* aspects of the minister's life. Of course, the church will be at the forefront of that investigation. It was the cornerstone of the man's life. The techs are already on their way here."

Emer opened and closed her mouth and then looked beyond me. "Carver, thank heavens, you're here!" She pushed Craig aside and walked toward the historian, who was still leaning against the garden shed with that cocky smirk on his face.

He straightened up as Emer marched toward him.

"Can you show the chief inspector the chapel ruins? Then

he might understand why it is so important to not associate the minister's death with what's going on over there. I believe if he sees the ruins close up, he will understand." She turned back to Craig. "If the chapel ruins get a poor reputation for being associated with the murder, we could lose our chance of being made a national historic site."

"I don't see how," I said, speaking up for the first time since Emer had arrived.

She blinked at me as if she was noticing me for the first time. "Fiona Knox, what are you doing here?"

"She was here to talk to me," Malcolm answered.

I glanced over at the church sexton, surprised that he had come so quickly to my aid when he'd appeared so irritated with me less than an hour ago when I'd refused to turn over the minister's medallion to him.

Emer narrowed her blue-violet eyes as if she didn't believe him.

"Is there anyone else at the church I should let know what's going on?" Craig asked.

She shook her head. "No. Everything can go through me. I'll relay whatever you tell me to the church elders."

He nodded. "That works for me."

Just then, two men in uniform carrying black backpacks and bags came around the side of the church.

"If you will excuse me," Craig said, then walked around to confer with the two techs. He pointed at the garden shed and the rain barrels as he spoke.

Emer made a motion like she was about to run her hand through her perfectly styled hair and stopped herself just in time. "This is just awful," she said. "Poor Minister MacCullen and poor St. Thomas's. This is such a bad mark on the church's good name."

"I don't think you have to worry about how this will hurt the church's reputation," I said. "Yes, it's a tragedy, but a church as old as St. Thomas's must have weathered many scandals and storms in its day."

Malcolm nodded. "Aye, that she has. Listen to the lass, Emer; this too shall pass."

Carver folded his arms over his chest. "I'm not certain of that."

"I don't understand how it can hurt the chapel ruins' chances of being declared a site on the national register," I said. "Aren't most of the sites on the register sites of violence? Garrisons and castles and the like?"

Carver arched an eyebrow at me. "You seem to be very interested in all of this for an outsider."

"You're an outsider too," I countered.

"Ah, but I'm being paid to be here. I am certain that you are not, and from the conversation I heard earlier, I believe the chief inspector would much rather not have you anywhere near his murder investigation." He smiled. "Or am I wrong?"

I scowled in return. I couldn't believe I'd thought this man was handsome the first time I'd seen him in the Twisted Fox. Any attractive qualities he'd had melted away in that moment.

Craig rejoined us. "The techs are working, so Emer"—he turned to face her—"if you would like me to see the chapel ruins to better understand what you're talking about, I have the time."

She clapped her hands. "Thank you, Chief Inspector. I'm sure that when you see what we are doing here, you will understand how important this is to the church and to the village as a whole." She waved to Carver. "Will you lead the way?"

"Certainly," Carver said, and pivoted in the direction of the ruins.

We walked through the daisies again. I plucked one of the daisies from the field and tucked it behind my right ear.

Craig glanced back and didn't seem the least bit surprised that I was following the trio to the chapel ruins. I was grateful he didn't tell me to leave and stay out of police business.

Carver stood by the four-by-fours holding up the one remaining wall. "This church was built in the twelfth century. This was pre-Reformation, so the worshipers here were Catholic. The interesting thing I have found so far is that they seem to have mixed some of the traditional Celtic beliefs with the new Christianity. That wasn't uncommon. When Christianity came to what is today the United Kingdom, the missionaries and priests used many druid and Celt religious symbols to help them explain the trinity and other Christian concepts."

I thought about the dozens of tiny triskeles carved into the menhir back in the garden. Uncle Ian had told me that the symbol represented the trinity, but in the Celtic world it had represented the cycles of life: birth, life, and death.

As Carver spoke, Malcolm walked through the daisies and stood on the edge of the conversation.

Carver ignored the newcomer and continued his lecture. "If you will look here, there is a triskele carved into the stone. Clearly it was carved when the building was constructed centuries ago.

What I think is significant is that triskeles are much more commonly found in stone in Ireland. This is the first one that I have seen in Aberdeenshire or even in Scotland as a whole."

Again, I thought of my menhir back in the garden. I wasn't going to tell Carver Finley that the same symbol was carved into the stone there. The last thing I wanted was for the eager historian to come poking around my garden.

Craig was watching me. I knew he was remembering the carvings on the menhir too. I gave him a small smile, and he nodded in return. I blew out a breath, knowing that meant he wasn't planning to tell Carver about my stone.

However, since the two had the same carving on them, I couldn't help but wonder if they were connected in some way.

"I believe," Carver went on, "the existence of the triskele carvings gives this site historical significance, and it should be preserved for future study. At the forefront, this one remaining wall needs to be shored up and preserved. That's where most of the money for this project will go. I do believe it has a good chance of being a national historic site."

"But not if the site is tarnished with the minister's murder," Emer said.

Craig looked as if he was about to say something, but before he could, Malcolm pointed at the pit where I had fallen. "Doesn't look to me like you are keeping a very clean job site. That dirt is so uneven."

Carver pressed his lips together. "Fiona knows that pit very well. I found her lying in the middle of it not too long ago."

My face flushed red, and I cursed the fair Scottish complexion I'd inherited from my father. "I tripped and fell in."

"Were you hurt?" Emer asked, sounding concerned. I wasn't certain if she was more concerned about me or about any lawsuit that I might bring against the church had I sustained an injury.

I shook my head. "I'm fine. Just my pride was bruised, but my coat might not recover."

Emer nodded and appeared relieved.

"It is helpful for me to see this site," Craig said. "So thank you so for showing me. Many of the files we found in the church office were about the chapel ruins. It appears to me that the minister had been trying to jump-start this project for several decades before it came to pass."

"It was Emer who made it happen," Malcolm said.

Craig and I both studied the woman. "How so?" Craig asked.

"Malcolm, really, I am not single-handedly responsible," Emer protested.

The old sexton shook his head. "Don't be modest. Ye are responsible for it. Without you, the minister would never have been organized enough to raise the funds. Emer is a whiz with money. The church was very lucky when she agreed to be our treasurer."

"How long have you been church treasurer?" Craig asked.

"Two years," she said. "The previous church treasurer had been in the position for nearly twenty years until he stepped down. I have a background in accounting, so when the minister asked me to step in, I was happy to do it."

"Are you an accountant?" I asked.

Emer glanced at me. "I was when Douglas and I lived in

Aberdeen, but when we moved to the village so he could take the head teacher position, I gave up my accounting job in the city. I much prefer to do volunteer work now for the community and the church. I believe it is my place as first lady of the school."

First lady of the school? That was a title I had never heard of. I didn't think it was a British title either.

"Craig!" one of the crime scene techs called from the edge of the ruins. "We are all done here. Didn't take very long."

Craig nodded and turned to Emer and Malcolm. "I'll let you know if anything of significance comes from what we found here today."

Emer nodded, and Malcolm frowned. Carver was walking around the ruins as if he had lost interest in the conversation.

Together, except for Carver, we returned to the community garden. Malcolm and Emer went back inside the church, and I stood at the edge of the daisy field, feeling torn over all I'd heard. The only outcome I was sure of from my visit to the church was that I had found the place where the minister had been killed. That was more than Craig and the police had discovered, but something still felt off. There was something about the chapel ruins that made the hair on the back of my neck stand up. I was forgetting something.

Craig walked over to me. "Are you all right?"

I looked up at him. "I'm fine. Why do you ask?"

He smiled. "Because you are biting your lower lip."

I realized he was right. I hadn't even known I had been doing that.

"Fiona, go home," Craig said. "Or go back to your shop. You're not needed here."

I bristled at his comment. I always wanted to help and be useful.

Craig seemed to sense my sudden shift in mood. "You did the right thing by calling me. I'm sorry if I was short with you when I first arrived. I just don't want anything to happen to you. You're a special woman, and it would be a great loss if anything bad happened to you. It would be a great loss to me."

"To you?" I whispered.

He nodded and reached toward me. Craig adjusted the daisy over my ear and brushed the side of my face with his hand as he did it. "There. We don't want your flower to fall out, do we?"

"No, we don't," I said, barely above a whisper.

Chapter Twenty-Seven

As I walked through the cemetery and back to the street, my ear tingled from the chief inspector's touch. I wished I could have said that his presence didn't have such a visceral effect on me, but if I had, I'd have been lying.

I walked through the cemetery gate and spotted Emer and her husband standing in front of the village school. It was the middle of July and school was out for the year, but I guessed the head teacher had to go to the school often even when there were no children there.

Emer waved to me, and I relaxed. I was happy to see she remained friendly despite what had been discovered in the community garden.

Emer smiled warmly as I approached. "I hope I didn't come on too strong back there. Douglas is always telling me that I need to think before I speak. Isn't that right, honey?"

Her husband was studying the tops of his shoes. "Yes, dear," the man muttered.

I frowned. I had seen Douglas only a couple of times, and he had never once looked me in the eye.

I waved away her concern. "The minister's death has been a shock to everyone, and I know you worked with him closely. I'm very sorry for your loss and for the loss of the church."

"The church will survive. The presbytery is sending out the general presbyter in the next week. He will fill the pulpit until we can find a more permanent interim. I don't think anyone in the congregation will be in a great hurry to replace the minister until some time has passed. Emotions are just too high right now."

I nodded.

"I am sorry that I wasn't able to stay longer at your flower shop opening, Fiona," Emer said. "How's business been?"

I bit the inside of my lip. "We've only been open for a couple of days."

She nodded. "It's hard to start any new business, and the old flower shop that was in the same location wasn't able to make a go of it because Bellewick is so small. If you need any financial advice, I'm happy to help any way that I can. Like Malcolm said, I'm quite good with numbers."

"Thank you for the offer," I said with as much grace as I could muster.

"When things settle down," she went on to say, "I want you to know that I will talk to the church elders about purchasing our altar flowers from you. I can put you in touch with the other churches in Aberdeenshire as well. I believe that is a great place for you to start and expand your business. From there it could lead to weddings." She paused. "And funerals."

I swallowed at the mention of funerals. "That's so very kind of you."

She smiled. "And you are always welcome on Sunday mornings. We would love for you to join our congregation. I know you might have been hesitant before, but . . ." She trailed off.

But I didn't have to worry about that anymore, I thought.

"Emer, I need to go back into the school to talk to the custodian," Douglas said, speaking for the first time. His voice was scratchy, like he didn't use it frequently.

Emer's eyes widened slightly. "I thought you wanted me to talk to him."

He stared at his wife. "I never said that."

Emer forced a laugh. "Then we will both go, love." She turned back to me. "I'll be in touch, Fiona, about the flowers."

I thanked her and watched as she and her husband walked up the school steps. Emer opened the door for her husband, and before they went inside, the head teacher looked back at me. The man's eyes were puffy and bloodshot, like he had been crying. It took me a long while to get the image of Douglas's sad eyes out of my head.

Before I returned to the flower shop, I decided to go to the laundromat to deal with my dirty coat. I wasn't too worried about how much it would cost to clean the coat. Raj charged me way less than he did most of his customers because he and Uncle Ian had been such good friends.

And I had ulterior motives. After the encounter that morning at the Twisted Fox, I knew that Claudia Kenner worked at the laundromat.

The walk back to the main part of the village gave me time to think. It was time for me to catalog the suspects I had for this murder.

I started with Seth MacGregor. The dropout medical student/staunch environmentalist had a couple of motives going for him. There was the grudge he held against Minister Mac-Cullen for ruining his chances of getting into St. Andrews when he was young that had ultimately, according to Hamish, resulted in his grandfather's death. It seemed odd to commit murder now, since so much time had passed. And there was his gambling problem, which was the more likely of the two motives. Even so, it was a bit farfetched even to me, and I had a big imagination. I knew I would need much more than that to convince the chief inspector that's what had happened.

My next suspect was sexton Malcolm Wilson. He was at the church all the time, so he certainly had had the opportunity, but I couldn't think of his motive. He didn't seem to be broken up by the minister's death, and he had seen Minister MacCullen every day. To me, he seemed like a man who took pleasure in his work and ignored everyone else around him, including the outspoken minister.

Another suspect with opportunity and no real motive was Carver Finley. As he'd told me at the chapel ruins, he'd had no reason to kill the minister. In fact, the minister's death made it more difficult for him to do his assessment of the chapel ruins because so many in the congregation were against the project to begin with.

The most likely suspect was Remy Kenner. Everyone in the village agreed that the man had a temper and would be the type to commit a murder if he was angry enough. He had been seen at the docks with the minister the day the minister died, and it had appeared that the two men were in the middle of an argument. Whatever that argument had been about could be Remy's motive. I wished I had thought to ask Chief Inspector Craig about how the questioning of Remy had gone when I was still at St. Thomas's. But I knew that if Craig had been mad at me for wandering off while waiting for him to arrive to see the rain barrel, he would be furious if he knew I was making inquiries about Remy, who he'd already told me was a dangerous man.

The laundromat was on the shopping district side of the troll bridge near the creek. It was also on the street with the village's one and only grocery store, a small Tesco that would have been considered a convenience store back in the United States. Superstores like those in the U.S. were becoming more common in the cities in the United Kingdom, but not in the small villages like Bellewick.

When I pushed the laundromat door open, I spotted Claudia's young son, Byron, on the floor playing with a collection of plastic dinosaurs and blocks. He held the T-rex out to me and roared. I made a face of mock horror, and the little boy laughed.

The chemical scent of soap solvent hit me as soon as I stepped into the building, but it wasn't an entirely unpleasant. Claudia sat at the counter that divided the dry-cleaning portion of the business from the main room where washers and dryers tumbled. Half of the machines were in use. I had learned that there weren't many people in the village who had their own washing machines, and other than the Twisted Fox, Raj's Laundry was the best place to gather village gossip. But whoever had put their laundry in the machines had come and gone.

Claudia's eyes were bloodshot from crying. She stood when

I walked up to the counter. Without a hello or any type of friendly greeting, she said, "Take you coat off. I will put it in to soak. I think, with the wool fabric, it would be best if we dry-cleaned it."

I removed my dirty coat, taking the time to make sure there wasn't anything in my pockets, and then I handed it to her. "That's what I was thinking too. If you can't get the mud out, I understand."

"I can get it out. Raj taught me all his tricks for stain removal, and he can remove any stain you can think of. I'm not worried about a little dirt."

I nodded and was happy to see that she could chitchat with me. Maybe she didn't hate me.

She looked down at my mud-covered jeans as well. "I should clean those too."

"I would love you to. They are my favorite jeans and ones I would never be able to find in the U.K."

She made the gimme sign with her hand.

"But I don't have any other clothes. I will have to bring them another day."

"Don't wait too long," she said. "The longer a stain stays on a fabric, the harder it is to remove."

"I'll remember that," I said.

"Rrr!" the boy called from the front of the store as he flailed the T-rex back and forth.

Claudia looked at her son and smiled. Tears rushed to her eyes, and she fell back into her seat. "What am I going to do? Can you tell me what I should do?"

I was surprised by her sudden shift in mood. I'd thought

I would come into the laundromat and she would throw me out because she blamed me for her husband being questioned by the police. I'd never thought she would ask for my help.

Her tears came in a rush, and I couldn't understand her garbled speech between the tears.

The little boy continued to play while his mother cried, like nothing out of the ordinary was happening. That's what broke my heart the most—the little boy was used to his mother's tears. He probably saw them as normal. I guessed that in the Kenner home, they were.

"Claudia," I said. "I want to help you, but you have to tell me what happened. Why don't we sit down?" I pointed at a folding table and chairs near the front window.

She wiped at her eyes. "All right." She came around the counter and took a seat.

I took the one across from her and waited. It would do me no good to press her. No amount of prying was going to get it out of her.

She took a shuddering breath. "I love Remy. I have always loved him, even when we were children. We both grew up in the village. He was so handsome and thrilling."

I nodded.

She folded her hands on the tabletop. "He has a temper. He always has. He had one as a child, and it's only gotten worse as he's gotten older."

I didn't like the direction this was going.

"He's not always kind to me. He's never hurt our son," she added quickly.

227

I wondered if she added that last part a little too quickly. I waited.

"I knew what he was like when I married him. I never thought we would have children, so I thought that would be okay. Then I got pregnant. I was happy and terrified all at the same time. It was all right to start, but our son is starting to notice things now. I went to Minister MacCullen about it for guidance. I needed to know what the best thing to do was, not for me but for Byron."

I raised my eyebrows. It made sense, if she was a member of the church, that she would go to the minister for guidance.

"What did the minister say?" I asked.

"He advised me to leave Remy." A tear rolled down her cheek. "I have tried many times to leave my husband before and always failed. The minister knew this, and he said this time I had to make the decision and stick with it. I wasn't sure that I could. I wasn't sure that I was strong enough, but I agreed to do it. Like he had many times before, he said that my son and I could stay in the church until we got our bearings."

"Were you at the church the night of the storm?"

She nodded. "Yes. Remy found us there. He was furious with the minister. He said that he would make him pay for stealing his family. Minister MacCullen told him to leave and never come back. Finally, after what seemed like hours, Remy left. The minister said he locked the church up tight so that my son and I were safe. There was no way Remy could reach us. We slept on cots in one of the Sunday school room and shivered all night through that frightful storm."

"Did Minister MacCullen stay with you?"

She shook her head.

"So Remy could have gotten to Minister MacCullen."

She wouldn't look at me. "I don't know what happened between Remy and the minister when Minister MacCullen left the church. I wish—I wish—Minister MacCullen had never left. Maybe if he had stayed inside the church, he would still be alive."

"You think Remy killed him?"

"I don't know."

"You're with Remy now," I said.

She stared at her hands. "When I heard the minister died, I went back to him. Minister MacCullen was my safety net for leaving my husband. With him no longer there, I had no power to stay away. And . . ."

"And what?" I leaned forward.

She swallowed. "And I thought if he could kill the minister, what would he do to my son and me? Maybe it was better to go back to deal with his day-to-day anger than face that kind of fury."

Tears gathered in the corners of my eyes, and my heart broke for the mistreated woman across from me.

"I'm just torn up inside. On the one hand, I can't believe that Remy would do such an awful thing; on the other, I can. Remy has been tangled up in many dangerous things since he was a teenager."

"Like what?"

She shook his head. "He made bad choices. Thought there were easier ways to make money than through hard work. I only hope he didn't make the worst choice and murder the minister, because if he did, it would be my fault that the minister is dead. I couldn't live with that guilt." Tears rolled down her pale cheeks. "Minister MacCullen was always so kind to Byron and me."

I was beginning to wonder at the paradox of the minister. He'd been the hard man who wrote scathing letters that stopped Seth's chances from being accepted to St. Andrews and the man who'd left unwelcome notes on the door to my flower shop, but he'd also been the man who cared deeply for the history of his parish and wanted to save the old chapel ruins and the man who had counseled a young wife and mother to leave her abusive husband. I did not know whether he fit best in the category of good or bad. Perhaps he was like everyone else and a mixture of the two. It was the decent folks who pushed the bad back to let the good out. Whoever had killed Minister Quaid MacCullen had let the bad win.

"What are you going to do now?" I asked.

She looked up to me for the first time. "I don't know."

I was about to suggest she go to Raj about her predicament. He and Presha were both kind and compassionate. They would know what to do to help Claudia and her son.

But before I could say any of that, the front door slammed against the wall and Remy Kenner stormed inside.

Chapter Twenty-Eight

"Byron, come here," Claudia shouted to her boy.

The child clutched his dinosaur to his chest and ran to his mother. She jumped from her seat and scooped him up into her arms.

"Claudia, we need to go home." Remy glared at his wife with so much malice I couldn't understand how he could claim to love her.

Claudia inched behind me with Byron in her arms. I took that as my cue to speak up. "Claudia can't go with you right now."

"Who are you?" Remy demanded.

"I'm a friend."

"It's Fiona Knox, Remy," Claudia said, barely above a whisper, but it was loud enough for him to hear. "She inherited the land from Ian MacCallister."

I inwardly groaned. *Thanks for throwing me under the bus, Claudia.*

Remy curled his lip, showing off his crooked teeth. "You're who sent the police after me. The old trolls at the docks told me they told you about the spat I'd had with the minister."

I swallowed but held my ground. "It sounded like a lot more than just a spat," I said. "Especially considering the minister was dead a few hours later."

"I didn't kill him, and Neil Craig knows that. If he thought differently, I would be in jail right now, wouldn't I?"

I realized he had a point. Craig would never have let him go if he thought Remy was the killer, especially knowing what a dangerous man he could be.

"What's your alibi?" I asked.

"Alibi? Alibi? Does this little girl here fancy herself as some kind of detective?"

"Remy, please," Claudia whimpered.

Remy snapped his fingers. "I have had enough of this, Claudia. Let's go."

"I can't leave. I'm working." She shifted a little further behind me, using my body as a shield.

"You're not working here anymore. Now get the boy and let's go. We are leaving Bellewick for good. I have more opportunities for my business in Aberdeen."

"What business?" I asked.

"My business is none of yours," he snapped.

"I—I don't want to go with you, Remy." Her voice shook. "I want to stay in Bellewick. I—I have friends here."

"Friends," he scoffed. "What friends? Who would want to be friends with a pathetic person like you?"

"I'm her friend," I said. "And so are Presha and Raj."

He snorted and took a step toward me.

As much as I wanted to step back, I held my ground. "She doesn't want to go with you. I think you should leave."

"You have no place to stand between me and my wife." He raised his hand as if he were about to hit me.

"Do you want to go back to the police station in Aberdeen?" I asked, lifting my chin. "Because believe me when I say that if you hurt either of us, that's where Chief Inspector Craig will send you, right to jail."

He took another step toward me, and I braced myself for the blow that was sure to come. The entire time, I stared Remy in the eye.

To my surprise, he took a step back. "Is this what you really want, Claudia? To destroy our family by breaking it in two?"

"I'm not going with you, Remy. I can't put my son or myself through this any longer." Her voice was stronger now, and she stepped out from behind me, if only by two inches or so. It was a start.

"That is what you want?" he asked again.

"Yes, it's what I want," she said, barely above a whisper.

"Fine. You will be sorry someday." He spun around and walked to the door, which slammed closed behind him. The door shook so hard, I thought for certain the glass would shatter.

I helped Claudia and her son gather their things and lock up the building. I sent Raj a text telling him we were closing for the day due to Remy's impromptu arrival. He suggested I take Claudia and her son to Presha.

Claudia remained silent and looked over her shoulder every few feet on the short walk to Presha's Teas, and I didn't press her to speak. It seemed she was still in a bit of shock that she had stood up to her husband, but she was also terrified. Even though she had found the strength to stand up to him today, I knew it would take a long time for the poor woman to recover from the decades of abuse she'd suffered.

I hoped she would find the strength to keep her promise to herself and stay away from Remy. It was a choice that Claudia had to make, and no one else could make it for her. Even so, I couldn't help but think that Minister MacCullen would have been proud of her in the moment that she told Remy she wouldn't go with him. Thinking that made me like the man just a little bit more.

Presha was waiting for us outside her tea shop with a tartan shawl in her arms. As soon as Claudia came within range, Presha wrapped the shawl around the other woman and Byron. Byron giggled when the rough fabric grazed his round cheek. "Itchy," he said.

Presha laugh. "The Scots make tartan for warmth, not softness." She squeezed Claudia's hand. "I have tea and biscuits and scones and milk waiting for you all inside.'

Byron clapped his hands at the mention of biscuits. I got that; it was the same reaction I had anytime biscuits were mentioned, especially Presha's shortbread, which melted in your mouth.

Presha guided Claudia into the tea shop and smiled at me as Claudia and Byron went inside. "Would you like to stay? It sounds to me that you have had quite an eventful few hours."

"You can say that," I agreed. "But I think I will head back to the flower shop and then stop at the Twisted Fox and check on my sister before heading home. This is her first night waitressing for Raj. I just want to make sure she's doing okay."

"I'm sure she will do fine. She is a bright and delightful girl who is good with people and friendly. That is half the battle when it comes to food service. You don't need to mother-hen your sister, Fiona. She is an adult."

"I'm not mother-henning her," I said.

She raised a black eyebrow.

"Much. I'm not mother-henning her *much*."

She laughed and patted my arm. "And don't worry about Claudia. I'll take good care of her and Byron. That was a brave thing you did, standing up to Remy Kenner like that. Raj told me what happened at the laundromat. When things calm down a bit, you will have to tell me the rest of it in detail, but first go check on your store and your sister. You will feel better when you see how well Isla is doing."

I chuckled. "You understand me so well, Presha."

She winked and went inside.

I stepped onto the sidewalk and blinked when I looked down the street just in time to see Seth MacGregor strolling down the cobblestone street like he didn't have a care in the world. I might finally have my chance to find out why he was in Bellewick.

I followed him at a light jog, but when I was within ten yards, I slowed my pace so that I remained the same distance behind him. I matched him stride for stride.

Seth increased his pace as we made our way down Prince Street, the narrow lane where the Twisted Fox and my flower shop stood. I wasn't surprised when he made a beeline for the Twisted Fox.

Just before the pub, Seth ducked into the alley. Thankfully, there was no one on the street to see me run after him. I jogged into the space between the buildings, but slowed my pace in the darkened alley, and came out the other side of it. I held on to the side of the stone and peeked around the corner of the building to see Seth.

Seth was waiting out the back of the Twisted Fox near the dumpster. There was a large tear in the right pant leg of his jeans. I couldn't help but wonder what kind of scrape he must've gotten into to tear the denim so badly.

I was about to confront him when the back door of the Twisted Fox opened and my sister came out of the building.

She was wearing a black Twisted Fox T-shirt with the fox-head logo on it and skinny jeans that hugged all her curves. A white apron was tied around her waist. She'd piled her blonde hair on the top of her head with a bright red ribbon, and pretty tendrils of it fell and framed her round face.

When she saw Seth there, she squealed and ran toward him. To my astonishment, Seth caught her, picked her up, and twirled her through the air before setting her down. My mouth fell open as she kissed him on the mouth.

When I gathered my courage to look back at them again, my sister had let go of Seth and was glaring at me. "Fiona! What are you doing?"

Busted.

Chapter
Twenty-Nine

"What am *I* doing? What are *you* doing?" I pointed at Seth, whose ears were the brightest shade of red I had ever seen. Brighter even than the ribbon in my sister's hair.

My sister grabbed Seth's hand. "We're together."

"Together? How? What on earth is going on? How did you even meet?" I knew I was yelling. I knew I was overreacting, but it had been a very long day. I had found a crime scene, fallen into a pit, been threatened, and oh yeah, there was still a murderer loose in the village. Maybe I wasn't in a good place to be rational about my little sister having a new boyfriend *who was also a murder suspect.*

She tightened her grip on Seth's hand. "We met in Aberdeen a few days after I arrived when I went into the city for shopping. I was at the mall, and there he was! It was kismet, Fi. There was instant chemistry between us, and then I learned his connection to Duncreigan. How can I deny fate?"

"It's not fate, Isla. You don't even know him. You don't know his past." I stepped all the way out from behind the building. As I did, the smell from the dumpster became more potent.

"If you are talking about his gambling problem, Seth already told me about that." She looked up at him in admiration. "He told me the very first time we met. It's hard to find an honest man." She turned back to me. "You should know that."

I winced. I knew that was a pointed remark referring to my ex-fiancé. "That's a little harsh, Isla."

Her cheek pinked just a little, but she didn't take the comment back.

"Seth," I said. "This is what you are doing in the village? You're here to see my sister?"

He nodded.

"Then why on earth did you run from me?"

"I panicked. I knew you would ask me what I was doing here, and we weren't ready to make our relationship public just yet."

I rubbed my forehead. "Have you seen Hamish since you've been in the village? He still believes you are in medical school in Aberdeen."

He lowered his head. "I know. I've been working up the nerve to visit him and tell him that I don't want to be a doctor anymore. I'm going to tell him soon, I promise. I think I am more of a free spirit. I can't be chained to a schedule."

Great. Just what every big sister wants her baby sister to be with, a free spirit. If I let this relationship go on, I knew my parents would kill me. And I would be the one who would be blamed for it.

"I want to follow other pursuits," Seth said.

"What other pursuits?" I asked.

"I'm still dabbling, trying to find my way."

It took everything in me not to roll my eyes. "Are you going to return all the money you borrowed from Hamish to pay for school, then?"

His face turned bright red to match his ears.

"Never mind." I waved my hand. "That's none of my business. That's between you and him."

"Thank you, Fiona," he murmured. "I will tell Hamish soon."

I wasn't sure I believed him. "You should do it quickly. He knows that you're in the village."

"How?" Seth yelped.

"After you ran away from me, I spoke to him to ask if he knew you were here. I also told him that you might be tangled up in Minister MacCullen's murder. He's very worried about you."

"What? Why would you tell him that? I didn't kill anyone!"

I raised my eyebrows. "Then what were you doing at the docks the evening before the minister died, while the minister was there arguing with Remy Kenner?"

"I—I wasn't there with the minister or Remy."

"The old men there saw you. They have no reason to lie about it."

He lowered his head. "I wasn't there to meet the minister." He glanced at my sister. "Isla and I had planned to meet up, but when the weather started to turn bad, I texted her that I thought it was a better idea if she went home. I didn't want her to be caught in the storm." He wrapped his arm around my sister's shoulder. "I don't know what I would do if something happened to her."

Because you've known her for all of two weeks, I thought. I bit the inside of my lip to hold my sarcasm back. My smart mouth wasn't going to help anyone.

"Fi, it's true," Isla implored me with her large, dark-blue eyes. "I have the text to prove it if you don't believe us." She looked up at Seth. "He was going to take me for a romantic walk on the beach."

I thought of the pebble-covered beach. It was much more likely that one of them would have turned an ankle on that uneven surface than that they would have had a romantic interlude. Again, I kept those thoughts to myself.

"Since you were at the docks, you are a suspect," I said.

"But why? I don't have any reason to kill the minister."

"Hamish told me about the acceptance letter to St. Andrews . . ." I trailed off.

He blinked at me. "That was over ten years ago. Why would I care about that now?" He held on to my sister's hand. "Isla is all I care about."

He had a point, and my list of suspects was rapidly dwindling. I still didn't know why Craig had released Remy. Did he have an alibi?

Still, I wasn't giving up that easily that Seth could be guilty. "What about your gambling?"

His ears turned just a tad redder. It was quite impressive, really. I just hoped they didn't catch on fire. "What about it? I'm in recovery. I go to meetings."

"Maybe the minister confronted you about your addiction," I said. "And you didn't like it."

"And I killed him over it? Why? Everyone knows about my issues with gambling. It's not a secret. Who could he tell? Isla already knew."

"Fi, you are being very judgmental," my sister said. "Why can't you just be happy for me that I found someone to spend the rest of my life with?"

"Wait." I held up my hand. "The rest of your life? What do you mean?"

"Fiona," my sister said. "Now that you know about Seth and me, we have more news." She looked up at Seth, and he gave her a slight nod.

I had a feeling that I wasn't going to like what she was about to say.

"Seth and I are going to get married!" she exclaimed with bright eyes.

I drew in a sharp breath, and my gaze fell to her ring finger on her left hand. There was nothing there.

Isla noticed my line of sight, because she said, "He will get me a ring just as soon as he has the money saved up. Right, honey?"

Seth's Adam's apple bobbed. "Right, my love."

I waved my hands back and forth in a universal stop sign. "Isla, you can't marry a man you have only known for two weeks."

"He's the one, Fi. It was love at first sight."

Seth's Adam's apple bobbed up and down double-time.

I took a deep breath. "Isla, why don't we go home and talk

about this? I'm sure Raj would let you out of your shift under the circumstances. It's been a crazy few days. You just graduated from college. You need to find out what you want from your life. It's not the time to become trapped."

"Trapped? Getting married is not becoming trapped. Just because it didn't work out for you."

I closed my eyes for a long moment. "Please, Isla."

She grabbed Seth's hand. "I'm not a child, Fi. You have treated me like a child my entire life. Seth and I are getting married. There is nothing that you can do about it."

"I just think you need to be practical." It came out as a whimper. "No offense to Seth, but he doesn't even have a job. He doesn't have a plan or—"

"What? Like Ethan had a job?" she asked. "You really aren't in a place to question my choices in men, are you?"

I felt like I might be sick.

"Let's go, Seth." She pulled on his arm and pushed her fiancé through the back door of the pub, and then turning back to me, said, "I'm going to stay with Seth tonight, so don't wait up."

My heart fell to the bottom of my shoes. "Isla, I—"

She slammed the heavy metal door before I could finish my sentence.

My arms dropped uselessly to my sides. All I could hope for was the world's longest engagement.

Chapter Thirty

P art of me wanted to follow Isla into the Twisted Fox, but I knew we were not in a good place to discuss this latest development in her life, and I certainly didn't want to make a scene in Raj's pub.

Instead, I removed my shop keys from my pocket and walked next door to the Climbing Rose. I let myself into the shop through the back door. Ivanhoe meowed at me, and his gray-striped tail slid back and forth on the weathered hardwood floor, making his annoyance clear. I had left him for too long alone in the shop.

I scooped up the cat. "Sorry, Buddy." I rubbed my cheek in his velvety fur.

Carrying Ivanhoe as I went, I swept through the store and was relieved to find nothing appeared out of the ordinary. Even better, there wasn't a mysterious note lying in wait for me. I was really tired of those notes.

I texted my sister and told her I was sorry and only surprised by the news of her engagement. My sister was engaged. It was hard for me wrap my mind around that. One of the best things about my sister was her willingness to take risks and jump into whatever she felt passionate about, but it was one of the worst things about her too. I knew that if she would take the time to think about it, she would see what a bad idea it was to be engaged to a man she had just met in a foreign country. Knowing Isla, she would move ahead full throttle until something really awful happened, and when it did, I'd have to pick up the pieces.

I rubbed my forehead, feeling a headache forming right between my eyes. Ivanhoe leaned against my shoulder and meowed.

"I think it's time to go back to Duncreigan too," I told the cat.

I gathered up his bed and half the toys I had brought to the shop for him that morning. The other half could be his shop toys, I thought. I slung Ivanhoe's bag of goodies and my tote bag over my shoulder, tucked the cat bed under my arm, and picked up his carrier, where he was impatiently waiting for transport by giving off a howl-like wail every two seconds.

"I know, I know," I said. "You are going to be just fine. Don't worry." When I managed to get through the front door, I had to set the carrier and cat bed down so I could lock up the shop. As I did, I heard a scraping sound to my left in the direction of the alley.

I froze with my key in the lock. "Isla?" I asked. "Seth?"

No one answered.

I must have imagined the noise. My nerves were all but completely frayed. I shook my head as I locked the door and said to Ivanhoe, "I think I might be losing my mind."

"That may be," an elderly woman said to me as she made her way down the street carrying two full shop bags. "You're talking to yourself," she added as she passed.

"The cat," I called after her. "I was talking to the cat."

She didn't so much as look over her shoulder when I said that. I picked up the cat carrier and the cat bed again and made my way to the public lot near the troll bridge. I walked by the open door of the Twisted Fox and heard Celtic music playing and laughter. I peeked inside but didn't see my sister or Seth in the dimness.

I continued down the street past the bakery, which was long closed for the day, a Bank of Scotland branch, and a tiny clothing store that mostly sold clothing suitable for fishermen. In all likelihood, it was the only clothing shop that could make a go of it in such a tiny fishing village. When I walked by the clothing store, I heard the scraping again, and I spun on my heel, determined to catch whoever or whatever was responsible for the sound. As I turned, I could have sworn a shadow disappeared between two of the tightly packed buildings.

Was I being followed? Was it Remy Kenner? I felt a chill run all the way down my back and into my legs. Should I go down the alleyway and see if I was right? Or should I run? I remembered what Craig had told me about Remy, about how dangerous he really was and that he was a drug dealer. He wasn't someone I wanted to mess with alone.

I ran.

The cat carrier bounced painfully against my leg as I ran, and Ivanhoe yowled all the way down the street. I ran over the troll bridge, like I was being pursued by the bridge troll himself, and into the parking lot.

A boys' football team, or soccer team as it would be called in the States, were standing in their uniforms and shin guards around two parked vans when I came flying into the lot like my tail was on fire. I pulled up short and stared at them redfaced. I gasped for breath, and Ivanhoe hissed in his carrier.

"Stop looking, children," one of the adults said. "It's time to get into the vans so we can head to the match."

The boys and I continued to gape at each other.

"Into the van with you," the adult ordered. "She's an American. She's going to do all sorts of odd things. It's not polite to stare."

The boys broke eye contact with me and piled into the two waiting vans.

I stood by my Astra and caught my breath, holding Ivanhoe's carrier to my chest. I needed to get a grip.

"Was there a reason that you were running away from me?" a voice asked.

I spun around, and Ivanhoe yowled.

Carver raised his eyebrow. "I assume there is a cat in that box."

"Were you following me just now?" I asked.

"I was."

My mouth fell open. I hadn't expected him to just come right out and say it. "Why?"

"Because I wanted to talk to you, but you ran away from me like your tail was on fire." He cocked his head, and his thick blond hair fell to one side. "What's got you spooked, Fiona Knox?"

I ignored his question. "What do you want?"

He smiled. "I was hoping to catch you at your shop this evening. I wanted to talk to you about Duncreigan."

To buy myself some time, I opened the passenger side door of my car and set Ivanhoe's cat carrier inside. He yowled as I shut the door after him. "What about Duncreigan?" I walked around to my side of the car, and Carver followed me.

"You and I both know it's a *very* special place, and I would very much like to visit it to see what its historical significance is to the area. Raj mentioned to me that there is a standing stone there. In my research of the area, this stone has not been documented."

I inwardly groaned and wished that Raj hadn't mentioned anything about Duncreigan or my godfather's garden to the historian.

"I think I could tell you a lot about the stone, perhaps even date it, if I was allowed to see it."

"I know that most menhirs can't be dated exactly. No one really can know who erected them."

He smiled. "I see you have done a little research into this, so you are curious about it, aren't you?"

His open curiosity had me on edge. "I appreciate the offer, but I don't need any help."

"Minister MacCullen didn't seem to think you were up to the task of caring for the garden. He spoke about it in church." He tapped his index finger on his cheek. "It was the Sunday that he chased you away from the church. That must had been humiliating for you."

My face felt hot. "Well, you have probably heard by now that the minister and I didn't see eye to eye on a great many things. I wouldn't judge what I was capable of by his low opinion of me." I swallowed before I lost my courage. "And what's your opinion of the minister?"

He shrugged. "As long as he funded the chapel project, I didn't care one way or another about him. Do you still think that I killed him?"

"I never did," I said, speaking the truth. It seemed to me that the minister's death would only have been a burden to Carver when it came to funding his research. He wouldn't put that in jeopardy.

"That makes me happy that you don't think badly of me, Fiona, because I do want the two of us to be friends." He leaned in close to me, and I stepped back, bumping into my car. He stared at my throat. "That's an interesting necklace you have on. A triskele. Just like the ones found at the chapel ruins."

Instinctively, I reached up and grabbed the pendant hanging from my neck.

"Where did you get that?" he asked.

I frowned. "It was a gift. I don't know what my necklace has to do with anything."

"I just find it curious that of all the Celtic symbols, it would be this one that you would wear. Must have some significance to you. Am I right?"

I put my hand on the handle of the car door. "I really have to go. My cat is hungry, and I need to get him home to feed him."

Carver smiled. "We don't want a hungry cat on our hands, now, do we?"

I started to open the car door, but he blocked me from opening it. "How much do you know about Duncreigan, really?"

"Please just let me go."

"It seems to me there is much you could learn about the garden." He lowered his voice. "About yourself, if you would only let me see the standing stone."

I yanked the car door open at this point, which cause him to stumble away from me.

"Don't you want to know what you're up against?"

I was about to duck into the car when his words stopped me. "What I'm up against?"

"How can you know how to use the garden properly if you don't know where the magic comes from?" He lowered his voice. "Because the garden does hold magic, correct?"

"I'm sorry, but I have to go."

"I *need* to see the stone."

I jerked back.

"Everything okay here?" A voice asked.

I turned to see Kipling walking toward us with a determined gait. His hair was perfectly styled, and the numerous brass metals and buttons on his uniform had been polished until they sparkled. I had never been so happy to see him.

Carver scowled and took a step back from me. "We're fine, Officer."

Kipling glanced at me, and I smiled at him. "I was just leaving."

Kipling nodded. "It would be good for you to go home, Fiona. I saw Remy at the station just before he was questioned. He's not too pleased with you right now. I'd give him a wide berth if I were you."

"I'm planning on it," I said. I planned to give Carver a wide berth too. "I had better go. My cat is in the car."

Kipling nodded and stepped away. He was scanning the parking lot for something or someone. Remy? I wondered. I didn't plan to hang around and find out who it was.

Carver stepped back from the car and let me climb in. Before I shut the door, he said, "Fiona, the stone must be studied. I will get to it eventually."

"It's on private property. The stone can't be researched without my permission," I shot back.

He smiled and stepped back from the car. "I don't think you've met a researcher as determined as I am before. You may say no now, Fiona Knox, but remember that I won't give up that easily. I will have a look at that stone with or without your blessing."

I slammed the car door shut and shifted into gear. I had heard enough.

I drove out of the village before I allowed myself to breathe again.

Chapter
Thirty-One

I vanhoe and I got home just as dusk was settling. Half of me was wishing that Hamish would be at the cottage when I arrived. The other half of me was not. What could I tell him? The good news was that Seth didn't appear to have murdered the minister, but we were all about to become family?

I thought I needed to digest this bit of news before I shared it with anyone. That especially was true when I thought about my parents. My mother would hit the roof. She hadn't been happy when I'd said I planned to stay in Scotland permanently, and now it was possible that both her daughters would live on the other side of the world from her.

I ate a quick dinner of cereal and chocolate milk. Ever since I had been working at the flower shop, my diet had become whatever I could find in the cottage—which wasn't much— and whatever was the day's special at the Twisted Fox.

In the last couple of weeks, all I had wanted was the cottage back to myself, but now that Isla wasn't there, it was too quiet. It was Ivanhoe and me and the twenty-some shipping boxes sent overseas by my mother. I glanced down at the cat. "Just between you and me, I miss her."

He mewed. He missed Isla too.

"Don't tell her I said that, okay?"

He wrinkled his little pushed-in nose.

Since I had moved to Scotland, I hadn't bothered to purchase a television. This was one of those times I wished I had one. I could have used the background noise. Maybe a sitcom would have kept my mind off of my troubles.

Even though I didn't know what to do about the murder or about my sister's engagement, I could at least start organizing the cottage. I was tired of tripping over the boxes from back home. It was time to claim the cottage as my own. The best way to do that was to finish going through my godfather's possessions and decide which of those to keep and which of them to donate to charity.

I went into the small bedroom, where I found my sister's clothes strewn across the bed and her makeup all over the top of the dresser. Clearly she had discarded four outfits before she settled on what she was wearing that day.

I shook my head and pushed my sister's clothes aside and dropped her makeup back into her makeup case. It didn't all fit. Isla should really buy stock in Sephora.

Like most homes in Europe, the cottage didn't have a closet. Instead, there was a free-standing walnut wardrobe across from the bed. There was only enough room in the small space to open the doors, with an inch to spare between the wardrobe and the end of the double bed.

When I was a child, I had been convinced that the

wardrobe would be my ticket to Narnia after I had read *The Lion, the Witch, and the Wardrobe*. I had even gone so far as to hide in the wardrobe for hours when I was nine. I'd curled up in the back and squeezed my eyes shut. I'd willed myself to wake up in Narnia and ignored the frantic shouts of my parents and Uncle Ian, who were searching all over Duncreigan for me.

It was Uncle Ian who had found me in the end. "What are you doing in there, my love?" he'd asked.

"Narnia business," I had said.

He had laughed his deep laugh. "You are a treat, my love. You are a treat. I'm so glad that I am your . . ."

My mother, with baby Isla on her hip, had come in the room then and yelled at me for hiding from them.

I opened the wardrobe again that night and pushed my godfather's clothes aside until I could see the back of the furniture.

Ivanhoe stood at my feet. "You won't tell, will you?" I asked the cat.

He mewed.

I knocked on the back of the wardrobe, just in case. It wouldn't hurt to double-check. Just like when I was a child, a portal to Narnia didn't open. It was a great disappointment. I had never been readier to run to a magical kingdom far away.

Ivanhoe mewed again, as if he were reprimanding me in some way.

"Hey, I'm the Keeper of a magical garden. It's not too far a stretch to believe that Narnia might be real, too."

He cocked his head as if to say, "You're kidding me, right?"

Below where I'd knocked on the back of the wardrobe, I spotted a square wooden box. When I was a kid, my godfather had said that was where he kept all his favorite things. He'd told me he would show me what was in the box someday, but he never had. I had forgotten about it until now.

I bit the inside of my lip. I wasn't sure I was ready to face whatever memories the box contained. Perhaps it would just be better to sort through my godfather's clothing so I could put my own clothes in the wardrobe. However, the strange encounter I had had with Carver in the village parking lot had me on edge. I was curious about the garden and my godfather. I wanted to understand my connection to both, but this was something I was determined to find out on my own. I wasn't going to go to Carver for help. Ever.

"This day has already been a disaster. I can't see it getting any worse," I told the cat. "Let's go for it."

He meowed encouragement.

I scratched his head between his folded ears. "I'm glad that you at least are on my side."

I pulled the box out of its place and set it in the middle of the bed. As I did, a cloud of dust flew up in my face.

Ivanhoe sneezed, and I coughed.

The box was locked, but I found a silver key taped to the bottom of it. The tape was brittle and fell apart in my hand as I removed the key. I brushed the remainder of the tape from the key.

"Now or never, right, Ivanhoe?"

The cat meowed. I took it as encouragement to open the box.

The key fit effortlessly into the lock and turned. I lifted the box's lid, and another cloud of dust enveloped the cat and me. Ivanhoe shook a dust bunny from his head and then batted it away.

I peered inside and gave a sharp intake of breath. The box was a time capsule. On the very top was my godfather's degree from St. Andrews and his acceptance letter into the Royal Army. I set those aside. The next item was a framed photo of Uncle Ian holding me when I was a baby. I recognized it because I had the same one packed away in one of the boxes in the main room. I set the photo upright on the narrow nightstand.

I found more old letters and trinkets from my godfather's early days in the army. Beneath these, I found a manila envelope. I opened it and found a group of yellowing photographs from my godfather's school days at St. Andrews. I recognized the places in the photographs because my parents would always take Isla and me there when we visited Uncle Ian. It was the place they had met, and they always wanted to go back.

Most of the pictures were of my godfather and other male students, and my father was in many too. They were either fooling around or smiling brightly at the camera, their arms wrapped around each other.

The very last photograph in the bunch was the surprise. It was my godfather and my mother. She was sitting on his lap with her arms around his neck. My father was in the picture, but he was off to the side looking at my mother and Uncle Ian with a frown on his face.

Something was off here. Why was my mother hugging Uncle Ian and not my father? Why was my father the one off to the side in the picture? Shouldn't my godfather be the one looking in on my parents' relationship? I flipped over the photo, and the date on the back was the year before I was born. I recognized my mother's handwriting. It was clear and precise. She had always preached about good penmanship to my sister and me. Beneath the date she had written, "Claire and Ian," with a heart around the two names. My father wasn't mentioned at all.

I picked up the manila envelope and blew into it. There was a note crumpled into the bottom of it. I removed the note, which was again written in my mother's hand on her personal stationery. She didn't write letters very often any longer, but I knew the stationery from when I was small. Once, when I was no more than five, I had taken half a dozen sheets from her stationery box and drawn tulips and daffodils on them. Mom had scolded me when she found out I had wasted so much paper.

I unfolded the note and read.

I named her Fiona like you asked. She may not be your daughter in name, but she always will be. I know it's been difficult on all of us, but the solution we agreed upon is the best for the family. We are all family now because of Fiona.

I stared at the words again. *She may not be your daughter in name, but she always will be.* Countless memories flooded through my mind about my godfather and the garden. How everyone in the village had assumed I was a MacCallister when I'd inherited Duncreigan, how I'd been told I had the MacCallister black hair, and how so many had assumed that Uncle Ian was my father . . .

"Oh my God," I whispered as the truth settled into my heart.

I shoved everything back into the box except for the framed photo of my godfather and me. That I left on the nightstand. I put the box back in the wardrobe and hid the key in the nightstand drawer.

"Cleaning is overrated," I said to the cat.

Ivanhoe meowed in return. I was certain that meant he agreed with me.

Chapter Thirty-Two

The storm raged on around me. I counted One Mississippi, Two Mississippi, Three—

I couldn't even finish the third Mississippi before the crack of thunder seemed to split the earth in two. I was hiding between the oil barrels on the docks. Rain pelted my back and ran down the sides of my face into my eyes.

Two people, carrying something long and black, came out of the darkness. Whatever it was, it seemed heavy—they were inching down the docks.

"I don't—" one of the two people began to say.

"That's the problem. You don't think, and I have to clean up all of your messes. I wish once, just once, you would think out your actions."

There was a mumbled response, but I couldn't make out the words.

The stronger voice came back. "Be quiet. We need to finish here before the storm gets much worse."

Suddenly, I was no longer in my hidden spot between the

oil barrels. I was suspended in air, being swung to and fro wrapped in a canvas tarp.

The two voices were speaking again, but I couldn't make out the words they said.

"Here," one voice came in clear.

They dropped me on hardwood. I could smell fish and the sea. I felt like I was still at the docks, but I didn't know exactly where. I tried to cry out, but my mouth refused to open.

Suddenly, the tarp was stolen from me and I shot out of it like a bullet from a gun. With a splash, I was in the sea and I was sinking down, down, down to the bottom with the minister's face floating below me.

Finding my voice at last, I screamed and sat bolt upright in the middle of my bed in the cottage. I waited for my sister's return scream that told me I had scared her awake, but it never came. That's when I remembered she hadn't come home with me the night before. She was somewhere in the village with Seth. I didn't know if it was realizing that or the terrifying nightmare that caused my nausea, but I had to take several shallow breaths to stop myself from throwing up.

Ivanhoe stood at the end of the bed and arched his back in fear. I fell back on my pillow, breathing hard, willing myself to calm down and breathe more normally.

Had that been a vision or just an anxiety-induced dream? I couldn't be sure.

I'd had dreams before that were made up of the visions I had received from touching the menhir, but this vision didn't seem to be connected to the one I'd had of struggling in the mud with a knee in the middle of my back. In the past, my visions had been peeks into the future. Was I to be thrown into the sea like the minister had?

Ivanhoe padded across the bed to me and purred in my ear. I struggled to a sitting position and braced my back against the headboard.

Grabbing the cat, I pulled him close to my chest, and got ahold of my cell phone. The time read one in the morning. I groaned. I'd thought for certain it would be much later. I had a whole night in front of me to remember the dream.

Before I could change my mind, I called Chief Inspector Craig.

"Fiona, what's wrong?" His voice was groggy but alert.

"Did I wake you? I'm so sorry." I wished I could hang up the phone and pretend I'd never called him. What was I doing calling Craig in the middle of the night?

"Fiona, tell me what's wrong. Are you okay?" He sounded much more awake now.

"I-I'm fine."

"Where are you?" His voice was sharp.

"I'm at home, and I'm fine, honest. I just called you because . . ." I trailed off. How lame would it sound if I said I'd just called him because I'd had a bad dream? I had never been a damsel in distress, and I wasn't going to start taking on the role now.

"Is your sister there with you?" he asked.

"No, she didn't come home last night. She's with her fiancé."

"Her fiancé? Is this new? Did you know this was happening?"

"It's new, and no, I didn't know about it until I caught them behind the Twisted Fox together. That's when she told me that they were getting married."

"Who is she marrying? Is it someone from the U.S.? Did he fly over to see her?"

"Oh no," I said, becoming increasingly aware of how uncomfortable this conversation was making me. Calling Craig had been a bad idea, a very bad idea. "You should have talked me out of calling him," I whispered to the cat curled up in my lap.

He purred in response.

"What?" Craig asked. "What did you say?"

"It's Seth MacGregor."

"Seth MacGregor!" He was fully awake now. "How?"

"I don't know the particulars, but it seems that it was love at first sight. They've known each other for all of two weeks."

"Ah," he said.

"Anyway, that's why I've been seeing Seth in the village lately. He and Isla were trying to keep their relationship a secret from me. They thought I wouldn't approve."

"You've been seeing Seth in the village? Why are you just telling me this now?"

I inwardly groaned. I shouldn't have mentioned that at all, but at least there was no reason for me to connect Seth with the murder now. "It never came up," I said.

"How do you feel about Isla and Seth?" His voice was gentle, gentler than I deserved so late at night.

"She's twenty-two years old. There's really nothing I can do to change the situation. It's her life, and I have to let her live it."

"Are you talking yourself into that point of view?"

"Sort of."

"Is this why you called me, because you are dealing with your sister's surprise engagement? Because if it is, I'm flattered that you would come to me with your personal problems."

I was grateful that Craig wasn't in the room with me, because a blush crept up into my hairline.

"It's not the reason. I—I had a dream—a vision."

Craig was quiet for a long moment.

"Are you still there?" I asked the silence on the phone.

"I'm still here. Is it like the vision you had last time when Alastair Croft died?"

"Not exactly. I think I saw Minister MacCullen being dumped in the sea." Before I could lose my courage, I went on to describe the dream in more detail, but I left out the part about me being dumped in the sea. There was no reason to upset the chief inspector unnecessarily.

"You saw him be murdered?"

"I think he was already dead by the time my vision began. At least he was limp. A pair of hands threw him overboard into the waves."

"What did the hands look like?"

"I—I don't remember," I said, feeling disappointed with myself. I should have concentrated more on the details of the vision—if it was in fact a vision.

"Did you see any faces? Can you remember anyone that you saw?"

I thought back to the dream and shivered as I remembered what it was like to sink down into the sea.

"Fiona? Are you all right?" Craig's voice was urgent.

"I'm fine. The only face I remember is the minister's while he was sinking into the water." I shivered. "I'm sorry that I can't be more of a help."

"You are a help. It fits with what the coroner found."

"What do you mean?"

"You found the place where he died. The water in the rain barrels matched the water in his lungs, and now you have told me where he was pitched into the sea."

"That was fast."

"I pulled a few strings," the chief inspector said. "I think I agreed to buy the lab tech lunch for a year or something to give my case priority."

"You believe me about the vision?"

"Your visions have been right in the past. I'm not in a place to question them."

I felt myself relax against the headboard. It was impossible for Craig to know how happy it made me to hear that.

"Don't tell anyone, not even you sister, about this vision. I think it could be dangerous for you if anyone else in the village knows about it. A secret like that can pass like wildfire, and I can almost guarantee whoever killed Minister MacCullen will hear about it. That makes you a target."

I considered this.

"Please listen to me, Fiona. Concentrate on your garden and the flower shop. Leave the investigating to me."

I couldn't do that, but I didn't tell Craig that. "Why did you let Remy Kenner go?"

"How do you know that?"

Now I've put my foot in it.

"We have no evidence to tie him to the murder," he said finally, when I didn't reply. "And I know you saw Remy today—or I suppose it was yesterday now, since it's after midnight. I got a call from Presha."

"Oh," I said.

"She told me what happened. As much as I hate the idea of you being a target for Remy, you did the right thing by protecting Claudia and her son."

"Thank you," I whispered.

"My officers are looking for Remy now. Claudia has finally agreed to press charges against him for years of abuse. But this is why I don't like the idea of you being at Duncreigan alone."

I shivered. Remy knew where I lived. If he was mad enough, I could see him coming to Duncreigan.

He paused for a moment. "Do you want me to come out there? I can be there in thirty-five minutes. Twenty if I use my sirens."

"Please don't; it was just a dream, and Remy has probably left the village by now. He said there was some business for him in Aberdeen," I said, sounding braver than I actually felt.

"Selling drugs, I'm sure," Craig said. "He's been in the business for years. With Claudia willing to speak against her husband now, we might finally get to lock him up." He paused. "And Fiona, we both know your dreams are not just dreams. This sounds serious. What if it predicts the future like your other visions have? I don't like the idea of you out there alone."

"I'm not alone. Ivanhoe is there."

"Is he going to scratch the killer?"

"The doors are locked. There is no way anyone can get inside. I'll be fine." Another thought struck me. "I hope you weren't too upset by the news of Isla's engagement."

"What?"

"I—I just hope that you weren't disappointed she is with someone else."

"What are you talking about?" He sounded irritated now.

"Um." I should have stopped talking when he told me about Remy, but my mouth had gotten in the way again.

"Do you think I have romantic feelings for your sister?" There was disbelief in his voice.

"The two of you seemed to hit it off."

He laughed.

Again, my face turned bright red, and again, I was happy he couldn't see me.

"Fiona, I have no interest in your sister romantically. I only talked to her because I know you care so much about her."

"Oh?" Relief whooshed into my body like a large wave against the coast.

"It was *you* I was trying to impress. You're the one I have feelings for."

"*Me?*" I squeaked.

"Yes, you. It's always been you."

I was speechless.

"And if you need me, call me anytime."

"But—"

He sighed. "I don't say these things just because. Call me, Fiona. Any. Time."

"Okay," I whispered.

Chapter Thirty-Three

I woke up the next morning under a pile of clothes. I hadn't been able to sleep after my conversation with Craig, so I'd decided to start unpacking the boxes my mother had shipped to Scotland. So far, I'd found a number of tanks tops, shorts, and sundresses. Although those clothes had been great for my life during a sweltering Tennessee summer, they weren't the most practical fashion choices in northern Scotland. My mother had also sent my ice skates. I didn't see me using those anytime soon either. I stood up and dropped my ice skates into the closest open box. Maybe I should have been more specific when I'd asked my mother to ship some of my things to Scotland. Clearly, letting her choose at random hadn't worked.

I pushed the pile of clothes off me and onto the floor. Unpacking had been a very bad idea. The cottage looked worse than ever, but there was no way I could blame Isla for its current condition. I had to get out of the cottage even though it was only six in the morning.

I showered and dressed for the day. I checked my phone from time to time for anything from my sister, but there wasn't a single text from her in response to the dozens of "I'm sorry" texts I had sent. When I was ready, I gathered up my purse and a jacket and headed for the door. It was still before seven in the morning.

Ivanhoe followed me. "I'll take you to the shop tomorrow. There's too much going on right now, and I don't know what the day will bring. I don't want you to be stuck in the shop so long alone like you were yesterday."

He butted my shin with the top of his round head.

"No." I wagged my finger at him. "No amount of head butts are going to get me to change my mind."

He meowed plaintively, walked over to his cozy cat bed by the fireplace, and lay down with as much drama as any actress from the silver screen.

I wanted to go to the garden, but the memory of all I had learned from my godfather's wooden box washed over me. I wasn't sure I was ready to face my godfather—even if he was only in fox form. I needed more time. I would deal with the mess that I had made with my sister and then deal with Uncle Ian.

I didn't have to open the Climbing Rose until ten, so I still had three hours. The Twisted Fox opened at eight, but I didn't want to go there on the off chance I would run into Isla and Seth, and I wasn't ready for that.

I pushed open the door to Presha's Teas. Most of the tables were full of men and women in business suits, as well as construction workers. The inside of the shop was pleasantly warm, and a wave of scents washed over me. The dough of the scones, the spice from Presha's famous chai, and a hint of lavender. My stomach growled.

The tea shop was one of the most popular businesses in the village. The entire space was decked out in purple tartan and thistle. The only nod to Presha's own heritage was a shrine to Ganesh in the corner of the room.

Claudia and Byron sat at a small table in the corner—the little boy on his mother's lap was happily playing with his dinosaurs. I smiled at her, but she didn't return the gesture. I wondered if I should talk to her or leave her be.

Presha set a plate of scones on a table for a group of ladies. She waved at me and handed her tray to one of her servers. She wove through the tables toward me. "Fiona, it's not often I see you in the village this early. Haven't you told me many times that you have trouble waking up in the morning?"

I smiled. "Usually that's true."

She studied my face. "You didn't sleep well, did you?"

I raised my eyebrows. "How do you know that?"

"I just do." She smiled. "And the dark circles under your eyes were a giveaway."

I groaned. "Great."

She smiled. "You need some scones and tea, and you will be just fine." She led me to the one empty table in the shop by the front window.

I sat and had a clear view of the village. Mothers and fathers walked with their children, and villagers hurried off to work. Older ladies carried empty canvas bags to the market to do their daily shopping.

As the waitress walked by, Presha said, "Erin, bring us two scones and chai."

Erin nodded and returned to the kitchen.

"How are Claudia and Byron?" I asked, glancing over at them.

Presha smiled. "They will be all right. Claudia and Byron will stay with me until the mess with Remy gets sorted. After that, we will help them get back on their feet, won't we?"

I nodded.

"Between my brother and me, we can give her enough work to stay in the village." Presha folded her hands on the tartan table-cloth. "Now, tell me what is bothering you. Is it the murder?"

"Yes and no." I sighed. "Mostly right now it's my sister. We got into a terrible fight last night."

"Because of Seth?"

I stared at her. "How did you know?"

"I've seen them in the village together, and they appeared to be very much in love." She smiled.

My mouth fell open. "Why didn't you tell me?"

"It was Isla's place to tell you. I knew she would in time."

I inwardly groaned. I should have expected this answer from Presha. She'd had a similar answer when I'd asked her why she hadn't told me the garden I'd inherited was magical. She'd said it was my godfather's place to tell me, which had been tricky since he was dead.

I sighed. "She didn't come home last night. I know I over-reacted with her. I just was so surprised. She's only known Seth for two weeks. How can she decide that she's ready to marry someone in two weeks?"

Presha smiled but remained silent.

Erin returned with the chai and scones.

I reached for one of the scones and set it on a small plate in front of me. "It would never work for me like that." I cut the scone in half and slathered both sides with butter and strawberry jam. Usually I wasn't so liberal with the butter, but I was an emotional eater, so I gave myself a pass.

She studied me and said nothing as I added more jam to my scone. Finally, she poured chai in my waiting teacup and said, "Because you would never allow yourself to fall in love so quickly."

Maybe what she said was true, but that didn't change the fact that I was wired much differently than my carefree sister.

I shook my head. "I need to talk to her and let her know that I love her. Whatever happens, she will always be my sister."

"It seems to me that you already know what to do then. You came here for advice, did you not?"

I nodded. "And this." I held up the scone. "It takes the edge off."

She laughed. "All will be well with Isla, but you must let her live her own life. She may be happy with Seth. You need to let her find out if that is true for herself."

The door to the tea shop flew open, and Emer entered. As always, her husband Douglas was a few paces behind her.

I choked down my too-big bite of scone. I would have to take a far less aggressive bite next time.

Emer smiled. "Presha, do you have the biscuits ready for us?"

Presha pushed a cup of chai in front of me. "Drink this."

I didn't know how a cup of her spicy chai would make me stop coughing, but I dutifully took a sip. It burned my throat all the way down, but the coughing ceased.

"Yes, the shortbread is ready." She nodded to Erin, who hurried into the kitchen and came back a second later with three white bakery boxes.

"These will do so nicely." She nodded to her husband. "Douglas, you will take these?"

He stumbled forward and took the boxes before shuffling back to his place behind his wife.

"Would you like some tea before you go?" Presha asked.

"Tea would be lovely, but please make it to go," Emer said. "There is much to do today. I believe that Carver will be making his final assessment of the chapel ruins today. With that, we can apply to be a historical site."

Presha nodded at Erin. "Two teas in takeaway cups for Emer and Douglas, please."

The young girl spun on her heels in the direction of the kitchen again.

"None for Douglas," Emer said. "He doesn't drink tea."

I glanced at her husband, wondering if he would speak up for himself, but he stood still as a statue, dutifully holding the boxes, waiting for Emer to tell him his next move. I had heard of Stepford wives, but apparently Stepford husbands could be a thing too.

"Just one takeaway tea?" Erin asked, turning back around.

Presha nodded. "Thank you, Erin."

The girl nodded and made an about-face again.

Presha folded her hands in front of her. "What do you think the historian's assessment will be about the chapel ruins?"

"That it is an important historical site. That we have a good chance of being named a national site. Of course, to do that and preserve the ruins will require the church to raise more money." She pointed at the box of cookies. "Carver is making a presentation to the church elders today and explaining all that will be required. Most of the elders will be there—at least the ones who aren't working—and the biscuits are a peace offering."

"And the church is behind this?" Presha asked.

"They will be when I explain how important it is. Carver will be there to help as well."

I wasn't sure how much of a help smug Carver would be.

Erin returned to the front of the shop carrying Emer's tea.

"Thank you," Emer said. She smiled at Presha and me. "We should be off. It's a busy day."

I watched Emer and her husband leave, not for the first time thinking what an odd couple they made.

Chapter
Thirty-Four

P resha crossed her arms as she watched through the window as Emer and Douglas walked down the street. "I'm afraid it'll take a lot more than shortbread to convince the church elders to spend money on the chapel ruins, especially now with the minister no longer there to champion her cause."

"Malcolm gave me the same impression."

She nodded. "He would know. There are many causes that the church has already committed to provide funds for. Many people who rely on the church for its support. For some, it will be difficult to save a crumbling building when there are people here and now that are in more desperate need of the help."

I nodded. "I see your point."

"You should know that Ian was against the chapel ruins project, not because he didn't want to preserve that village history but because he cared deeply for the people who needed assistance from the church."

"That sounds like my godfather." When I said that, I thought back to the photos I had found in my godfather's wooden box. Presha had been a close friend of my godfather's, and she probably knew what I suspected to be true. I still wasn't ready to say it aloud, though.

I told myself to get through the murder investigation and then worry about the box. Instead I asked, "Do you know Emer and Douglas well?"

"I know them as well as I do any young couple in the village." Presha pursed her lips. "They've only lived here for two or three years. They came here from Aberdeen when Douglas took over the village lower school as head teacher. I'm not completely sure that he is happy here."

"What do say that?" I asked.

She stared out the window as if lost in thought. "When they first arrived, he was much more animated, but it seems now he lives in the shadow of his wife. Don't get me wrong, Emer is a wonderful person. She does much for the village and takes on many of the jobs that no one else would like, like being the head of the welcome committee."

"Has Emer changed too in the time she's lived here?"

"No." She shook her head. "Emer has always been the same." She handed a scone wrapped in a napkin to me. "Now, off with you. It's time you go and apologize to your sister."

"She owes me an apology, too." I had to admit, if only to myself, that my response was a tad whiny.

"She does," she said with a nod. "But no one should make an apology expecting one in return. That ruins it for both parties. It is better to say you are sorry and be at peace."

I smiled. "Presha, how did you get so wise?"

"Lots and lots of mistakes, my dear. More than you could ever count."

I wanted to ask Presha what those mistakes were, but I knew she would tell me if she thought I needed to hear about them for my own good. If not, I would never know.

Before I could reach the door, Remy Kenner stomped into the shop. "I'm here for my wife and son."

Claudia yelped and stood up, clutching a crying Byron to her chest. Most of the other guests in the tea shop stood up as well. It was clear that no one wanted to be in the middle of the Kenners' domestic dispute.

"You again!' Remy pointed a calloused finger at me.

I balled my fists at my side and was ready to defend Claudia and her son if the need arose, but before I could do a thing, Kipling and Craig, followed by two of Craig's constables, ran into the tea shop. The place was crowded, and many of the villagers, who were there that morning just to enjoy a simple cup of Presha's tea, pressed against the wall, doing their best to stay out of the fray.

Kipling pointed at Remy. "I told you I saw him in the village, Chief Inspector."

Remy gaped at him. "What is going on?"

Craig slapped cuffs on Remy's wrists and then shoved him in the direction of one of his officers. "Take him back to Aberdeen."

Kipling wrung his hands.

"You can't do this!" Remy shouted. "Claudia, how can you do this to our family?"

Remy was out the door with the two officers.

Claudia crumbled into her seat, still holding a crying Byron in her arms. Presha hurried over to comfort the woman.

Craig looked to Kipling, who appeared to be looking for a way out of the tea shop of his own. "Kipling, you did good work, seeing Remy coming into the village and notifying my department."

Kipling puffed out his chest, seemingly recovered from his fear from a moment ago. "I'm here to serve and protect." He walked to the door. "I'll go let them know at the pub that Remy Kenner has been apprehended."

Craig shook his head. "You do that."

Kipling left, and Craig turned to me. His face softened. "Why am I not surprised that you were here when we caught Remy?" He took a step toward me. "I have to consult with my officers about what just happened. I'll stop over at the Climbing Rose in a little bit. Will you be there?" he asked.

I nodded wordlessly.

He touched my cheek before he went out the door. I blushed, and I was certain that everyone in the tea shop saw.

Chapter Thirty-Five

I left Presha's not long after Craig did and went straight to the Climbing Rose. It was still an hour or so before I would open, but I thought I might as well get some paperwork done.

I walked down Prince Street and spotted my sister sitting cross-legged in front of my shop. When she saw me, she stood up quickly.

Happily, Seth was nowhere to be seen. I increased my pace.

Even before I made it to the store, she ran to me with her arms out.

I wrapped my arms around her. "It's okay. I'm sorry that I wasn't understanding," I said into her hair.

"I'm sorry I was such a brat, and I should have told you about Seth a lot earlier. It just seemed like such a fairy tale, I wanted to keep it to myself." She stepped back to look at my face but didn't let me go.

I wiped a tear from my eye. "Let's not talk about what we should have done or not done. You and Seth are a couple. I'm ready to move forward knowing that."

She wiped away a tear too. "Thank you, Fi."

Two elderly Scottish women walked by with empty shopping bags, heading in the direction of the market. "They are Americans," one whispered to the other.

The other woman nodded. "Aye."

I supposed that was explanation enough for our sisterly embrace.

I wrapped my arm around Isla's shoulder and removed the shop key from my tote bag with my other hand. "Let's go inside to talk."

"Yeah," Isla said. "I wouldn't want to be caught in the middle of the street being American." She giggled.

I smiled as I unlocked the door.

"No Ivanhoe today?"

I shook my head and pushed the door inward. "I wasn't sure what the day would bring, so I decided to leave him at home."

"Probably smart. I don't think he cares much for Seth." She smoothed her hair.

I dropped my bag on the sales counter. "Why do you say that?"

"When you left the shop yesterday and I was here alone, Seth dropped by."

"Oh?" I said.

"Ivanhoe scratched him."

I'd known I loved that cat for a reason. I made a sympathetic noise like I was sorry to hear that. The scratch must have explained the tear I had seen in Seth's jeans the day before. Ivanhoe must have put a lot of force behind his swipe at Seth to tear through the denim like that. "I'm glad he wasn't hurt."

Isla shook her head. "No, you're not, but thanks for saying that anyway."

"Where did you stay last night?" I asked.

"Raj let me crash in the pub. Let me tell you, sleeping on the pub floor wasn't that comfortable. I'm looking forward to getting back to my bed at Duncreigan."

"Your bed?" I asked. "We're going to have to talk about sleeping arrangements at the cottage if you plan to be there long term. We can go to Aberdeen this weekend and find you something to sleep on. Because I'm reclaiming the bed."

She frowned. Knowing Isla, she was counting on her ability to talk me into things to get me to let her reclaim the bed as her own. It wasn't going to work this time.

"You could have come home at any time last night," I added. "I know I had the car, but I would've driven to the village and picked you up at any time."

She nodded. "I know, but I wanted to think things through before I saw you again. I needed to come to some conclusions."

"What conclusions?" I tried to keep the surprise out of my voice and failed.

"I do love Seth. It's not an act."

"I believe you, but I do think you should slow down. Get to know him before you jump in with both feet." I had to say it. I was still her big sister.

"Fi, you and I are different. You always weigh the pros and cons of everything and still hesitate. I jump right in. Maybe my way is messier, but I don't have regrets for not going after what I want."

I bit the inside of my lip to hold back a smart remark. It wouldn't have done any good, because what she said was true. We were two very different people. We attacked problems differently, and maybe, I realized, that was okay.

"I need you to respect that," she said, sounding more like a grown-up than I had ever heard her sound.

I folded my arms. "I do respect that. I'm even a little jealous of it, *but* I think a little caution wouldn't hurt."

She nodded with a thoughtful expression on her face. "I know; that's why I told Seth we shouldn't call ourselves engaged just yet. Maybe we need to get to know each other a little bit better first."

I gave a small sigh of relief.

"I do love him, though, and know I will marry him someday. I guess you can say that we are pre-engaged." She beamed.

Being pre-engaged sounded like one of the dumbest ideas I had ever heard, but I could handle pre-engaged better than engaged. I was going to have to take it. "I think that's wise," I said sagely. "And I would wait until you know him a lot better before you tell Mom and Dad. There's no reason to get them worked up this early into it."

"Agreed," she said. "Although I am going to stay in Scotland for Seth."

"We can get you a cot for the cottage. You will love it."

"Are you sure you don't want to sleep on the cot and I get the bed?"

I narrowed my eyes at her. "Don't push it, Isla. Now, let's get ready to open the shop."

She saluted me and went to the workroom. A moment later,

she came back into the showroom with a watering can in hand and began to water the flowers.

A half hour later, the shop door opened. It wasn't yet ten in the morning, but I must have forgotten to lock the front door.

I walked toward the door with a glass vase of pink roses in my hands. "Sorry, we're—" I was about to say we weren't open yet, but it was Seth. I bit the inside of my cheek.

He ducked his head. "Is it okay if I come in?"

I was happy to see that he was a tad sheepish.

My sister rushed over to him and wrapped her arms around him. It didn't irritate me to see her do it this time. Well, it didn't irritate me as much.

"Don't worry, sugar," my sister said in her Tennessee drawl. "Fi and I talked it over and all is well. She understands now, and I'm going to stay with her while you and I get to know each other better."

I wouldn't have said that I understood, but I didn't see it helping anything if I argued. "What have you been up to this morning, Seth?" I asked.

"I was just up at Duncreigan, actually."

"Oh?" I wondered if *oh* was becoming my new favorite word.

He nodded. "I told Hamish that I dropped out of medical school and plan to get a job here in the village to be close to Isla." He looked at my sister lovingly and then back to me. "I told him that I would do my best to pay him back for all that he's loaned me for my education and I squandered. It might take some time, but I know it's the right thing to do."

281

"That's so noble of you, Seth." My sister gazed up at him with starry eyes.

He nodded. "I was thinking of applying at the school. There will be a custodian position open now that Remy Kenner has been arrested. I think I would do well at that, and it would give me time to find what I really want to do."

I blinked at him. *Remy Kenner was the custodian at the village school?*

"How did you hear about his arrest?"

Seth grinned. "I stopped in the Twisted Fox on the way here, and Kipling is in there holding court about how he single-handedly brought Remy to justice. I'm sure I wasn't the only in the pub who doubted that's how it went down."

"It wasn't," I said absent-mindedly. If Remy Kenner was as awful as they said, why had the school hired him to be a custodian around children? It just didn't make sense.

"You might be a teacher," Isla said.

He looked down at her again. "I do like kids."

She beamed.

I felt my stomach drop. I didn't know if my blood pressure could handle them talking about kids right now. I had only just accepted their pre-engagement.

"The only problem with the school job is I don't know if the head teacher would hire me," Seth said.

"Why's that?" I asked.

"Because I saw him buy drugs at the docks." He spoke matter-of-factly.

I dropped the vase of flowers onto the floor. It shattered,

and blossoms went every which way. I covered my mouth as I stared at the mess.

Isla ran around the counter to the workroom and came back with a broom and a dustpan. "Fi, are you okay?"

"I'm so sorry. I was just shocked by the news." I stepped out of the way so Isla could sweep. "Are you sure?" I asked Seth.

"Definitely. I saw him down at the docks."

Douglas had a drug problem. I thought back to all the times I had seen him. But how did that tie together with the murder? Poor Emer. It was no wonder she tried so hard to give the impression that everything in her world was perfect. If her husband had such a serious problem, it most certainly wasn't.

"When was this?" I asked.

Seth winced. "I'm sorry that I said anything."

I took a step toward him. "Answer my question, please."

He held up his hands. "Okay, okay. It was the night the minister was killed, in the early evening when I was waiting for Isla. It was before she texted me to tell me that she wasn't coming."

"Did you see who he bought the drugs from?"

"Sure. It was Remy Kenner, the school janitor."

Whoosh. The air went out of my lungs at that announcement. "Did Remy or Douglas see you?" I took a deep breath and waited for the answer.

"I think Douglas did, but not Remy."

I gave a sigh of relief. As much as I wasn't thrilled Seth was dating my sister, I didn't want anything to happen to him. If Remy Kenner knew that Seth could testify that he was a drug dealer, Seth could be in some serious danger, even after Remy's arrest that morning.

Seth's eyes went wide. "You don't think it's connected to the minister's murder, do you?"

"It might be," I said. "You saw Douglas buy the drugs from Remy the night that Minister MacCullen died. The old men at the docks also saw the minister and Remy arguing at the docks that night. It would seem too coincidental if the two things weren't linked. There's just one problem."

Isla dumped the dustpan of broken glass and mashed flowers into a trash can. "What's that?"

"The police questioned Remy about the murder, but they let him go. Craig said there wasn't enough evidence to link him to the murder. He was arrested today on domestic abuse and drug trafficking charges, not murder." I shook my head. "In any case, I have to call Craig about Douglas. I hate to do that to Emer, but it strengthens his case against Remy. No one wants him back on the street."

"I don't think you need to call him," Isla said.

I shook my head. "I have to. He needs to know all of this, and Seth, you need to talk to him too."

"No, really," Isla said. "You don't need to call him because he is right there." She pointed out the window.

Through the glass, I saw Craig walking to the Climbing Rose's front door.

Chapter
Thirty-Six

C hief Inspector Craig came through the door and looked at each of us in turn. "What's wrong? What's going on?"

"Why do you think every time I see you something must be wrong?" I asked.

"Your reputation precedes you," he said with a teasing voice.

"Well, it just so happens that today you're right, and Seth has something to tell you."

The chief inspector turned to Seth and waited.

As Seth began to tell the chief inspector about Remy and Douglas Boyd, the shop phone rang.

I hurried over to it. "The Climbing Rose Flower Shop, the finest flowers in Aberdeenshire. How may I help you?" I smiled. It was the first time I had been able to try out the greeting, and I hoped it didn't sound over the top.

"Hello, may I speak to Fiona Knox?" a woman's voice came over the line.

"This is she," I said, hoping I came across as bright and cheerful.

"This is Mary Macintosh. I was at your shop opening."

"I remember," I said eagerly.

Isla sidled over to me while keeping an eye on Seth and the chief inspector at the same time.

I mouthed an answer to her unspoken question, "It's the mother of the bride."

Her eyes went wide.

"When we met, I briefly told you about my daughter's upcoming wedding. I know this would be a quick turnaround, but my daughter will be up from London this coming weekend. I would love to show her your shop and discuss the possibility of you doing the flowers for her fall wedding. The flowers and arrangements in your shop were unlike any I have ever seen before. You have such a wonderful eye for color and attention to detail. I know that my daughter would be wild about your designs. Is that something you would be interested in doing?"

"I would be happy to do it," I said, trying not to show how eager I was. In my head, I was jumping up and down.

"I'm so happy to hear that. What about Saturday at eleven? Does that give you enough time to get everything together?"

"Saturday at eleven will be perfect. I will have a flower presentation for you and your daughter then. Does she have any favorite flowers?"

"Not particularly, but the colors for her wedding are purple and gold."

"That gives me a start. I can work from there. Thank you so much for calling." I gave Isla the thumbs-up sign.

"No, thank you. I know your flowers will be the perfect touch to my daughter's wedding." We said good-bye and I hung up.

Isla bounced over to me. "What happened?"

"I think we might have just booked a wedding."

Isla squealed and threw her arms around me.

I hugged her back but said, "We can't celebrate just yet. We have to wow the bride and the mother of the bride with our presentation on Saturday."

"That doesn't give us much time." She dropped her arms to her sides.

"I know. So we have to start working now."

Tears gathered in my sister's eyes.

"Isla, what's wrong?"

"I was just thinking, the best part of that was you said *we*." She sniffled. "Like you and me, like we are a team."

I hugged her. "You're my sister. Of course we're a team."

She brushed a tear from her cheek. "I'm glad."

"Now, let's get to work. We have a lot to do for this wedding presentation."

Craig snapped the small notebook where he had been recording Seth's story closed. "What's all the squealing over here about?"

"Fi got a wedding gig," Isla said.

I shook my head. "I got a wedding trial, a chance to pitch my work to a bride."

"Don't be modest. As soon as the bride sees what you can do with flowers, she is going to book you," Isla said.

"I think you will get it," Craig said.

I looked up at him for a moment too long. "Thank you." I turned away.

"Yes, well," Craig said. "I'm going to have a chat with

Douglas Boyd and see if he will corroborate what Seth said. If he does, it is very unlikely Remy will be getting out of jail anytime soon."

"Can I ask you a question?"

His brows went up. "Yes."

"Why have you told me so much about the investigation? Like at the docks, you told me about the marks on the back of the minister's neck, and you thought it was murder."

He sighed. "I'd hoped that by telling you little bits of the investigation, you would realize how dangerous it was and you would stay out of it. Clearly, that was a miscalculation."

I considered this. It *had* been a miscalculation on the chief inspector's part. If anything, what he'd told me had made me more determined to find out what had happened to the minister.

"Will you be staying here today?" Craig asked.

I looked up at him again. "What do you mean? I'm trying to run a business. Of course I will be here."

"Good, because even though we caught Remy, a murderer is still on the loose. Remy might have killed the minister, but until we are certain, I want you stay put."

I thought of the note that had been left on my to-do list the day before. I almost told him about it, but then changed my mind. If I told him, he would put me under house arrest for sure. "I'll be here," I repeated.

He lowered his voice. "Good. Because I don't want anything to happen to you, especially before I can take you out on a proper date."

I glanced at my sister and Seth, who were standing with

their heads together across the room. "Chief Inspector Craig, are you asking me out?"

"If I were, would you go?" he asked.

"Probably."

He smiled. "I'll take that as a yes, so yes, I would like to go on a real date with you. No murder talk, just you and me."

"I'd like that too," I whispered.

He glanced at my sister and Seth, who were still in their own little world; then he leaned forward and kissed my cheek. "Good." With that, he went out the door, leaving me standing in the middle of the Climbing Rose in a daze.

Seth left shortly after Craig, saying that he was going to look for a job. I was happy to hear that. Maybe being in a relationship with my sister was just the motivation he needed to get his act together.

An hour later, Isla and I were at the front counter sketching out a plan for the wedding when Kipling strode into the shop. I had many flowers on the counter and was trying to see what worked best for the purple-and-gold theme.

I wiped my hands on a cloth to remove the pollen left by the flowers. "Hello, Kipling, what can I help you with?"

He puffed out his chest. "Nothing. I'm here to stand guard."

Isla blinked at him. "He's kidding, right?"

"He better be kidding," I said.

Kipling shook his head stubbornly. "Chief Inspector Craig said that I was to keep my eye on you until the murderer is apprehended."

I groaned. And here I had trusted that Craig believed me that I would stay in the flower shop all day. "If Craig thinks I'm in so much danger, why didn't he pick me up and put me under house arrest?" I couldn't keep the irritation from my voice.

Kipling rubbed his chin. "I believe he gave that some serious thought but concluded that you wouldn't be open to that idea."

"He concluded right." I ushered Kipling toward the door. "I also don't need someone to stand guard over me. The Climbing Rose is in the middle of the village right next to the pub. There is no way the killer will try to confront me where there is so much potential for witnesses."

"The chief inspector thought it would be best if I kept an eye on you to make sure you are safe."

I groaned again. I was about to open my mouth to argue with him some more when Isla said, "Just let him stay, Fi. It's not a huge deal, right? Kipling won't bother us while we work. We can just pretend he's not here."

Kipling scowled at that last part.

She clasped her hands in front of her heart. "Besides, it's such a romantic gesture. The chief inspector wants to protect you. It's hard to find a chivalrous man like that in this day and age. I found one myself in Seth, of course." She sighed dreamily.

I grumbled something under my breath, but in the end, I agreed with her. I had too much work to do and no time to argue. I wanted my flower presentation for the Macintosh wedding to be absolutely flawless. I knew that if I bombed the flowers for this wedding, I might as well pack up my shop and return to Nashville with my tail between my legs.

Chapter Thirty-Seven

True to his word, Kipling stood guard over Isla and me all day. Honestly, it wouldn't have been so bad if he hadn't talked most of that time as well. The one thing I would have said about Kipling was that the volunteer police officer could talk. He wasn't as easy to ignore as Isla had thought he would be.

Kipling stood at the front window. "Looks like it's going to rain. It won't be as bad as the storm the night the minister died, but I would say at least four inches of rain."

I had to admit that in the last half hour, the sky had clouded over, but it looked nothing like it had the night of the storm. There was no wind to speak of, and that had kicked up the night of the murder.

Isla eyed him. "Are you a Scottish weatherman or something?"

He stood a bit straighter. "Nay, but I have lived in Belle-wick my entire life, and just like my grandfather and father before me, I learned to read the weather."

I had only a half hour left before I closed the shop. After that I planned to go with Isla—and probably Kipling—to the

291

Twisted Fox for dinner and call Craig to see when I would be released from my guard detail.

The phone rang for a second time that day.

I repeated my greeting—I was getting quite good at it.

"Hello, is this Fiona Knox?" a heavy Scottish voice said over the line.

"This is Fiona. How can I help you?"

"This is Malcolm from the church."

"Hi, Malcolm," I said, surprised. "Is anything wrong?"

"No, no," he said. "I will correct that. Nothing is more wrong than what happened to our poor minister. That's why I'm calling. We hope to have the funeral in two days' time, which is not enough notice for a normal flower supplier. Would your shop be able to take care of the flowers? We'll pay you, of course, and be ever so grateful if you would help us, since we are in a pinch."

"I thought Emer would be making the funeral arrangements."

He snorted. "She would like to think so, yes, but I am the one who worked with the minister day in and day out these last twenty years. I should be the one to plan the funeral." He sighed. "She won't let me take it all on, of course, but she said I could be in charge of the building and grounds. The cheek of her! I am always in charge of the building and grounds. In any case, that includes the flowers for the service. Can you help us out? We would be in your debt."

Two potential accounts in one day. Perhaps my business would survive in Scotland after all.

"I'd be happy to. I was just about to close up shop," I said.

Just like when I'd spoken with Mary Macintosh, I tried to measure my eagerness at the prospect of more work. "But I could come now if that works for you?"

"That's good of ye," he said, and ended the call.

"What's up?" Isla asked.

"That was the church sexton. He wants me to meet him at the church to discuss providing flowers for Minister MacCullen's funeral. If it goes well, it has the potential to lead to other arrangements for the church. Maybe even the weekly chancel flowers."

"Whoa," Isla said, giving me a high five. "Fi, that could be a huge account. I bet there are a bunch of special events and weddings in that big beautiful church. It could lead to more business."

"That's what I'm hoping." I grabbed my jacket from the workroom. "Can you lock up and go straight to the Twisted Fox? I'm a little worried about leaving you here alone. I guess the chief inspector's paranoia has rubbed off on me."

"Let's close now, and you can walk me to the pub, but I don't like the idea of you walking to the church alone either. The chief inspector has me spooked too."

"Not to worry," Kipling said. "I'm going with Fiona to the church."

I held up my hand. "Kipling. Really. There is no need for you to do that. That wasn't part of your assignment. You were supposed to watch over the store, nowhere else."

He shook his head. "If something happens to you, the chief inspector will have my head on a platter."

"He does have a point, Fi," my sister said. "And besides,

I would feel a lot better if I knew he was with you. Otherwise I don't want you to go."

I folded my arms. "Okay, fine." I pointed at Kipling. "But I don't want to hear a peep out of you when we're talking about the flowers."

"What would I have to say about flowers?" he asked. "I don't know a rose from a daisy."

We followed Isla's plan, locked up the shop, and walked her to the pub, and then Kipling and I made our way to the church.

On the way, Kipling talked constantly. This didn't bode well for him not talking during the flower consultation.

We didn't even make it off Prince Street before it started to sprinkle.

"I told you it was going to rain," Kipling said in the middle of his diatribe.

I grunted in return.

By the time we reached the front door of the church, it had begun raining in earnest. I put my hand on the door handle, ready to pull it open and take cover inside, but nothing happened. I yanked on the door again. Again, nothing. It was locked.

Kipling held his hand over his forehead to block rain from running into his eyes. "I thought Malcolm said to meet you here."

"He said the church. I just assumed he wanted to meet inside. I don't have the church number to call him." I banged on the door again, but there was a hollow *thud, thud, thud* and then nothing.

The sky got darker by the second. There wasn't any overhang

to take cover under. "There is another door to the church around back by the community garden. If he's not there, we can head back to the pub. I'm sure Malcolm would understand because of the rain."

Kipling shrugged.

I led him around the side to the community garden. Rainwater gushed through the gutters of the old shed into the two remaining barrels.

Beyond that, I could see the field of daisies bent over against the force of the driving rain.

I walked through the vegetable garden to the back of the church. Kipling was right behind me. He wasn't talking now. I supposed he had given up since I wouldn't be able to hear him over the rain pounding onto the roof of the church anyway.

I tried the back door handle. It was locked, just like the front door had been. I raised my hand to knock on the door.

There was a loud bang as I knocked on the door again. The sound was much different from the hollow thud I'd heard before. I turned behind me to see if Kipling had also heard it, and found him crumpled at my feet holding his shoulder. Blood oozed out from between his fingers.

"I've been shot," he said.

I stared at him, and blood seeped through his uniform. "You're bleeding!"

He groaned. "You have to get out of here."

"I'm not leaving you here," I yelled against the rain.

"You have to. The chief inspector said I couldn't let anything happen to you."

Another shot rang out. I ducked down over his body, and

the stone on the corner of the church splintered and showered us with tiny shards of granite. I didn't know how I could get out of the situation. Kipling was a small man, but I couldn't carry him. I pulled out my phone and called the police.

As quickly as I could, I explained what was happening and where we were. The police would be there soon.

There was another shot. I couldn't tell where they were coming from. I pulled Kipling around the side of the building. It was no use moving him any farther. He was dead weight.

"Run, Fiona. Please just run for help. You have to get out of here."

"Help is coming!" I promised. I stared to run through the cemetery toward the front of the church, but I saw a form moving through the graveyard in the rain, which was now coming down in sheets. I couldn't make out who it was before another bullet pinged off the closest headstone.

I spun around and ran in the opposite direction toward the chapel ruins. I ran through the daisies, crushing them in my haste. The rain became heavier when I reached the edge of the ruins. I heard another shot, which spurred my forward. I knocked into the one remaining upright wall of the chapel ruin. Pain shot through my whole body as the stone dug into my ribs. I couldn't stop to collect myself. I ran on, and again I tripped over the edge of the pit and fell face first into the mud.

The rain pelted my back, and I was wet and cold. It was dark, somewhere between night and day. I lay on my stomach in the mud. Painfully, I reached my hand over my head, and my knuckles scraped against rough stone.

"There you are. Have you decided to choose your own

grave? That was thoughtful of you." The voice came from above me, but I could not distinguish if it was male or female. I wanted desperately to turn onto my back so I could see who was speaking. I tried to roll over, and pain shot through my right side. I wondered how I had gotten that injury.

The vision! I was living the vision I'd had in the garden. And in that vision, I had been about to die.

"I would prefer if you not move. It will make this much easier for both of us," the voice said.

I felt the sharp pressure of a knee in my back. Fear coursed through my body. I knew I had good reason to be afraid. A very good reason.

Hands, strong hands, were around my throat. They were squeezing tighter and tighter. I gasped for air.

"This won't take long. Try to relax." Again, the voice's gender was unclear. I could barely hear it over the pounding rain.

Two hands were squeezing tighter and tighter. It was just like my vision. I didn't want to live out my vision.

"I thought the note I left for you in your shop would scare you away, so it would not come to this," the voice said. "You should have heeded my warning."

The note. Whoever was trying to kill me had written the note, the note I should have told Chief Inspector Craig about, but it was too late now, far too late.

Suddenly, there was a scream and the hands let go.

I gasped and held my face out of the mud. As quick as I could, I crawled out of the pit. I wiped mud and rainwater from my eyes so I could see what was going on.

Kipling lay in the mud, groaning. It must have taken all

the strength he'd had to walk over to the ruins and pull my assailant off me. He had saved my life. A life that had been about to be taken by Emer Boyd.

"Leave him alone!" I shouted at her.

She turned her gun on me. "He's not much of a threat anymore, so I will happily shoot you first."

I turned and ran deeper into the ruins.

Emer had plenty of opportunity to shoot me in the back while I ran, but she must not have been a very good shot because she missed every time. Her hitting Kipling by the church doors must have been blind luck.

I crouched behind a crumbling stone.

"Come out, Fiona. Don't you want to talk about the church flowers?"

Nope, not really.

"You seem genuinely surprised to see me. Who were you expecting? Remy Kenner? The drug dealer who ruined the new perfect life that I was trying to build for Douglas and me?"

The new perfect life. That was all Emer seemed to care about, perfection or the appearance of perfection.

"My husband went through all our savings spending money on drugs, mostly prescription pills, but since he met Remy, harder things. I knew he should never have given Remy the janitor job, but he did. It wasn't long before Remy figured out Douglas's weakness for pills. Douglas went through every penny we had. Finally, when the money was gone, I thought it would be over, but I was wrong. Douglas began stealing from the school to feed his habit. Do you know what would happen if the school board found out? He would be out of a job and my new life would be destroyed. So I did the only thing that made sense. I *borrowed* money from the church's chapel restoration fund. I was the church treasurer, after all. I know how to hide what I did, and I paid back the school. The only wrinkle was Minister MacCullen wasn't a trusting man and double-checked my accounting. He noticed a problem and confronted me. I went to him and told him about my husband's issues. I told him that I would pay every penny back. I begged him to have mercy. He had mercy for Remy's wife and child and let them stay at the church; why couldn't he have mercy for me? No amount of pleading and begging did any good. He didn't care. He planned to expose me and my husband to the congregation. That was his mistake. I wasn't going to let that happen."

So she had killed him.

"So I killed him." She laughed. "It was quite clever of you to tie my husband and Remy together. When the police came to talk to Douglas this afternoon, I knew you had been behind it."

The funny thing was that she was wrong. Seth had been the one to unravel the connection between Douglas and Remy, but I didn't see any reason to correct, her since she appeared to be dead set on killing me at that moment.

She came around the side of my hiding stone. "There you are." She smiled.

"What did you do to Malcolm?" I asked, praying that the old man wasn't yet another one of her victims.

"Malcolm?" she laughed. "He's tucked away in his little cottage now, sipping tea. I was in the church when he called you. I told him to go home and I would take care of the

flowers. I take care of everything, don't you see? I do it best."
She raised her gun. "I'm tired of this conversation."

I leaped up and ran around the chapel's one remaining wall
and stopped just behind the four-by-four holding up the wall.

Emer came around the side with the gun out in front of
her, ready to shoot.

I kicked the four-by-four with all my might. The wood
shifted, but held. Before I could change my mind, I charged
the four-by-four again. The pieced of wood gave.

Emer screamed as the wall landed on top of her.

Epilogue

My godfather had been buried in St. Thomas's cemetery, and his grave was still fresh. He had been gone only a few months, and it took time for nature to reclaim land that she had given up. Grass was starting to make its way over the grave, but it was still only timid shoots. In a year, the raised earth would fall inward toward his vault and casket and the grass would be green and lush at the foot of his stone. I didn't know if the pain would be worse then, when he was settled into the earth, than it was now, when it was still fresh.

A GOOD MAN was carved into the stone below his name, his rank in Her Majesty's Army, and his birth and death dates.

When I died, would A GOOD WOMAN be carved into the stone? I wasn't sure it was a title I deserved. I didn't know what my life would bring. I had a lot of opportunity for mistakes in the future, and my mistakes seemed to have been increasing since I'd moved to Scotland. It had been in self-defense, but Emer Boyd was in the hospital recovering from several broken bones from a wall falling on her. It was a wall *I* had made fall on her.

At least Kipling would be all right. He had just been released from the hospital that morning for his gunshot wound, a wound Emer had given him. He was a hero for saving me like he had, and he loved the outpouring of praise and attention the village was giving him. As much as it was deserved, I suspected we would be hearing about his heroics for a long time to come.

As for me, I would have to learn to live with what I'd done to Emer somehow. I wondered how my godfather had lived with all his baggage from war. It couldn't have been easy.

It couldn't have been any easier for him to give up his daughter to another man. Or at least, I hoped that it had been difficult to give me up. I knew he had, but I didn't understand why or why he and my parents had chosen to lie to me about it my entire life.

Chief Inspector Craig stood next to me, holding my hand. "You okay?" he asked.

I nodded and moved away from my godfather's stone. Craig, still holding my hand, came with me.

There were many MacCallisters buried in the church cemetery, dating all the way back to Baird, the first MacCallister to have called this village home. I touched Baird's stone, and the grime and moss stained my fingertips, but I didn't care. Baird was the one who had started it all. In a way, his deal with the sea was what had put me in this very place right now. It reminded me how every decision a person makes has a lasting impression, not just on their own life but on the lives of those who come after them. Baird was the reason I was the Keeper.

I knew I had to take that into account when making my own decisions. What I didn't know yet was everything the garden could and was meant to do. Yes, my godfather—my birth father—had left me instructions, but I was realizing there was much he had left unsaid. Not just about my birth, but about the garden itself. Uncle Ian had said that the garden was used to help. Perhaps it could help more than I already knew. I suspected that the garden held many more gifts than just the ability to give me visions when I touched the stone. Those gifts and how to use them, I needed to learn, and I would in time—without the help of Carver Finley. It was true that he might be able to tell me quite a bit about the menhir, its history and purpose, but after the encounter in the parking lot, I didn't trust him. I hoped that after the chapel project was complete, he would forget about our little village and move on. A small voice in my head told me that he wouldn't.

I had to protect the garden, because someday I would pass it over to another. The responsibility of that suddenly felt heavy, and Craig and I walked out of the cemetery without uttering a word.

Finally, when we were a block away, I spoke. "This must be one of the oddest first dates that you have been on."

He smiled down at me. "It's not often a woman asks me to go to the cemetery with her." He touched my cheek. "But I'm happy you did."

I pressed my hand over his on my cheek for just a moment and then turned away. "I have to call her."

"I know. Do you want me to give you some privacy? I can go to the pub while you talk it out with her."

I shook my head. "No." Craig was the only one I had shared my suspicions with. I hadn't even told my sister. He was the only one I trusted until I had my own emotions about my birth sorted out.

Epilogue

As we walked back to the Climbing Rose, I removed my cell phone from my coat pocket and called a number I had memorized at the age of three. Somewhere on the outskirts of Nashville, the phone rang on my family farm. It rang and rang. I was patient. I knew my parents were out doing chores, and they set the phone for the highest number of rings before it turned over to voicemail to make sure they could reach it in time. They didn't always make it, but most of the time they did.

This call might be one of those rare times when they didn't make it. I knew there was just one more ring before it turned over to voicemail. I was almost happy for that. I didn't know that I was ready to have this conversation with my mother. Maybe I'd been wrong in my conclusion. A tiny part of me hoped that I had.

"Hello?" My mother asked in her native Tennessee drawl. Usually, hearing my mother's voice put me at ease, but not today.

"Mom?" I asked, pausing in the middle of the sidewalk. Craig stood with me, still holding my hand.

"Fiona, sugar, how are you? I hope Isla is being a good houseguest for you."

"Isla is fine." I didn't think this was the time to tell my mother that my sister had fallen in love with a medical school dropout and was pre-engaged with no plans to return to the States. Not that my mother could argue. It seemed to me that when she was studying abroad in Scotland, she had fallen in love with a local as well, possibly two locals: my father, who I had called Dad my entire life, and my godfather, who very well could be my biological father.

Epilogue

"Mom . . ."

Craig squeezed my hand.

She sighed deeply. "Oh, honey. I was hoping this day would never come. I've been waiting for your call."

And that's when I knew I was right.

Acknowledgments

I have always thought that gardens and flowers hold a little bit of mystery and magic. Like Fiona, I am my happiest and most at peace when I am in my garden. It has been my joy to bring flowers, magic, and mystery together in the Magic Garden Mysteries, and I am so grateful to my dear readers who make every one of my stories possible. It would be impossible to do what I do without you.

Even though I have written these stories, they weren't published alone, and I have several great people to thank for making the magic garden possible. First, as always, thank you to my super-agent Nicole Resciniti for her unfailing support and friendship. Thank you also to the team at Crooked Lane Books, especially to my editors Anne Brewer and Marla Daniels.

Thanks also to flower arranger Helen Grannetino for giving me a lesson in making beautiful bouquets and arrangements. Fiona Knox's flower shop is better for it.

Thanks so much to my assistant Molly Carroll for her help with this novel and for the assistance of friends Mariellyn Grace and David Seymour. A special thanks to David for helping to plan the murder in this book.

Acknowledgments

Love, as always, to my family: Andy, Nicole, Isabella, and Andrew, for their love and encouragement.

Finally, to my Heavenly Father, thank you for flowers of all colors, shapes, sizes, and scents. The world is made richer by each one.